Echoes of the Drum

Debra Bruch

Bruwicked Productions • South Range, Michigan, USA

A Bruwicked Productions Original

Bruwicked Books

Copyright © 2021 Debra Bruch

ISBN: 978-0989802222

Take an exciting sojourn into the ancient past of North America. Located at the Keweenaw Peninsula of upper Michigan, this remarkable historical fiction novel brings to life the making of Lake Superior, the Clovis people and Woodland people as they confront glaciers, mammoths, and the power and beauty of the land. Written by award-winning author, Debra Bruch, enter the ancient world of myth and intrigue, where prehistoric people struggle to live and love, spanning the time when the world was born through the ice age to 5000 BCE. Discover the origins of humankind through the eyes of our unknown ancestors.

Many Thanks and Acknowledgements!

Community of Christ Earth Stewardship Team

Dr. Theodore J. Bornhorst
Who sent me his pdf files about the formation of Lake Superior.

Dr. Susan R. Martin
Who turned me in the right direction about PaleoIndian. Her book,
Wonderful Power, *was significant.*

Dean and Bobbie Ann Robinson
Dean, who knows Clovis history and sent me on that track. Bobbie Ann, who listened and supported me throughout the writing of the book.

Bruce Crockett
Who kept me on the right reason I was writing the thing.

Peggy Gorton
Who patiently listened when I blocked, then started again.

Bob and Carol Wenc
Who helped me find a title for the book.

Shannon Lucenko
Who gave feedback on the beginning pages.

Michael and Karen Sharp
Who supported me throughout the writing.

Christina Brochu
Who supported me throughout the writing.

Our Indigenous brothers and sisters can teach us much. If we would listen.

Table of Contents

Preface

Echoes of the Drum is an historical fiction novel. The research was not only from books and articles, but I even looked at YouTube's videos about how ancient people may have processed leather and rawhide. For my main research for Clovis includes B. Fagan, *Ancient North America* (London, 2005). G. Haynes, *The Early Settlement of North America: The Clovis Era* (Cambridge, 2002). G. Haynes (ed.), *American Megafaunal Extinctions at the End of the Pleistocene* (New York, 2009). D. Meltzer, *First Peoples in a New World: Colonizing Ice Age America* (Berkeley, 2009). S. Mithen, *After the Ice: A Global Human History 20000-5000 BC* (London, 2003). Despite the amount of evidence of Clovis points, nothing is known of their culture. Later PaleoIndian culture, however, has more evidence, and the sources are *PaleoIndian Archaeology: A Hemispheric Perspective* by J.E. Morrow and C. Gnecco, (U Press of Florida, 2009), and *Across Atlantic Ice* by D.J. Stanford and B.A. Bradley (U of Calif Press, 2013). The main resource I used for Part II's Woodland was *Wonderful Power: The Story of Ancient Copper Working in the Lake Superior Basin,* by Susan R. Martin (Wayne State University Press, 1999) mainly because it was about prehistoric people living specifically in the Keweenaw.

Research in our pre-history can go only so far. The Prologue chapter is as factual as I could get and I was surprised by how Lake Superior, and consequently the Keweenaw, was formed. Everything I read led me to believe that we have not changed very much, despite our ancestors' characterizations in movies and television. Our understanding of our world has changed, societies changed, technology has certainly changed, but our human needs of belonging, tribal peace, our need for love and acceptance, our hearts, our thinking, use of language (mostly), and our creativity have always been in play. We were fully human with different worldviews, beliefs, and norms since our beginnings. I have a deep respect for Indigenous American thinking and I hope that came across in this novel. At the same time, I also respect that, as humans, we have a dark side and so there's pettiness, greed, oppression, and prejudice we struggle to overcome.

The narrative voice in *Echoes of the Drum* is both contemplation and an expression of archeological and anthropological scholarship. I am influenced by: Joseph Campbell, *The Masks of God: Primitive Mythology* (New York: The Viking Press, 1959), Will Durant, *The Story of Civilization: Part 1: Our Oriental Heritage* (Vol. 1. 11 vols. New York: Simon and Schuster, 1954), James George Frazer, *The Golden Bough: A Study of Magic and Religion* (Collier Books Publishing; Abridged edition, April 1, 1985), Wilfred L. Guerin, Earle Labor, Lee Morgan, and John R. Willingham, *A Handbook of Critical Approaches to Literature* (2nd ed. New York: Harper & Row, 1979), Susanne K. Langer, *Philosophy in a New Key: A Study in the Symbolism of Reason, Rite, and Art* (Cambridge, Massachusetts: Harvard University Press, 1942), Stephen C. Pepper, *World Hypotheses: A Study in Evidence.* (Berkley: University of California Press, 1942, 1970), Jack Scarborough, *The Origins of Cultural Differences and Their Impact on Management* (Westport, Connecticut & London: Quorum Books, 2001), and Philip Ellis Wheelwright, *Metaphor and Reality* (Bloomington: Indiana University Press, 1962).

The characters, tribes and tribal names are fiction. Their cultures are fiction as well as their basic beliefs, relationships with each other, and their actions. I'm also influenced by my own life-experiences of having a close connection to the earth and have communicated with trees and animals. This includes camouflage. So I see a reality in it all. My hope is that you will enjoy reading the novel.

-- Debra Bruch

Prologue

Creation

Chapter One: Fire and Rock

Inhale. In the Dark, the eternal breath embraced the first stardust. A soup of chaos ensued within a miniscule of space – a cacophony of breathing bits of stardust dead to themselves, knowing nothing, seeing nothing, feeling nothing, being nothing. Millennia passed and the sound of breathing began to vibrate the bits. Through eons passing, the vibration steadily increased.

Exhale. Whether by design or chance, the vibrating eternal breath sparked the Light. Suddenly, in an instant, the Light fired Life into the dust, overwhelmed the Dark, and exploded outward, forever creating a series of transformation when life will change itself into Becoming and then death, then transformation again.

Stardust became dust, then dirt, then earth. Inhale. Exhale. Transformation through eons of time no longer eternal. Next: fire, air, water, then plants and animals. Then humankind. The breath of Light embedded Life in all, through all, and around all. Earths, stars, nebulae, galaxies, blood and bone, green and rock. Space where Life dances and creates. Dances and creates. The dance is not yet finished.

At birth, Earth experienced a series of events forever defining Lake Superior and the surrounding land, including Michigan's Keweenaw Peninsula: that finger of land jutting up into the bottom center of Lake Superior.

Over four billion years ago the earth was hot and unformed. Violently the Precambrian earth heaved without thought or desire except to Become. Long before life could set hold, continental plates of earth rose and hardened, and with unimaginable violence, those plates crashed together and fused. Millions of years past by before the earth plates fused the area called the Great Lakes Tectonic Zone. Today, we see Archean Eon rocks over three billion years old. Many of the rocks are volcanic while some are sedimentary, having been born from sand, mud, and gravel. Other rocks are granite that intruded into volcanic and sedimentary rock as molten and then solidified deep beneath the surface. The Earth loves diversity.

Eon after eon passed while Earth slowly breathed. She cooled on the surface, the rains came, and Light breathed life. But underneath laid a hot cauldron, straining to be released.

The Lake Superior and the surrounding area was a flat, shallow sea. Life formed. A lava burst containing iron created rock. Its force formed rock ridges. But the area continued to be mostly flat. Early Proterozoic life formed as algae and bacteria, the earth moved and deposited sedimentary rock into a large shallow sea that was then covering much of the upper North American plate. Some contained iron and most of the iron ran south of the Keweenaw from Marquette to Ironwood to Duluth. An event tilted the rock and can still be seen at Jay Cook State Park south of Duluth. Millions of years of erosion wore down the rock. The sea receded, leaving traces of sea life we can still find.

Earth was not finished. A slow but catastrophic event formed the foundation of Lake Superior and consequently the Keweenaw Peninsula. Under tremendous pressure, about 2.2 billion years ago during the Proterozoic Eon, the earth became so hot that the magma beneath the mantle created a plume and rose upward, cracking fissures in the mantle.

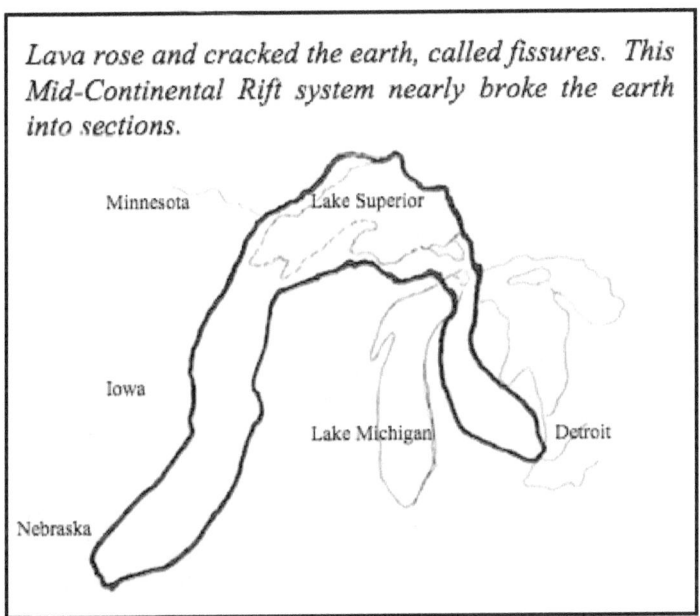

Lava rose and cracked the earth, called fissures. This Mid-Continental Rift system nearly broke the earth into sections.

A little over a billion years ago, the fissures widened and formed the Mid-Continental Rift system that threatened to splinter the North American plate. It ran from Kansas up through Minnesota, across the center of Lake Superior west to east, and down near the center of Lower Michigan to north of Detroit. The Rift did not separate the plate, but set off a series of events forever connecting Isle Royale and the Keweenaw to Lake Superior.

The Mid-Continental Rift created a geological weakness in the earth. And because it was centered across the middle of Lake Superior, the rift created the phenomenon that formed Lake Superior, the Keweenaw, and it's surrounding land. Centered in Lake Superior, lava punched up through the existing rock with incomprehensible violence, creating geysers shooting hundreds of feet into the air, then falling and slowly spreading out several hundred square miles onto a flat, barren plain. Now called the Portage Lake Lava Series, lava spewed upward about twenty times during this era, coating the surface with basalt rock.

Between the lava geysers and flows that lasted millions of years each, lava paused, again lasting millions of years each. *Inhale – Exhale.* Lake Superior is rimmed with this basalt rock. From the air, you can see the same parallel basaltic lava flow deposits forming the Keweenaw and Isle Royale.

Finally, the earth calmed herself after another two tectonic plates crashed and fused. The rift became inactive and lava flow ceased altogether. The plume underneath Lake Superior settled. But the earth had spewed so much heavy basalt from underneath the crust to the surface during the Portage Lake Lava Series that the earth sank along the Rift's axis. Without the plume pushing up, the land lowered, compressing the rock and forming a bowl, in turn pushing up the bowl's edges. Over the span of a billion years, the earth inhaled and exhaled when pressure pushed up the edges and, relaxing, erosion, rivers, and streams brought sentiment and rock, mostly sandstone.

The geologic drama formed faults in the crust of the earth that further defined Lake Superior and the Keweenaw. One powerful movement cracked the edges of the basin and formed the Keweenaw fault that travels along her spine. Another movement pushed rock up against the Keweenaw fault and jutted high above the land creating sharply defined cliffs. Stand high on Brockway Mountain and you stand on top of those cliffs.

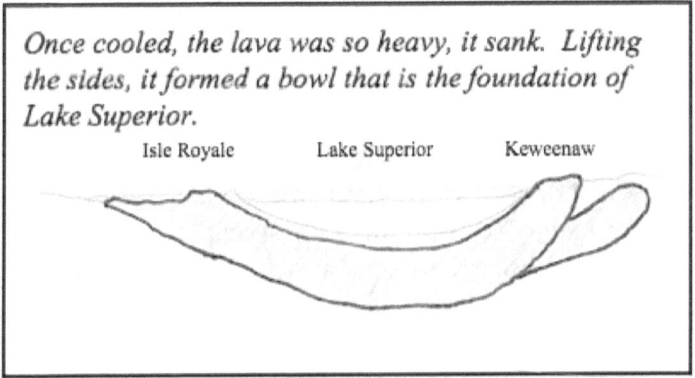

Once cooled, the lava was so heavy, it sank. Lifting the sides, it formed a bowl that is the foundation of Lake Superior.

Isle Royale   Lake Superior   Keweenaw

The movement also hit the fault near Isle Royale that formed the Isle. Today, ribbons of basalt rise from Isle Royale, down to form the western central area of the bowl of Lake Superior, and up the Keweenaw. Eventually the area stabilized. Hard rock formed the edges and the basin of Lake Superior, while soft material, caused by erosion and streams, eventually blanketed the basin.

The final creation happened during the past two million years. Finally, glaciers carved out much of Lake Superior's soft rock, creating the land around Lake Superior. Time and time again, glaciers breathed, excavating Lake Superior's center basin of its softer sedimentary rock. Glaciers pushed the sediment up over the hard edges of the bowl and formed the land around Lake Superior. The Huron Mountain range was nearly as tall as the Alps today until the glaciers filled the valleys and the erosion of millions of years took its toll. Finally, that too became peaceful. About 10,000 years ago the last of the ice melted and Lake Superior was finally shaped and at rest.

Nobody knows how or why a geologically small bubble of copper came to the Keweenaw and not elsewhere around Lake Superior. The fissures of the Mid-Continental Rift released sulfur that purified the copper. The fissures also allowed the molten copper metal to find a home inside the Keweenaw Peninsula. Bands of copper two to eight miles wide resided in the earth's fractures. But the richest copper was housed within the smaller fissures or veins. Glaciers scraped the rock and deposited drift or float copper on the surface of the land. Some silver and iron were also carried into the Keweenaw Peninsula. Isle Royale contained enough silver to warrant notice.

And so the earth deposited her fire-colored metal into the Keweenaw. It is, indeed, the largest deposit of native copper on earth. Once at peace, the land became home to a wide variety of flora and fauna. The Keweenaw grew thick with pine, walnut, beech, cedar, fir, ash, and birch. The wolf, bear, deer, moose, fox, bat, and beaver came to thrive on this small piece of land. Finally, people came and left both their footprints and their blood. They were a curious species and wondered at the hard fire discovered within the earth. They were a hardened people, a determined people, and a compassionate people, fiercely protective of each other living amongst the rock, water, trees, and animals, and surrounded by alternating harsh weather and paradise. The people who came to live here were undoubtedly forged by this land called Keweenaw. This is their story.

Part I

Clovis
11,200 BCE

Part I Dramatis Personae

Dorn......................A young man

Burgo ....Dorn's best friend

Kathe .... Leader of the tribe and Dorn's father

Sariah .... Kathe's mate and Dorn's mother

Calla   .... Healer and Woman Beside Leader

Huko .... A man of the tribe and a great warrior

Apia .... Huko's mate

Rochek .... Huko's son

Leah .... Dorn's love interest

Jefers .... Man of the tribe

Sofoa   .... Jefers' mate

Fila .... Woman of the tribe

Cakana .... Leah's friend

Gala .... Leah's friend

Pitra   .... Dorn, Burgo, and Leah's friend

Dabra .... Apia's friend

Garath .... Man of the tribe, and Rochek's friend

Joga, Dirk, Lio, Bulak, Kobo, Sham ....

        .... Men of the tribe

Chikel .... A child of the tribe

Lalkpo .... Man of the Others

Chapter Two: Home

"Ema! Appa!!" Scared, Dorn cried out for his protectors. He was thirteen and nearly Man, but his sister died last winter and he felt lost.

His tribe had been traveling north toward the base of the Laurentide ice sheet where beasts traveled. The glacier forming Lake Superior slowly breathed life into the earth, so slowly to seem beyond time. Definitely beyond Dorn's perceptions. West and north of their travels as close as Ontonagon, Michigan was the ancient Lake Duluth. Later, receding glaciers opened outlets for Lake Duluth to lower her water level and outline the western arrowhead shape of Lake Superior.

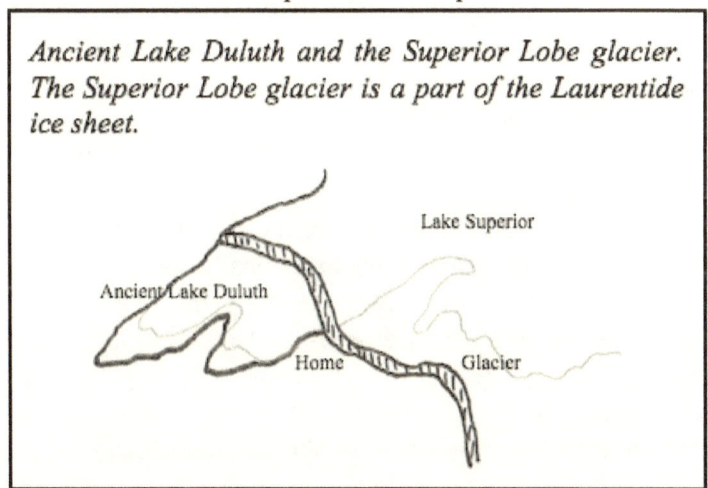

Ancient Lake Duluth and the Superior Lobe glacier. The Superior Lobe glacier is a part of the Laurentide ice sheet.

East of the tribe was what became known as Lake Algonquin. During this geological time, the ancient Lake Algonquin was nearly horseshoe shaped. The

Laurentide Ice Sheet marked its northern boundary covering northern and eastern Upper Peninsula and parts of Ontario. The lake's western boundary began at the glacier near Gwinn in Michigan's Upper Peninsula, down into what was once the western edge of ancient Lake Chicago (now Lake Michigan but was more narrow and shorter) up again hitting Traverse City and Petoskey to near Mackinaw. Then the southern boundary traveled back down the eastern edge of Lower Michigan to south of Alpena, then east into the northern part of now Lake Huron and back northeast well into Ontario to the ice sheet. The great Superior Lobe of the Laurentide glacier covered the Keweenaw in ice over a mile high at this time.

Once the Superior Lobe of the Laurentide ice sheet retreated north into Canada around 10,000 BCE, the water found different outlets that merged the ancient lakes and lowered the water level, uncovering and defining the now known land and creating Lake Superior as well as the other Great Lakes.

In the distance ahead where the glacier had paused to inhale, Dorn saw rows of mountains covered with green. Dorn's tribe headed to the foot of the mountain range and as he stepped, the earth beneath his leather shoes became more and more wet. His feet fell on pebbles and sandstone covering a large plain where the glacier had exhaled. The air was cool but the sun was warm and his heart lifted.

"Dorn! Calm and grow!" shouted one Appa of the tribe, Jefers. He reminded Dorn to become Man and Dorn quickly stepped up to his challenge. He was well formed physically but his mind had yet to enter maturity. To all youngers, all upper-generational men of the tribe were Appa and all upper-generational women of the tribe were Ema. All older members protected the youngers as much as life and living allowed. Dorn knew his birth Ema and Appa, of course, but listened to and relied on all.

Tribal members communicated with words more than gestures, but sometimes both would be spoken together. According to Raymond Scupin in *Cultural Anthropology*, people had developed the physiology of speech-making by 100,000 BCE, a good 80,000 years before Dorn's living. That would be about 80,000 years for humankind to develop the capability to tie highly symbolic meaning to the spoken word. Along this line, humankind also developed symbolic thinking. This stimulated creative thought and wonder about the world as well as the ability to see beauty. By the time the Clovis people lived, humankind's ability extended to art, music, and an engineering explosion of creativity to make a large array of tools.

"You scared, little boy?" mocked Rochek who quickly walked beside Dorn. "I'll protect you, little boy." Rochek was two years older than Dorn and had gone through his manhood initiation rite the summer before. Dorn suddenly became ashamed of himself but said nothing. Burgo, Dorn's best friend, pushed himself between Dorn and Rochek, forcing Rochek off-balance enough to nearly fall.

"Don't let him get to you," Burgo said. "He's not worth it."

"Thanks," muttered Dorn.

Rochek gave them both an icy look, then moved away.

The tribe was a very small segment of people that later became known as Clovis who populated the North and South Americas. To calm himself in this unknown world, Dorn touched his toolkit inside his knapsack. His toolkit held the items of Man: his bone knife, hammer/cutter for making points and rock or bone tools, and stone spear points, a braided rope made of plant fibers, a piece of flint, a small season stick to carefully track his growing every fall, a small flat bowl made of wood, and the small wooden artifact given to him at his passing to person and member of the tribe.

A child's birth is celebrated and given a name, but the child is not deemed person until he or she reaches six years old. Most children do not survive during this harsh time of humankind. At six years, the child is named Human and a boy is given an amulet made by his birth father for protection for the rest of life. A girl is given a bola from her birth mother that hung around her neck for protection until her menses when she became Woman. Dorn's sister, Kale, had just turned Woman. She was with her friend, Gala, trying to find wood for burning for her sacred ceremony when they encountered a pack of very large wolves. Kale never returned.

It seemed to be months of travel and everyone was tired. The sun was nearing the west when the plain began to slope slightly upward. Enough to leave the swampy beach-like land behind and into a grass-filled plain. The leader, Kathe, stopped and told them to make camp for the night. Dorn's knapsack and water bag were secured to his chest. On his back was his large pack with flat leather bands on his shoulders that were tied to his knapsack and lower straps around his waist, and a large, flat leather band he placed on his forehead to help carry the pack. He untied the shoulder and waistbands so his knapsack could fall, and grabbing the headband, lifted the pack off of his back and placed it on the ground.

Burgo let go his burden with a heavy thud beside Dorn. Dorn looked at his best friend and muttered, "Why do we have to be here? I want to go home."

"This is home," Burgo whispered back.

Burgo was not as large as Dorn, but was just as strong and agile. "My feet are still wet," he complained.

The tribe numbered twenty-seven men, women, and children. The number of people was large enough to sustain with enough food. If the number of people were too small, they would not be able to protect each other and still get enough food. Having more than one family unit also ensured healthy procreation.

Eight dogs rounded out the cache of travelers. Each dog carried a burden on a travois – two wooden poles crossed at the top behind the dog's neck and attached to the dog with a leather harness around the neck and chest so the dog pulls primarily by the chest. Beneath the harness each dog sported a lightweight blanket to keep the poles and harness from rubbing. A healthy skin made up for the slight loss of staying naturally cool. Behind the dog the poles were secured together by a bundle mostly of buffalo hides for their shelters.

The men and children carried their load similar to Dorn's. But the women pulled a sledge of poles, hides, and food. Men did not pull a sledge because they needed to quickly break free of their load in times of danger. Being larger and stronger, men's tasks were to protect and supply food, and these tasks were sacred to them. Women were also able to protect and find food, but their kind of protection was different than those of men.

While men focused on the needs of the tribe as a whole, women focused on individual needs by addressing physical hurt with medicine, by making sure food and shelter were as good as possible, and by comforting in times of hardship. However, if a man saw his life purpose following a woman's sense of protection, or a woman to hunt and protect the tribe, that was acceptable. Each person traveled his or her own life path and each respected the abilities and tendencies of the others.

The tribe stopped for the night in a dry, flat area near a small creek. Someone chose a small area for a fire and the children began to pick up as many rocks as they could find nearby to ring the pit. Dorn and Burgo tended to the dogs and released them of their travois. The sound of the excited dogs kept all predators at bay. The men gathered together and decided the best way to set themselves to protect the tribe, and then about half hunted for firewood and kindling with the older children. The women drew food from their packs and children helped carry. Most of the food was meat they had dried before they began their journey. Soon, Kathe used his flint stones and had a fire going.

By the time they had enough wood for the night, the sun was setting. Dorn stood with an armful of wood and marveled at the beauty of orange clouds shifting to blue.

"Oh Breath!" he exclaimed quietly. Burgo stepped to his side and also looked at the scene.

What? he motioned.

Look at all of this! "I wonder how. I want to know how."

"You wonder too much," scoffed Burgo. He then took the wood from Dorn and moved off to throw them by the fire and pick up his own bag.

"Maybe," he thought. "But I want to know." Dorn stood gazing at the sunset as it turned from orange to red and blue. Kathe walked up to him and immediately Dorn was embarrassed.

You will hunt with us, motioned Kathe. "When we find home."

Thank you, and Dorn bowed his head.

"You will be Man soon," Kathe said. Dorn was surprised at his candor and ventured a question.

"Am I ready?" he asked.

"Are you?" Kathe countered. "What is the most important to Man?"

Dorn knew the answer immediately. *To protect,* he motioned proudly.

To protect "what?"

People of the tribe.

"What else?"

Dorn became confused and was no longer sure of himself. "Dogs," he said.

"What else?"

Embarrassed, Dorn admitted he didn't know.

Look around you. "Everything." Kathe drew Dorn very close. "Wolf, bear, plant, rock. Everything."

"Protect that too?" asked Dorn.

"Yes."

"Protect them from what?"

Kathe paused for a moment, then took him by the shoulders and looked in his eyes. "You are my birth son," he said quietly. "When you can answer that question, you'll be Man."

"But the Man Hunt."

"The Man Hunt is only the beginning to becoming. It takes a long time to be Man. …. Come. You and Burgo stay near."

"Thank you Appa." It was an honor to be invited to stay near the men and a lot of questions ran through Dorn's mind as they walked to the fire.

To protect was the most important value to the tribe. Protecting requires caring about and for something outside the self. We still cannot survive without it.

Kathe called all members to the Breathing. They formed a circle around the fire, each facing outward and stood silently with respect as Calla, Woman Beside Leader, slowly walked the outside perimeter asking protection of the Unknown.

Awareness was the first requirement for complex life. Long before humankind, protozoan life did not engage in awareness, but rather responded to surroundings. But as life developed, response changed to awareness. Long before the Clovis people, ancient Humans became aware. Indeed, the need for survival forged awareness, for every moving creature must be aware of her surroundings to hunt and live. But unlike other moving creatures, Human awareness expanded. The nature of Humankind itself stimulated the need for explanation and at the same time survival honed their skills to be aware. Quickly during the era of early Human life, awareness birthed the perception of spirituality.

The tribe had no word for worship and no concept of religion. The closest they knew of spirituality was Breath, not relating to a god but to life itself and a deeply ingrained respect for living and the need for death. They sensed everything to be bigger than they but at the same time they knew they were connected to the earth and had no understanding of separation from their surroundings. They belonged as much as do the tree and deer, wolf and stone. They also knew their limitations as Human, and acknowledged that they need protection, for they knew they could control nearly nothing of their world. They addressed the Unknown wisdom of life, for they sensed everything to be alive. Tree and rock were as full of life and carried their own Breath as they and their four-legged brothers and sisters. Each and all had their own wisdom.

Oh Breath. Help us be thankful.
Oh Breath. Help us be strong.
Oh Breath. Help us to listen.
Oh Breath. Help us to protect.
Oh Breath. Help us be Human.

A porcupine has the ability to climb a tree, a deer to jump, a bear has teeth and claws, a wolf can run, and a moose has antlers for protection. Humans have none of these things. We have the ability to think and create until the fog lifts and we then know how to live. But that is our task: for each Human to discover his or her ability to live. And because one ability differs in type and competence from another, the Human tribe is absolutely necessary. From that necessity came rules and expectations in the quest for peace within the tribe. Each member complements the others and together in community Humans can protect, hunt, and live.

Oh Breath. Help us to live.

Calla carried the mandaka as she chanted. The sacred stick was an heirloom passed down from generation to generation. A task, action, object, word, or totem was sacred because they believed each helped either the individual Human or the tribe to connect to the earth.

The sacred served as a conduit from Human Breath to the inner Breath of all. They believed that without it, they would perish, for they would no longer be able to walk their path to becoming Human. They would no longer understand their belonging, they would be disconnected from the very earth they depend upon, and their sense of protection would be lost.

Oh Breath. Help us be one.

Feeling fear is not sustainable, and creative knowledge backed by experiences of visions and dreams conquered fear during the course of humankind. Later, scientific knowledge further diminished fear by opening opportunities to dissuade the course of fearful possibility. By the time of Dorn and Burgo's living, humankind had learnt to recognize patterns and to explain their world in creative ways. This way, we lessened our fear of the world whilst at the same time be diligently aware of our surroundings.

Rain was not in the air, so the tribe did not bother to construct their shelters. Dorn pulled his bedding of bear and wolf skins from his backpack and laid it on the ground near Kathe and motioned to Burgo to join him. When his friend hesitated, Dorn gave him a face that clearly insisted. Suddenly, Huko grabbed Dorn's bedding and threw it toward the women.

Go! he motioned.

Kathe dropped his own bedding and quickly stepped to Huko. They silently stood face to face. The encounter seemed like eternity to Dorn.

"My birth son," Kathe said quietly. Dead silence as the tribe watched. The custom for everyone to voice an opinion was strong in this people. But once the leader made a judgment, all were expected to follow without complaint. They believed the tribe to be more important than the individual and Kathe was well aware of his role.

Finally, Huko quietly said, "Not man."

Kathe paused and considered Huko's objection. He then turned to Dorn and said, "Truth. Your time will come Dorn." Disappointed, Dorn picked up his backpack and knapsack, moved away from Huko, and picked up his bedding. Burgo sauntered over to Dorn.

"That was fun," he said.

"Shut up."

They walked to the opposite side of the fire and lay out their bedding.

"Who wants to be with them anyway Dorn?" *Look at them.* "They're too serious. No fun."

Dorn's birth-Ema, Sariah, closely watched the encounter and saw Dorn's disappointment but did nothing to comfort. She knew that to grow partly means to learn to handle not getting what he wants and interference would damage Dorn's growing as well as embarrass him.

The men huddled close and obviously in debate. Dorn wondered why Huko seemed angry all the time. Some of the women went over and sat next to them. It was time for closeness. The men quickly stopped the debate and no doubt talked about the path tomorrow.

Burgo shook Dorn out of his reflection and turned his attention to the younger generation. *Look*, he motioned. The girls noticed Burgo's attention and giggled to each other. One caught Burgo's eye, and he felt as if he would melt.

"Why do they grow that way?" pondered Dorn.

"Who cares?" counted Burgo. "I like it."

"They're so different."

"They are. It's a mystery really."

Then Leah came into view. Every time Dorn saw her, he couldn't help but feel protective. He wasn't yet fourteen, but imagined her black hair against his skin. Her skin was darker than usual, and he found her to be magnificently beautiful.

Suddenly a sharp pain. Laughing, Burgo had punched him and Dorn doubled over.

Desperately trying to hide his pain, Dorn gasped, "Why you do that?"

"I did you a favor."

"You worm."

Burgo stood up. "I'm hungry. Come on, stand up." Dorn just looked at him from the ground. "Come on." Burgo helped Dorn stand and they moved away from the campfire toward the dogs who had returned. "You can play with the dogs. Make you feel better."

"You're not my friend."

"You're figuring that out just now?"

Dorn and Burgo took their bedding and dragged it nearer the dogs. Dorn laid out his bedding, sat on it, and gazed over again to the women and girls. He was proud to protect them. He knew that ultimately that was his role in life, to protect the tribe.

The children handed out the food to both humans and dogs. Nobody ate until Kathe began. It was a time to remember the sacrifice the deer made for their living. Even the dogs were silent.

As he was chewing, Dorn felt a faint whisper of wind lift his hair. He was grateful for the dried meat, but was looking forward to the tribe finally settling down and finding fresh meat.

The men were quietly in disagreement. Huko pointed south. "We've come too far. It's getting colder here." *We will die.*

"Stop it," said Kathe. "You'll put fear in the people."

"You don't know what you're doing. Your arrogance will kill all of us. We must return."

"And have our women be slaves? No."

"They won't be slaves."

"They won't be human. They won't be women."

Look at us! "We are stronger. We should rule over women," countered Huko.

"You find none of that in Earth. The four-legged don't separate their kind. If we did that, it would cut our tie with Earth."

"You're wrong," said Huko. "I side with Takara."

"Then why did you leave with the rest of us?"

Without answering, Huko saw the women coming, moved away from Kathe, and pondered silently. He looked over at the women and found Calla staring at him. He felt she knew his deep secrets and he didn't like it.

After traveling a few days, the tribe could see the glacier now called the Superior Lobe. Blue/white in color, they could see the deep cracks on his face as he sloped slightly north and climbing so high his height was out of sight. The west side also sloped. They could not tell that the east side also sloped hundreds of miles away. The Late Wisconsin Laurentide ice sheet held about 2.6% of the world's water. The area of the Laurentide ice sheet called the Superior Lobe that the tribe encountered began to move south 30,000 to 27,000 BCE. By 26,000 BCE, the ice kissed the land upon where the tribe stood. By 21,000 BCE, he rested at his southern border near

Ohio. The Superior Lobe then retreated to the world the
tribe knew around 11,200 BCE. Twelve hundred years
later, Lake Superior and the surrounding land would rest
and be as we know it today.

The people of the tribe looked at the glacier and were
both awed and frightened. They had never seen such a
massive and overwhelming entity before. It reminded
Dorn of the vastness of the sky and the beauty of the
sunset. He knew to respect him.

"What is he?" asked Burgo.

His question remained unanswered, but that evening,
the tribe talked at length. They decided to travel
forward, more out of curiosity than courage. If the entity
were to hurt them, even kill them, they thought to be
killed by such an entity would be a good way to die. The
glacier was not a god to the tribe, but an entity of nature.
They decided to name the glacier Laskibiski, meaning
earth-whiterock.

The tribe decided to head northwest toward the
glacier's western slope near what is now known as
Ontonagon. The glacier had already pushed up and
formed the land, but there came a time when the tribe
walked on short grass dotted here and there with maple,
pine, and birch trees. The land near the glacier needed
time to build her soil and seed with grass and trees. Near
the glacier, the tribe could see the barren moraines of
rock and dirt. They could not know that the moraines
marked a time the glacier paused to deposit his rock,
when he knew a balance of climate. It was that pause of
rest from inhale to exhale. The tribe stopped at a large
meadow of short grass without many trees. The few
trees that dotted the landscape did not block their view of
their surroundings.

Standing on high, level ground, the tribe recognized home. North, sunlight reflected off the south face of the glacier and onto a narrow body of water as black as dusk. Water was trapped in a vastly deep and long and narrow crevice of the Superior basin. The wind picked up the water's surface and it tumbled into the rocky shore. Beneath the glacier, large rivers of melting water carved the earth to give depth to the lake as well as facilitating the glacier's movement. As Dorn looked closer to the deep water's edge, he could see that the water had broken rocks upon the shore and ground them into small, sometimes sharp bits. But the rock stained the water red from iron, and the shoreline was also stained red. Dorn picked up a rock that has been shorn in two, wondering where the red came from.

"Even rock can be moved and broken."

Fearful, Dorn turned and saw his father. *You startled me,* he motioned.

"If I startled you, then you need to be more aware," Kathe said.

Yes Appa.

"Your life could depend on it." Kathe touched his shoulder and walked off to be with another member of the tribe. Dorn watched him and marveled at his father. But the Earth soon refocused Dorn's attention. He placed the rock back to where he picked him up.

Off to the northwest they could see ancient Lake Duluth. Her cold dark blue water already teemed with fish. Nobody knows how or why fish came to travel the streams to make the ancient lake their home. To the immediate south and east, the forest grew more and more dense. They believed the earth would provide for them there.

The sun told the tribe it was late afternoon and everyone was exhausted. They decided to spend the night on their bedding and take their time tomorrow to set up Home. The next day, there was an air of excitement when they woke to the warm sun and cool breeze. After food, Kathe called everyone together and all the members of the tribe decided who would be where and where the center of Home would be. The consensus did not take long. Three men went hunting together into the forest, leaving the dogs behind, whilst the rest of the tribe set up Home. Only Calla did not participate in building shelters. She roamed the area with the mandaka to bless the space, quietly calling on Breath and ritualistically inhaling and blowing. When she passed nearby, people would pause in silence out of respect and awareness until she passed.

The kind of shelter that early humankind built depended on terrain, natural resources, and engineering knowledge. Evolution targeted and enhanced a species' attributes for successful living. The outer appearance of *homo sapiens* did not change and evolve very much like other species who had their own attributes. But the brain evolved quickly. Challenges and problem solving differing in need and intensity developed the human brain over hundreds of thousands of years, and the more complex the problems, the more acceleration of the evolution of the brain. In technologically developed areas, we see this demonstrated today in very young children who know how to navigate a computer whilst their great-grandparents struggled to turn one on and place a cursor.

The tribe stood on the cusp of the upper Paleolithic and Mesolithic eras. (Depending on the source, some would say they lived in the Mesolithic era.) The Pleistocene Epoch lasted until about 10,000 BCE but the giant fauna like the nearly eight-hundred pound American Lion (*Panthera Leo Atrox*), the short-faced bear (*Arctodus simus*) standing six feet on all fours, the Dire Wolf (*Canis Dirus*), and the American Cheetah (*Miracinonyx*) were still roaming the earth during the tribe's living, although they had been vastly reduced in number. By 10,000 BCE these giants were gone. The tribe experienced summer and winter, but the climate was much colder than today by about nine to eighteen degrees Fahrenheit or five to ten degrees Celsius. Overall, summer and winter were more in balance than today because today's continental climate happens without glaciers. Glaciers tended to block the low-lying cold air from coming south, so despite the overall lower temperatures, summers were cooler and winters were warmer than today in North America. Also, ice trapped earth's water, so rainfall was significantly less than today. With a stream nearby, short grass, level terrain high enough to see their surroundings, and forest in the near distance, the spot was paradise to the tribe.

Once in a while during their journey, the tribe would find a small cave, but all were inhabited by bats, along with the smell and filth. They knew the best shelter for them was a tipi shaped structure, that the tribe called *wagino*. Children found rocks to outline the tribe's main fire pit. Dorn, Burgo, and other older youngers searched and found pointed rocks and started to dig postholes. The adults untied all of the long, flexible posts and set them around near where the shelters would be.

The first shelter built was for Fila and her family. She was pregnant and the travel was difficult for her. Sofoa pulled Fila's bedding from her poles and Fila could then lie down whilst other members of the tribe built her shelter. Being pregnant, Fila connected to creation that was sacred to the tribe. Indeed, Fila reminded the tribe of the value of woman and their place as part of the creation of Earth itself. While Fila knew of her role, she also knew that she could not survive without the community of the tribe, so she was always grateful for their concern and help.

Sofoa looked at Fila being helped with petty distain. She has yet to have a child and believed the others saw her as worthless, even though most did not. She looked at Apia, Huko's mate. "She is weak," Apia whispered.

Working together, the tribe tied and placed poles in the holes as they lifted them upright. Then they filled in the rest of the poles, bound together with leather ropes. Finally they placed thin, finished skins on the poles, securing them with porcupine quills, and leaving a flap at the top they could move to release smoke and another flap for a door. Together, the tipis surrounded the tribal home hearth, leaving a large area around the fire pit. The tribe placed bedding on the floor of each tipi, and then Dorn and the others dug a shallow trench with an outlet around each in case it happened to rain. Women and children walked near the forest to gather wood for each home and for the fire pit.

Look! motioned Burgo. The three men were returning, carrying a deer. Tonight would be fresh meat. They did not gut the deer before bringing him home, as the tribe used nearly all of him in some fashion or another.

They traveled about two-thirds of the distance between the forest and the camp when a small pack of wolves stepped out of the forest. Dogs saw them first and alerted the tribe of danger and began to approach the wolves. But the men called them back. The tribe shouted to the men and they walked more quickly. They did not run and neither did they drop the deer. Meanwhile, the men took up their spears and approached the incoming men. The wolves were not dire wolves but smaller yet still dangerous. The wolves hesitated. They had never seen nor smelled human before and did not know how to attack or if they should attack. But they knew the humans were in their territory and they smelled the kill. The three managed to get to the tribe before the wolves broke into a run. The women took the deer and tied it tightly to the trunk of a nearby tree. Men and dogs against wolves. The wolves broke into an attack run but the men stood their ground. Dogs obeyed and stayed.

Huko picked up a stone, placed it into his sling and threw as hard as he could. It landed center nose of the Alpha who went down but got back up, dazed. The other wolves, confused, stopped their run and that's when the dogs hit them. By that time, the men were nearly on top of the wolves as well with spears hitting home. It did not take long for the wolves to surrender and run back into the woods. The Alpha was dead as well as about half of the small pack. The tribe knew that they would not come back.

The dogs sustained a few punctures, but the only serious hurt they got was a dog who was slashed by a wolf's teeth. But the women knew what to do and eventually the dog could run again with his scarred shoulder. The women released the deer from the tree. They tied it in case the wolves overran the tribe. By tying the deer to the trunk of a tree, the wolves would not have been able to take the entire deer. But the wolves hesitated. The women then tied the deer to a branch to dress it. A few men took the dead wolves and tied them to be dressed as well.

Kathe walked up to the dead Alpha wolf. "This was not necessary," he said. "There's enough for everyone, brother wolf. It seems that we all have something to learn in order to live together."

Huko moved and stood at Kathe's back, but did not surprise Kathe. "There's more to all this than what you see," said Huko.

Kathe turned to face Huko. "What do you mean?"

"The wolf is not human. The wolf has his nature and we have ours. You don't seem to see that," said Hugo.

"Is it the nature of human to want more than what he is?" asked Kathe.

Huko paused and stared at Kathe. "My name is Man. And I will be who I am." The two again stood up to one another.

We are all connected, replied Kathe.

Your blindness will get us all killed Kathe.

"Huko, if we separate from the Earth, we will no longer be human."

"Being human doesn't mean we are the same as all the rest of Earth, Kathe," Huko countered. "We are made to walk different."

"Of course we're different," said Kathe. "Just as the wolf and the deer are different. But I think you mean to rule over wolf and deer just as you mean to rule over woman. But all beings in life are fulfilling their purpose and we need to honor that. Everyone – wolf, deer, tree, human – remembers their purpose. We all must remember who we are and become awake from this sacred dream so we can return home. If we do not honor connection to Earth, we become lost."

"Ack." And Huko walked away.

Meanwhile, Calla took her mandaka and whispered words to the animals so their breath would return to the earth in peace. Each member of the tribe touched each animal to honor their sacrifice. They knew that without sacrifice by their four-legged brothers and sisters, they would perish. The tribe felt no guilt in killing to eat. Their rites destroyed a sense of guilt that could be a consequence of their awareness. Humankind sees all four-legged people of the Earth kill in order to eat and they know death and sacrifice is part of a sacred circle of life. Being connected to the Earth partly means that whilst other people – that is, other species – do not seem to be aware in the same way as does humankind, they know that they themselves are aware and they sense a great responsibility in their awareness. Just as the great mammoth keeps the Earth in harmony with her unheard but deeply vibrating voice, so does Humankind's awareness of Earth's circle keeps the Earth in harmony. Because of this responsibility, the tribe takes the rites and perceptions of their relationship with the Earth very seriously. By concerning themselves with the welfare of the earth, humankind can continue to be awake and connected. For in the welfare of Earth lies their welfare.

The tribe gutted and skinned the animals. They kept the stomach of the wolves and carried the intestines into the forest to dispose of them. They then untied a wolf, cut off his head, and laid down the carcass for the dogs to feast. They would dry the rest of the wolf meat for the dogs. Brains were always kept for tanning.

When skinning, they left a thin layer of meat against the skin enough to assure they did not cut the skin. It also makes it easier to flesh. They loosely rolled and tied the hides, placed them in the stream, and placed rocks on top of them so they would stay under the water and not float away. The women had time to address the deer and wolf meat before needing to attend to the pelts. Dorn, Burgo, other older male youngers, and some of the men walked to the forest to cut or find thin trees branches to build several racks for drying meat and working the pelts. They stripped the poles of bark and branches.

The tribe used as much as possible of every animal they killed. Sharpened, antlers were good weapons and awls. The pelts of the wolves would be for decoration and bedding and, with the hair removed, anything other hides can give. Deer hides gave the tribe their clothing, tipi covers, shoes, straps, and just about anything else. Rawhide means they stopped the tanning process after a soaking and they can shape the hide to make bowls, containers, cut and sew to shoes as soles, drum heads, and knapsacks. Once dry, rawhide items are hard.

Hooves gave the tribe glue, bladders and stomachs were used as medicine or bags for food or water, tendons were made into sinew for thread and string, including stitching up wounds. Bones transformed into plates, spoons, scrapers, needles, and weapons. Teeth placed in a dry bladder tied to a stick made a rattle for babies.

Accumulating items is deeply ingrained within the human psyche. The tribe lived at a time when settling down for a long period of time was not yet possible. Now that they found home, however, they could stay in one place long enough to make and keep items they need to ease their living and express their artistic bent as well as to survive. Later, with the advent of agriculture and increased population, the Neolithic people could stay in one place. Then, items eventually became a sign of prosperity and wealth. A sense of worth related to quality and number of items came into being as well as the path Humankind walked into creating economy along with class structures and discrimination.

But despite the Clovis people populating both North and South Americas, they had not yet entered the Neolithic age. Items were seen as tools, and because creating them was very difficult, people of the tribe simply cooperated with one another. The women decided which tools were needed with input from the men who told them their needs for weapons. This was because weapons and the use of tools to make them were but a fraction of the overall needs of the tribe. That way, also, men were free from such decisions. The tribe saw the items as communal until something was given to an individual, like bedding, a replacement part of a tipi, or a rattle. But more likely than not, whatever they made belonged to the tribe and anyone could take and use. Underlying every item, the tribe knew gratitude for the Earth from whence it came.

That first night, the tribe feasted and danced. They did not have a concept of prayer. They danced knowing their breath belonged to the Breath surrounding them. They danced for home.

And for the first time, Dorn and Leah gazed through the fire and smoke and saw each other with an intimate sight. Burgo noticed, leaned over to his friend and said, "You're done for now."

Without taking his eyes off of Leah, Dorn replied through clenched teeth, "Shut up."

Chapter Three: Leah

"Oh breath! Are you sure?" asked Burgo.

"Yesssss. I'm sure. Now will you or not?" asked Dorn.

Early summer was wonderful to the tribe. By now, their home looked lived-in. They had dug a shallow, narrow trench around the perimeter of the camp and placed sharpened poles pointing outward. They dug another trench slightly on the outside and placed poles to support the fence poles. Children played inside their fenced home. Here and there were racks for drying meat and working hides as well as other smaller racks for drying clothes and anything else they needed and wanted to do. Women had scoured the land and found plants for medicine and food. Burgo had made a drum out of rawhide and a small hollow tree he found in the forest. Fortunately, it had not yet begun to rot. Cutting to size, removing the bark, and smoothing the outside and inside gave it a pleasant sound. He took a leg bone and wrapped and tied a soft piece of pelt on one end for a drumstick.

Downwind, women and children had created another fire pit and were braining hides again. The smell was pungent. They had a large turtle shell to use for braining and cooking. They kept the brains of a deer and boiled them in water by placing hot stones from the fire in the water. Braining a hide was necessary but as usual with all stages of working hides, it was labor intensive.

Some had found broad-blade grass south of the camp and Leah was making a basket, along with others. Dorn couldn't keep his eyes off of her.

"You do this," said Burgo, "and you'll be throwing away a lot of fun times."

"Are you kidding? It'll be nothing but fun times."

"Oh, I see. It's all about you then."

"I'm a man now and I got needs." Leah looked their way and they both quickly moved out of sight behind a tipi. They both leaned back side-by-side against the tipi and sighed.

"Have you ever even talked to her?" asked Burgo.

"Of course I've talked to her."

"Really?"

After a pause, Dorn replied, "No, but I've talked plenty with my eyes. Plenty."

"And now you plan to mate with her."

"You don't understand, Burgo. I have to. I HAVE to."

"You're not a man yet Dorn!"

Dorn lifted his arm and showed Burgo his armpit. "See? I got hair. I'm a man."

Burgo quickly grabbed a couple of hairs and pulled them out. "Not anymore."

"Ah BREATH!! You worm. You worm!" Dorn hissed in pain. "I hate you."

"And I hate you too." The two again leaned against the tipi they were hiding behind and paused, looking at the sky that was a darker blue during that time of Earth.

"So you gonna do this or what?" asked Dorn, still looking at the sky.

After a pause, Burgo sighed. "Fine. But I don't think the elders will let it happen Dorn."

"Okay. Let's do this."

The two snuck around to the opposite side of the camp from Leah.

They paused and Dorn looked at Burgo. "What?" asked Burgo.

"You gonna get it or just stay here kissing grass?"

"Oh." Burgo snuck around and into his tipi and picked up his drum, then back to Dorn. "You'll make a fool out of yourself, Dorn," Burgo said, making one last effort to save his friend. "She won't want you."

"She wants me." Burgo looked at him. "What? She wants me."

"Okay. Let's say the sun won't come tomorrow and she wants you. The elders have to agree and they won't." Dorn just stared at Leah across the fire pit. Burgo gave in. "Fine."

Burgo stood and stepped from behind the tipi. With solemnity and great importance he slowly walked to the fire pit, slowly and steadily beating his drum. Dorn stood and stepped in sight. Once Burgo arrived at the fire pit, he turned and pointed to Dorn. Dorn slowly, in rhythm to the drum, walked to Burgo.

By this time, they had the attention of the entire tribe. Burgo then pointed to Leah and Cakana stepped forward. Burgo rolled his eyes. *No* and pointed to Leah again. Leah stepped forward. *Yes.* She turned to her friends, then turned back. Slowly, she walked to the rhythm of the drum toward Burgo and Dorn.

About half the distance, the elders came out of shock. They quickly moved between Dorn and Leah before she closed in. Chaos. Calla quickly took Leah to her tipi. Burgo stopped drumming and an elder took his drum. "What I tell you?" Burgo accused.

"What? No! Wait!" Dorn pleaded.

Kathe pointed to his tipi. *Go!* Dorn gave up and started walking to the tipi. Burgo tried to mingle with others but Kathe caught him by the back of his neck and shoved him toward the tipi. Calla walked back to the others and they talked a long time whilst Leah and Dorn/Burgo were left alone in their separate tipis. Rochek tried to get near enough to hear, but he couldn't. This was a meeting of elders and he could not be a part of it.

Dorn and Burgo were silent for quite a while. Finally, Burgo said, "I'm hungry. What about you?" Silence again.

"How can I be so stupid?" Dorn asked.

Burgo thought and said, "Just your nature I guess."

Kathe and several other male elders entered the tipi. Dorn and Burgo stood up. "Appa, that was all my doing."

"Sit down." Burgo sat down.

"Burgo had nothing to do with it. It was my idea."

"Sit ... down," Kathe commanded. Dorn sat down.

"So you want to mate with Leah," stated Kathe.

"Appa, I have to!"

"Did Leah know before today?"

"No," said Dorn. "No," Burgo echoed.

"A man and a woman will mate ...." Kathe began.

"But Appa! I'm a man!" Dorn raised his arm to show the hair in his armpit. "See?"

"Oh Breath," Kathe sighed. The other elders tried not to smile. Burgo wanted to disappear.

Dorn stood to reveal more hair. "I can show you more!"

"SIT … DOWN!!" Dorn sat down, along with his unfulfilled proof.

"The tribe says no," Kathe said firmly.

"But Appa! Someone will mate her! I know it!"

"No."

"Look at her! Who doesn't want that?"

"I don't," said Burgo. Everyone stared at him. Finally, Burgo said, "Well, I DO. Who wouldn't? But Dorn here …"

"Be quiet," Kathe commanded.

"Okay."

Kathe quietly said, "Dorn, we have the way to live for a reason. Just as a wolf pack has a life together so do we, and the way we live is for survival as well as becoming human. We are Clovis. We are tribe."

"You don't understand," choked Dorn.

"We understand more than you know," Jefers said.

Kathe continued, "The tribe says no … for now." Dorn perked up. "But there are some very hard rules for you son. You may be with Leah, talk to her, do things with her…. But you may not have her."

"I … I can be with her but not have her?" Dorn stammered.

"Yes. Do you understand?"

"No! I don't understand!"

"You will not touch her, Dorn. There's no argument or other thinking with this. Do you hear me?" asked Kathe.

"I … I … yes."

"Burgo, you will be with them whenever they are together."

"Me?" Burgo asked.

"Yes Burgo. You. If they cross the line, you are to tell me or any elder. You are responsible. Do you understand?"

"Okay," squeaked Burgo.

"But Appa," Dorn whispered. "Someone else will have her."

"That will be her choice," Kathe whispered in return. "But neither Leah nor you are woman and man yet. You will abide by our law in all things."

"What if she chooses someone else?"

"Then she chooses someone else."

Dorn felt defeated and slumped. Early humankind learned Law concerning relations, for they discovered that interbreeding was dangerous. The tribe did not remember when the Law about mating was first formed, but it was as ingrained as was awareness of their surroundings. Both tied to survival. The Clovis people had much similarity but not quite the complexity concerning these laws as did the ancient Australian Aborigine that was studied and revealed – and deeply respected by the Aboriginals – by Ronald M. and Catherine Berndt, who were cultural anthropologists from the University of Western Australia. Humankind could only mate within their generation. Nobody could mate a blood relation. And absolutely nobody could mate with a girl who had not come of age. Neither could a boy mate until his initiation rite when he comes of age. For this reason, every three years, the tribes gather together for the tribal festival. But Kathe and Calla's tribe were already mixed by unfortunate circumstances. Monogamy was not considered during early humankind; it wasn't a known word. People could mate with more than one.   Except for this tribe, women usually outnumbered men. It was a dangerous life for a man.

"Let it be said. Let it be done," Kathe commanded. "If you ever misuse a sacred way again, you will be banished from the tribe. Do you understand?"

"Yes. I understand," Dorn said.

"Burgo?"

"Okay."

Kathe motioned them to get up. "Come. You know what to do."

Early humankind knew how to handle infractions and justice in order to keep the tribe together in unity. For such a minor infraction, Dorn, Burgo, and Leah were required to be a part of a ritual to expel them and then to accept them back into the tribe. The purpose was to satisfy any and all bad feelings tribal members might have toward them and to demonstrate consequences. Nobody was afraid of the consequences of the boys' actions, but had someone gotten hurt, the custom was much more harsh.

Dorn and Burgo walked to the center hearth and stood there. Members of the tribe got spears and surrounded the hearth. Any person who did not want to participate did not have to do so. Someone beat a drum and that began the ritual. Tribal members used the back of a long spear and hit the two boys, but not hard enough to seriously hurt them. They drove Dorn and Burgo out of the fenced-in home with shouts of "Get out!" "We don't want you here." And "You were wrong!" etc. People of the tribe did not walk past the entryway. Once outside the fence, Dorn and Burgo turned and bowed to them. They then walked to the forest. Soon, Kathe, Dirk, and

Jefers joined them and stood next to them. They said nothing.

Then it was Leah's turn and they did the same to her. She entered the woods a ways from the boys. Calla and Sariah joined her. The drum continued to beat.

The men then left Dorn and Burgo alone and returned to the compound. After a while, Burgo quietly spoke up. "At least you get to be around her."

"This is the worst day of my life."

"Hey, Dorn. She wanted you. Remember?"

That perked Dorn up. "Yeah! She did, didn't she? She was willing to mate with me!!"

"Yeah! So now you can really talk to her and be around her. That's not so bad. Just don't touch her."

"Yeah. I can do this."

"Okay, Kathe is back at home. Let's go," Burgo said.

The two friends slowly walked back to the compound, and just outside the entrance, bowed. The drum stopped and then silence. Everyone was waiting. Then the drum began again and the boys entered the compound. This time, people surrounded them and one-by-one, Dorn and Burgo apologized. Each person placed a hand on his shoulder, chest, or head. Most of the tribal members said something usually positive to them, but that was not required. Sariah told Dorn that he was a good human. Huko called both Dorn and Burgo an idiot. Rochek did not participate but smirked at them.

Once the tribe was satisfied, it was Leah's turn. Calla and Sofoa returned to the compound. Then Leah. Drums stopped, then started, and Leah apologized. Afterwards, the incident was considered finished by tribal custom, even though Dorn, Burgo, and Leah felt badly for a while.

That evening, Dorn and Burgo sat together in silence, watching the reactions of the people. The elders acted like nothing happened. But Leah had been crying and her friends tried to make her feel better. Calla and the other women elders had said the same thing to Leah as did the men elders to Dorn and Burgo.

The next day, Burgo sat next to the center fire to make an atlatl. The atlatl lengthened the throwing arm so when hunting he could throw a spear harder and at a longer distance. He was shaping a stick that had a natural cradle for the short spear and was using his knife to cut a notch. He had learned to throw very accurately, but had lost his atlatl when it fell into a river while they were traveling north.

Leah was getting ready to help with braining a hide. That morning, a couple of women continued to boil the brains until they could break it into small pieces. When the mix became a lightweight goo, it was ready. They were waiting for it to cool. The hide also was ready. They had scraped both sides so the hair was gone. Once the brain mixture was cool, Leah and other women smeared the goo into the hair side of the hide that was laid out on the ground.

Dorn finally got up from his depression and saw what Leah was doing. He quickly walked over to Burgo and grabbed him, lifting him up. "Come on, let's go." Burgo's stick, knife, and protective piece of leather scattered. Burgo broke Dorn's grip on him and stepped back.

"Will you just stop?!"

What?

What! Burgo picked up his stuff.

"Leah's over there," pointed Dorn.

"Really? You want to mess with that stuff?" Burgo asked, meaning the brain goo.

"Leah's doing it so I want to."

"Oh. I see. You want to mess with Leah." Dorn stood there helpless. "Come on then."

They walked over to Leah, Burgo sat down to watch, and Dorn helped himself to the goo. A woman smiled knowingly at Dorn, stepped out of the way, moved to another hide, and let Dorn help smear the brain water on the hide next to Leah until they were done. There were four hides, so it took a while. They said nothing to each other, but Leah was obviously happy he had come over.

Garath poked Rochek and got his attention. "Look at the fool," he said.

Rochek saw that Dorn was near Leah and his blood began to boil. "That boy will not see the light of day," he muttered.

"What are you gonna do about it?" asked Garath.

"Dunno yet. But the time will come for me and I'll take it then." Garath and Rochek moved away and went about their business before anybody noticed that Rochek wanted Leah. It was forbidden. Both Rochek and Garath were two years older than Dorn and had gone through their initiation rites together, so they were considered men and were not allowed to speak to girls. Of men, only the elders could speak to them. But Dorn and Burgo were not yet men, so they could speak to Leah and her friends.

When finished, Leah and Dorn folded the hides tightly, put them in a tipi structure out of the weather, and placed rocks on top. Dorn didn't go into the tipi. While the others took a piece of soap and walked down to the stream, Dorn and Leah stood face to face, silent for a long time, brain water dripping from their hands.

"Hi," Leah ventured.

"I saw you over here. I was over there," Dorn said, pointing.

"Oh breath," muttered Burgo.

"I was here…." Leah said quietly.

"… I know. I saw you.… I'm sorry about last – "

"— I'm not."

"You're not?" Dorn's heart leaped.

"No."

"Why not?" asked Dorn. Leah laughed a little out of embarrassment. "I'm sorry. Didn't mean …."

"Calla said we need to see each other. I don't see you and you don't see me."

"I see you!" Dorn said a little too loudly.

"Dorn. No, you don't. Calla said it will take time," Leah said.

"Oh.   Whatever you say."   They stood in silence staring at each other.

"You do know you two are all wet, right?" Burgo asked.

"Oh," Leah jumped, giggling. "I suppose we should…"

"Yeah, okay," Dorn said grinning.

Leah moved away to walk to the stream. Dorn stood his ground, quietly admiring her. "Move," Burgo said shoving him from the back.

"Okay. Okay."

"You're an idiot, you know that?" Burgo asked as they walked to the stream. "'I was over there.' Really?"

Dorn stopped and slowly turned to Burgo who also stopped. "Peuckle me." They both laughed at that and continued toward the stream. Women were returning from the stream and looked at them with amused interest.

Burgo said, "We're going hunting with the elders when they go."

"You can. I'm staying here."

"No, you're going hunting."

"Why?"

"Because I want to go that's why. And I can't go unless you go and it's my turn to do what I want."

"Yeah, it's your turn. Your turn to do what I want," Dorn replied.

"Funny. You're funny Dorn."

They got to the stream and Leah had already washed her hands. She saw Dorn and threw the soap at him. He saw it coming too late and it hit him in the face. In trying to catch it, Dorn got brain goo all over his face. Leah, embarrassed, laughed and quickly returned to the camp while Dorn awkwardly picked up the soap and washed.

The elders saw what was going on, but had learnt the art of disguising whilst seeing so the youngers didn't know. That seems to be a human art learned later in life after having children, and still resides in mothers' memory. They also understood that human emotions needed to be tempered in order to live peacefully in a tribe. More importantly, perhaps, is the affect of the discipline of human emotion has on human development, to help a human walk a healthy path for oneself.

That afternoon, Dorn saw Leah talk to Dabra and they then talked to Calla. They gathered women and girls together and they went out to pick up stones. In an out-of-the-way area inside the camp walls they started to carefully build a stone structure. They placed the stones carefully, trying to fit each stone to be supported by the stones underneath. The stones rounded the walls into a roof and enclosed a space, making a circular structure with a hole big enough to allow people to enter. Once the stones were up and securely supported by each other, they made clay with the soil near the stream, short grass, and water. The women carefully smeared the clay onto the cracks of the stones both inside and out. This way, the structure was secure and safe. There was no smoke hole, as they did not plan to have a fire inside.

Dorn and Burgo did not know for whom the structure was being built, but they recognized their actions as intimately Woman. They did not inquire or even talk to each other about it. Dorn got his atlatl and some short spears and he and Burgo went outside the camp. Burgo sat and finished his atlatl whist Dorn practiced throwing. Burgo finished the cradle notch, smoothed it down with a porous rock, wrapped the handle with a thin leather strap, and tied a weight next to the cradle to put some extra strength in his throw.

That evening after food, Leah surprised Dorn. She brought Pitra who agreed to be their physical bond. Pitra was man woman and a gentle and kind human. Born male, she and the elders knew very soon during her growing that her breath did not follow the male path. Now grown, she stayed and worked with the women. They considered a neumeen to bring luck to the tribe, and the women welcomed a person having more physical strength than usual to help.

Pitra did everything a woman did except the most intimate of woman activities. So she did not help build the stone structure and even though she understood, she felt badly. She tried not to show it, but being unable to be a complete woman sometimes made her feel lonely and an outsider. No member of the tribe indicated anything but belonging to her, but not being able to mate or bare children or be included in the women's intimate activities sometimes brought feelings of seclusion and regret for who she is. Leah knew Pitra would be completely trustworthy, and her proposal to Pitra made her very happy at a time when her differences made her sad.

Leah sat Pitra down in the circle and told Dorn to sit next to her. Leah then sat on the other side of Pitra and held her hand. Dorn soon held her other hand. Burgo rolled his eyes, but secretly was very happy for his friend. From then on, the four of them were often seen together and Dorn and Leah touched Pitra in ways they wanted to publicly touch each other, usually holding hands or leaning on each other. After a few weeks, Leah could tell that this opportunity felt good to Pitra and told her that whenever she needed a closeness that she would give that to her. Pitra never misused her role and became more and more wise and discerning concerning these very human needs. She liked her becoming and the tribe thought it was good too.

Once everyone was comfortable around the main campfire that evening, Calla decided to tell a story about their heritage. They had heard it several times, of course, but it never got old to them. Calla stood, her long, braided hair shot with gray made her look wise. She wore a long leather tunic and pants as did the other women, but hers was decorated with colored stone that were traded over a long period of time amongst the tribes. Later in the living of Humankind, such an array of emerald and ruby stones would make her tunic nearly priceless. But at that time, people did not care of such things. (Men wore a short tunic and pants.) Calla bored a hole through each stone, then sewed it on the fringe of her tunic. She was beautiful. She began, "A long time ago, all people of Earth had one language, and all of us could hear and understand each other. The tree people, the grass people, all the plant people, the stone people, the winged, the four-legged – like Breath, all knew the same language.

"But then Raven came and called, and Humans could no longer hear the language of Earth. Humans thought themselves superior because they thought they were smarter than everyone else. They could take what they want, when they want, and forgot to ask. They could no longer see people of Earth or hear them cry as they took. The four-legged, the winged, plants, and rocks knew the way of the heart and mind and were sad because the Humans could no longer hear.

"So the wolf said, 'I will live with them to help them return to the Way.' And wolf became dog to Humans. Dog listened to the heart of Humankind and quickly knew Human language, but Humans still struggle. All our brothers and sisters of Earth still know the language. They have their wisdom, and dog and all others want to teach us the First Language again. Once in a while, dog teaches the Way of kindness to open up the heart and listen and a Human learns to hear.

"By respecting them, by calming our mind with gratitude and kindness, and opening up our heart as we stand before Earth people, we can learn this language again. And we can speak to the other Earth people, and we can listen to their wisdom. They are our teachers, and by watching and honoring them, we can go back into the

Way and walk our path toward becoming." She then sat down and the tribe talked quietly amongst themselves.

Huko stood. "Why do we teach our children such things?"

Kathe stood in reply as well as Calla and he and Calla approached Huko. "What do you mean?" Kathe asked with anger in his voice.

Calla quietly interjected, "So they can walk their path to becoming."

"Becoming? Becoming what?" asked Huko impatiently.

"Becoming Human," said Kathe.

"Don't be stupid!" Huko said. "We're all human! We're already human! We're Clovis. We're the people of Earth!"

"You mean people over Earth," Calla said quietly.

Huko stood his ground. "Of course I mean people over Earth!"

Kathe grew angry. "What is this, Huko? Why do you need to dominate? Why do you want to put yourself in that place? You must know what it means ... to say that women are lesser, that our four-legged brothers and sisters are to be killed without gratitude. Are you so very blind that to dominate, to set yourself higher, will eventually lead to death for us? I've seen you, Huko. I've seen you kill without thanks, just kill as if you wanted to kill, as if you think it makes you a man. You kill our Mother Earth without thought, without awareness. You take away your own humanness. You destroy your own heart when you dominate and take."

Huko moved close to Kathe. "I know who I am. I know where I belong."

"Everything belongs, Huko," Calla said quietly. "Everything has a purpose. I think you forget that."

"You can't fool me, Calla. I am Man. I am Human. And I have the right to take what I want."

Calla said, continuing to be quiet, "But what kind of Human are we to be Huko? Are we really to take what we want? Without thinking? Without caring?"

"Yes!" Huko said. "We need to rule this Earth! If we don't, we will die. We're weak, Calla."

Calla replied, "We're weak because we've lost the first language and we need –"

"There is no first language!" Pointing at Kathe, "You want us to remain weak!" Huko declared. "You want to rule us!"

"Is that what this is all about? You want to be leader?" Kathe asked.

Huko stepped back and quieted. "No," he said. "I want us to live. I want us to take what we need without all this magic and superstition. We are Human and we already rule. But you don't know that. You are stuck in your own mind."

Kathe stepped up to Huko. "You are arrogant," he said. "You will walk a path so far from Human that you will give sickness to Earth. If not you, then your children's children if they become like you. You will take what you want without the wisdom our Way teaches. You will take what you want without care and someday you will no longer be Human."

"No," Huko said. "I want us to survive. I want us to live. I want us to be fully Human."

"Your way is not the Way," Calla said.

"Your way is saying that a dog is better than us!" Huko bristled.

"No, I –" Calla began

"Necan, come here!" Huko called. A dog came to him. "To you, we are like bugs in his coat." He grabbed the dog and held her tightly. "What's the first language, Necan? What can you teach me Necan?" The dog whimpered.

"You're hurting her!" a child cried.

"Huko, no," Calla said quietly.

"Hurting her? I'll kill her!" Huko exclaimed, drawing his knife and putting it to the dog's throat. The children became upset and started to cry.

Kathe drew his knife. "No!"

"You see what you have done? You've made our children weak!" Huko said, angrily.

Apia, Huko's mate, stood and took the dog away from Huko, letting her go. "Enough of this," she said. "You will never make them understand."

"I will teach my children the other way," Huko said. "I will teach them how to be Human."

"Is it worth upsetting the balance of the tribe?" Kathe asked.

"I am Human. And I am better than a dog," Huko said quietly. He and Apia then went into their tipi. Rochek followed.

"Let's go," Kathe said. The tribe then went to their own hearth.

"He doesn't know his own power," Calla quietly said to Kathe once alone. "His way leads to destroying Earth. Then we will die. His children's children will die and we will be no more."

"As long as there are Humans who know the Way, we will heal."

"Perhaps."

A few days later, a few women and most of the men as well as Dorn and Burgo started their day's travel toward the glacier. Some of the dogs traveled with them to carry bedding on a travois and to help with the hunt. Like the others, Dorn carried his knapsack, atlatl, short spears, long spear, and water container. It was time to begin to prepare food for the winter and that was a lengthy and labor-intensive process. For the first time since being a united tribe, they were trying for a mammoth. It was a dangerous venture.

Just outside the camp, Leah and Pitra came up to Dorn and Burgo. *Protect yourself. Protect the others*, Leah motioned. She then gave Dorn a small amulet she made out of bone. She had carved a pine tree on it. He thanked her and put it in his knapsack. Leah then hugged Pitra and Pitra hugged Dorn.

Thank you, he smiled.

"Yeah. I'll be okay too," Burgo said. "Thanks a lot."

"Shut up Burgo," Dorn replied. The two friends continued the journey with the men and women to hunt. Dorn turned and stared at Leah walking back to the compound with Pitra. Burgo grabbed him and pushed him along with him. Both were looking forward to the hunt.

Moving away, Huko came up to Dorn and walked with him. When separate enough from the others, Huko quietly said, "That's ridiculous."

"What is?" Dorn asked.

"You want Leah. She wants you. So just take her."

"You mean ....?"

"I mean take her. She's a woman and you want her so just take her," Huko said emphatically. "What you're doing is embarrassing the tribe."

"But the tribe said no, and I'm not a man yet –"

Hitting him on the back, Huko said, "You look like a man to me." He then walked more quickly and joined the other men.

But Leah was not yet a woman. The stone structure was a sweat lodge and it was Leah's, friend, Cakana, who went through the sacred ceremony. She had her first menses that ended a few days before and it was her initiation ceremony into Woman.

The travelers came upon rolling hills of tall grass near the glacier. They saw a large herd of mammoth in the near distance and decided to move toward the glacier to prepare for the hunt. Nearer the glacier was rock and dirt that was the moraines. Once on the moraines and out of sight, they gathered together without building a fire and sat down. Without standing, Kathe picked up some black dirt and let it flow out of his hand. He chanted:

Oh Breath, let Earth provide for us.

Oh Breath, thank you for the sacrifice.

Oh Breath, protect us as we strive to live.

The others then repeated the chant quietly together. "It seems like Laskibiski will not hurt us," Kathe said, meaning the glacier. "This is a good sign." Suddenly, Jefers quietly said, "What's that?" alarmed. The others did not stand but laid flat on the ground, trying to keep out of sight on a barren land. They told the dogs to be silent. The dogs were well trained for hunting, and silently laid down with the travois still on their backs. They saw a creature rise from the foot of the glacier and walk toward the trees. It was long and tall, with what looked like scales along its back and sides, spikes down its back, and the head of a mountain lion. Its head had horns, and the long tail ended in copper. The tribe saw the copper as a fire. It roared "MIPEASHU! MIPEASHU!" The tribe couldn't see who or what the monster was roaring to. Slowly, it went into the trees.

Suddenly, the sky changed to black, the wind picked up, and they were pelted hard with rain that came with a ferocious storm. Thunder roared and lightning danced against the glacier, making it look alive and glow. With Kathe's direction, they slowly crawled out of the moraines and, hunched, walked away from the trees into the tall grass. They untied the dogs from their travois and told them to lie down and be silent. They took half their bedding and spread it out on the grass, told the dogs to get on, then lay on the bedding and covered themselves with the other half of their bedding. It was tight but kept them out of the rain. The grass kept them camouflaged and the dogs kept them warm. They did not speak. All they could think about was the earth-being that came from under the glacier. After a while, they took some food out of their knapsacks, ate, and slept.

The next morning was a cloudy, crisp day. The tribe ate and rose. The men took off their tunics for the hunt. They did not want to overheat or become entangled. They noted where the mammoth herd was and prepared their weapons for the hunt. Each had a long spear, and an atlatl and short spears. A short spear was shorter than a spear but longer than an arrow. (Humankind had not yet invented the bow and arrow.) Every spear had a Clovis point – an arrowhead about four inches long and three-quarters of an inch wide at one end tapering to a point at the other – notched and tied. Each of the short spears also had a fletch of feathers. Dorn and Burgo knew to do exactly what they were told when they were told. There was no time to disagree, question, or debate. It was Huko's role to direct their movements and actions, as he was well known by the tribe to be the best hunter. Kathe had no problem with that. They stealthily moved through the tall grass toward the mammoth herd in the distance, leaving the women behind. About half the distance to the herd, they told the dogs to stay.

The women quietly and slowly took the travois and placed bedding on them. They then moved slightly into the trees out of sight of the herd. After placing bedding on the tree limbs to dry, they waited. All members of the tribe were downwind of the herd.

The tribe believed that the animal who sacrificed his life became aware at his end. He knew before he died that his purpose was fulfilled, and that belief helped the tribe know deep gratitude for Earth and for the animal. They did not hunt for sport any more than did their four-legged and winged brothers and sisters. They hunted to live. They found no pleasure in it, just necessity, and they were aware that their actions were a part of Earth's way of life. Most believed that if they became disconnected from creation too far, their skills would diminish, animals would refuse to sacrifice, and the tribe would die.

The men stayed low in the grass until they could manipulate the herd. They saw a young bull limping and obviously in pain. The tribe looked for any advantage and Huko motioned that he was the target. They got close enough to try to divide the herd.

All eyes were on Huko. Joga and Derk to the left. Kathe and Lio to the right. Huko, Jefers, Rochek, Dorn,

Burgo, and Garath up the middle. Huko gave the sign and they took off. The herd panicked and started running left. Derk hit the target in the front chest and that turned him toward the right. Whistle. Dogs came and chased most of the main herd away from the target. The target turned away from the main herd. Huko yelled to Dorn and Burgo to get between the target and the rest of the herd. Rochek found himself near Dorn and Burgo. Kathe hit the target in the leg. But the target was still among part of the herd. Whistle. Dogs ran back. Whistle. Dogs cut the target from the rest of the herd who ran toward the main herd. Dorn and Burgo had to scramble to keep from being trampled. Lio, Joga, and Derk hit the target, making him blind with fury. Desperate to get back to the herd, he suddenly seemed to become enemy instead of prey, turned around and charged Dorn and Burgo. Dorn went right and Burgo left. The others hit the target. The target went after Dorn who ran toward the main herd. But Dorn could not outrun the mammoth. Rochek seemed to try to help Dorn, but he tripped him, unseen by the others. Dorn stumbled to the ground, including his weapons, but he got up, turned, and grabbed the tusks and hung on with arms and legs while the mammoth tried to throw him to gore him. Out of his mind with anger, the mammoth passed near Burgo. But by then, Burgo had his atlatl ready. Burgo stood his ground. Just as the target passed, Burgo hit him in the back of his hind leg, severing his tendon. The mammoth went down. Still fighting and trying to rise, he went after the others who kept hitting. But Huko threw his atlatl spear with all his might and the point went into the mammoth's heart. Kathe followed with his long spear. The mammoth was dead. A little dizzy, Dorn was finally able to jump off of the mammoth.

Kathe was red with anger. "You put the boys between him and the herd?"

Huko flared just as angry. "Of course I did!"

"Why?"

Huko hissed, "Look around you! Who could die first? A man or a boy?"

"I should have been placed there!"

"Don't be stupid!"

Dorn hit Huko in the chest. "You can't talk to him like that!"

"Why not?"

"He's ... he's my father!" shouted Dorn.

"SO AM I!" And Huko shoved Dorn hard enough to hit the ground. "Stay out of this!"

Kathe drew his knife. "I've had enough of you."

Huko stopped short and looked at Kathe. Then he laughed. Joga joined in laughing, then Lio. Kathe was confused. "Kathe, you see these two as if they are children," Huko said, quietly. "They're not. I put them between this one and the herd because they are the best runners here. As it was, he turned, and it was Burgo that brought him down. You're too old to have lived through that."

Kathe looked at Huko and put his knife away. "I'm sorry."

Huko then laughed with the rest of the men. He and Kathe clasped arms and Kathe laughed at himself. Huko said to Dorn and Burgo, "You both did well today."

Their attention then went back to the mammoth. The men became quiet. One by one, they touched the mammoth in gratitude. It took some time, but Huko cut open the mammoth and removed part of his liver. He took a bite, then went to Kathe, then the rest of the men who in turn took the liver and ate, then passed it back to Huko. The last were Dorn and Burgo, but being last did not separate them from the others and they felt a kinship with them. The dogs also were given a piece of the liver.

"Better luck next time," Garath said to Rochek. Rochek shrugged him off.

The women came to the scene, dragging the travois. They built a couple of tipis with the travois poles and set up racks for drying meat. They then got firewood and prepared a fire pit. The men put their tunics back on. Most would stay for a few days to handle the work.

All the while, a pair of eyes peered from the edge of the forest and saw all that happened. When the women walked toward the forest for firewood, the eyes disappeared.

Some of the men also walked to near the forest and dug a pit. The area was a home for mammoth and they wanted to be able to return with more ease than this first venture. Other men started to skin the mammoth and dress him. Dorn and Burgo helped dig the pit.

Out of sight, Rochek quietly walked to Huko and said, "Well played, Appa." Huko turned on him in anger and grabbed his hair, pulling him down.

"What is that supposed to mean?" Huko quietly growled.

"Nothing! I mean, you fooled them," gasped Rochek.

"Things are not always as they seem, Rochek. And sometimes they are." Huko then let go his hair and Rochek crawled away, but not in time for Huko's kick to the side of his chest.

The tribe did not always cook the meat. Once cooking became a staple in human living, tooth decay started to become a problem. But they did once in a while, especially after a fresh kill. But this adventure was to preserve meat, and that was a whole different ball of tallow.

Culture and individual preference determine how and what a person eats. During this age of humankind, accumulating food for future use was necessary but preserving food was difficult if not impossible. Besides drying meat, they ate putrefied meat and fish, and being contaminated by bacteria was not much of a health hazard. As for the smell, they were "nose blind". The tribe considered maggots and grubs to be a delicacy, and fried on a pelvic bone with fat over a fire was a treat. Their idea of preservation was to dig a pit and line it with birch bark. They placed the meat in the pit, then more bark, then stones, then dirt, and left it there perhaps for months before consumption. Being putrefied, the meat was soft and often fell off the bone. The tribe often did not cook it before eating it. Tastes like chicken.

Rancid fat is toxic however. The men cut off as much fat as possible when skinning the carcass and stored it in a rawhide bowl. The best fat came from around the organs, especially the kidneys. Later, women cut the fat into small pieces and placed it in a bowl over a low fire to slowly melt the fat. After several hours, the fat separated from the tissue and the women strained it into another bowl through a leather cloth in which they had poked small holes as a strainer. They set the cracklings aside to feast on later that night and carefully poured the liquid fat into small bladders supported by small wooden bowls. The women let the fat harden overnight. The next day, the fat was hard and white, and the women tied the bladders so air would have difficulty getting in. They mostly made the bladders out of cleaned, cut, and tied intestines. The tallow would last as long as a year and was a good source of nutrition, giving vitamins B6, B12, K2, potassium, selenium, niacin, phosphorus, iron and riboflavin. Women made soap and lotion out of stored tallow as well as using it for eating and cooking. Later, humans made candles out of tallow as well.

The tribe could not lift the mammoth, so they worked one side at a time. They skinned the animal and cut the pelt in pieces. They loaded some on a travois for the dogs to carry and Dorn, Burgo, and Jefers also carried pelts. The tribe and the dogs took the day-long journey back to camp with no incident. Jefers led the way and the two walked behind.

"I wonder what Leah's been doing," Dorn mused.

"Probably hugging Pitra," Burgo responded.

"Shut up."

"Thinking of you and touching Pitra here and here. And here."

Dorn dropped his baggage and tackled Burgo. They both fell on Burgo's baggage and tore the ties, scattering pelts as they wrestled. Jefers broke it up by smacking both their heads with the back end of his long spear. Dorn and Burgo suddenly thought more about that pain than the cause of the fight. "Hope you two are finished because we've got half a day left to get to home," Jefers said. "We don't want to get caught out here after the sun dies." Dorn and Burgo sullenly picked up the pelts and retied them.

At the mammoth camp, the men cut off a back leg and threw it into the pit. Some of the women covered it with birch bark, then rocks, then dirt. The other women began drying meat.

Dorn, Burgo, Jefers, and dogs arrived home at dusk. They unloaded the pelts. The rest of the tribe will take the pelts and begin the process of tanning it, leaving the hair on. Mammoth pelt was a very effective insulator from the cold that was soon coming.

Dorn looked around, then panicked. "Where's Leah? Where's Leah?" Sariah, Dorn's birth Ema, came up to Dorn.

"She's here Dorn. She's here. But she can't see you right now."

"Why not?" Sariah looked at Dorn, then it dawned on him. "She is? She IS?"

"Yes," Sariah replied. "She's in Calla's hearth now," and left him to attend to the pelts.

Dorn approached Burgo who was more interested in eating than anything else. "Burgo, she's doing it!"

"Doing what?" Burgo asked with his mouth full.

"Becoming a woman!"

That stopped Burgo. "She is? That means ... that means she's going to be a woman!"

"I always thought she was."

Just then, Pitra came to them. "You'll never guess what's happening! ..."

"Yeah, Pitra, we know. "

"You know! You know! Well, now I'm hurt. I wanted to tell you." Pitra then gave them both a bear hug.

That evening, the tribe did not take food to their individual hearths, but everybody ate together after cooking some of the meat. It was a festive time.

After eating, everyone gathered around the center hearth wanting a reenactment of the hunt, even though most of the hunters were still at the site. Burgo and others got their drums and others had hollow tree limbs that made different pitches when beaten with a hard stick.

Jefers stood and said, "We got to the great Laskibiski and he didn't hurt us. But then something came from the water under him. I've never seen anything like him! He was a dragon with scales and a long tail that ended with fire. He had the head of a mountain lion with horns and roared 'Mipeashu!' and in the trees we heard the sound of 'Bisi! Bisi!' and the trees moved as if they were walking. Not like moving in the wind." The tribe wanted to know what they did. "Nothing! He didn't know we were there, but right after he entered the forest from the water, a great storm came with water and wind and light and sound and I thought we were all going to die but we didn't." The tribe talked excitedly to themselves for a while and asked Dorn and Burgo if it was true and they said yes.

Once the crowd calmed down, Jeffers told the story of the mammoth hunt, with quite a lot of exaggeration that was fun whilst others made music noise with their instruments whenever they felt like it. Jefers described the hunt and held up the dog, Traco, as an important asset. Early humankind saw dogs as willing participants in the life of the tribe. They did not own them and had no word for ownership.

He mimed Kathe as slowly lumbering along as an old man and people were delighted at that, even though Kathe was not there at the presentation. Jefers mimed and yelled as Dorn holding on to the mammoth's tusk for dear life, and then Burgo making the shot. At that, Burgo stood and bowed and everybody clapped. Jefers then mimed the death of the mammoth and that sobered people because they knew the sacrifice. But then, Jefers yelled for more meat and the presentation was over and the festive atmosphere restored.

Humankind engaged in theatre, ritual, music, painting, and sculpture since we began to live as a community. Jefers' performance united the tribe as well as entertained. It is an asset of humankind to have an artistic and creative bent.

The tribe sat together and talked well into the night. They found it difficult to separate after experiencing such closeness. "Come on you two. To bed with you. We have a long journey ahead." Jefers said.

"Oh! Can I sleep with you?" asked Pitra.

Which one? Dorn asked.

"Silly. Both of you of course! I can't sleep with the women right now."

Okay. Come on. Burgo motioned. They all piled into Sariah's home.

The next day, Dorn, Burgo, and Jefers along with the dogs started the walk back to the mammoth camp. Pitra ran up to them carrying a basket. "Can I come? Sofoa wants the brains and I can do that." Jefers looked at his mate, Sofoa, and motioned that Pitra will come this round. Sofoa motioned back that it's okay.

"Ema!" Leah had never known her own Becoming like this before. "I'm scared."

Calla held her and soothed her fears. "The Earth has touched your womb, Daughter. You are becoming a creator."

"I hope I never go through this again!"

"I'm sorry child. What is happening now will return."

"Why?" Leah gasped.

"The Earth must rebuild you, Leah, until you can no longer create."

"Are you still able to create, Calla?"

"No. My time has passed. When you can no longer create, you will help those who can, and protect them and their youngers. It is a sacred time for women.... Here, it's ready. Drink this." Calla had made medicine from a poplar tree – the same ingredient as in aspirin – to relieve Leah's pain.

"Calla, Why does it hurt?"

"Many reasons, Leah. The hurt prepares you to birth a child. But the hurt is also needed for your becoming. You must become the best of human; and know that all of Earth – brothers and sisters, as well as humanity – experience pain from time to time. Pain is a part of life and it will help you see Earth and humans."

"Ugh," Leah felt pain.

Calla just chuckled. "You'll get used to it."

Two days later, Leah felt much better. It was time to experience the sweat lodge. Most of the women stopped what they were doing and attended to this sacred rite. An act is sacred when a human believes it will serve as a conduit from this physical be-ing to becoming aware of belonging to something larger and outside the self. To the tribe, that awareness connects to Breath and the sacred act opens the possibility that the human will experience Breath in all. By that experience, the human becomes acutely tied to the tribe, Earth, and all of creation.

Outside the lodge, the women placed stones in the central fire. Once hot, they will take them and place them in the center of the sweat lodge. Leah entered and sat opposite the doorway. Calla sat next to her. The only other person to go into the lodge carried in a hot rock and removed the cooled rock. Calla placed a bladder full of water next to her. She brought in an empty basket and the mandaka. She also brought in hallucinogenic tea that would help Leah find her inner self. Calla found mushrooms that the tribe calls ayahu in the forest. While other mushrooms are either toxic or edible, the toxic ayahu is mild when made as a tea. The ayahu mushroom has long gone extinct.

Leah and Calla settled themselves in the lodge. It became very dark when the flap was covering the entrance. "What is your role, woman?" Calla asked.

"To protect the tribe," Leah answered. Long silence. Then Cakana, Leah's friend, came into the lodge with a hot rock and placed it in front of Calla. Leah noted right away that Cakana's role in the rite was an honor to her. Calla threw a little water onto the rock and it steamed. When the steam happened, other women outside sat in a circle and sang to the beat of the drum. They will continue to sing and steadily beat the drum until Leah exited the lodge. Periods of silence in the lodge were necessary for Leah to delve deep within herself.

"What is your role, woman?" Calla asked again.

"To protect the tribe," Leah answered.

Hours passed with Cakana entering and exiting, and Leah became frightened because the constant steam became distressing to her body. But she did not complain. Calla noted her suffering.

"You are meant to suffer, woman. Suffering hurts, but it helps you Become. As long as you have life, you must suffer and be grateful for it. When you suffer, and you see its blessing, then you will be aware of another's suffering and you can bind with that person. You will be able to know that everyone else suffers too. I lost four babies before they could be called Human, and the suffering of that loss was very painful to me. But now, right now, I love you in ways I could not do if I had not known that loss. So knowing that, I can see suffering as a gift and be grateful for it."

"You wanted your babies to die?" asked Leah.

"No. You never want suffering or pain, or loss. I wish it did not happen. But it did happen and it does happen, Leah. It's a part of living within the Breath. Pain and suffering helps you know deeply within yourself, and you can connect with other people and even with creation. Gratitude also helps us become."

The steam kept coming and Leah was overwhelmed. Calla asked again, "What is your role, woman?"

"To be the tribe," Leah whispered.

"You are ready then." Calla touched Leah on her head with the mandaka, and Leah responded by vomiting. Fortunately, Calla was quick enough to place the basket under in time. Calla then had Leah drink the tea. "Now is the time for you to find yourself, Leah. Look for your earth be-ing and speak the first language." Calla laid Leah flat on the ground, took everything she had brought in, and left the lodge. She returned shortly and sat with Leah.

Dorn, Burgo, and Jefers returned with another cache of pelts and meat as well as Pitra with a basket of brains. Dorn noticed Calla leaving the sweat lodge and decided to sit and wait quite a distance away from the lodge. The elders noticed but said nothing. Fila gave him something to eat.

Leah was grateful that the steam was finished. She was also happy to be lying on the ground. She couldn't move and didn't want to. The darkness started to close in and then she saw light through fog. She was flying. Through the fog, she could see Dorn sitting on the ground and waiting, then the fog obscured everything. A red mountain lion walked through the fog toward her, then turned around and started to walk back. She saw herself walking side by side with the lion, then she changed to a raven that flew with the mountain lion. The red mountain lion then jumped and caught the raven who struggled then escaped and flew higher and higher. Suddenly, flying, she saw the glacier, then the glacier was gone and in its place was a vastness of water, then she saw buildings rising, then smoke. Everything was burning. Then she saw forest again and within the earth she saw veins of bright rust-orange metal. Finally, she heard one word: "Love."

Leah woke as if she had not been drugged. She saw that Calla had been sitting with her, but they said nothing. Both Leah and Calla knew that Leah's vision was hers to keep. Exiting the lodge, she saw Dorn stand and she smiled at him. The drums stopped. Leah felt gratitude and a closeness to the tribe she had not felt before now and she cherished it. The women came to Leah and embraced her. She spent the next day sleeping.

Dorn, Leah, Burgo, and Pitra spent most of their time together helping the tribe prepare for winter. Three mammoths sacrificed their lives for the tribe as well as several deer and a bear. Every tipi was well insulated with mammoth hides.

Dorn sensed a shift within Leah. She was Woman now and, well, different. Older but not superior. They still spent as much time as they could together and now that Leah was woman and Dorn was not man, both knew it was forbidden to touch.

One day, Calla came up to Leah with a batch of tea. Cakana looked at it and said, "Oh, I know what that is."

What? motioned Leah.

"Here," Calla said. "I will teach you how to make this. You are to drink a little every morning."

"Why?" asked Leah.

"There is a time for everything, Leah," Calla said. Cakana giggled.

"Well, how long must I drink this in the morning?" Leah asked.

"Until you choose, my dear. Sometimes a man will take what you don't want to give. It's every woman's right to say what happens to her and her body."

After drinking the tea, Calla left. Leah just looked at her. "What was that about?" she asked Cakana.

"You don't know anything, do you? Amazing!" Cakana laughed. "Mushrooms are wonderful!"

It then dawned on Leah what Calla meant. Rochek might try. She wanted only Dorn.

Rochek knew the change in his fortunes. He was free to interact with Leah. Several times, he gave Leah small presents: a bouquet of flowers, an amulet, a bracelet. Leah was kind, but said no each time, and each time Rochek grew more angry, although he didn't show it.

Leah, Dorn, Burgo, and Pitra were in the forest gathering wood. Rather, they pretended to gather wood, and decided to set up a camp for the night. The next day, the four friends wandered the forest, and felt a closeness to the trees and wind. "Where are we?" Pitra asked.

Dorn became alarmed that they had wandered far from their makeshift camp. "Dunno," Dorn answered.

"Are we lost?" asked Pitra.

Leah laughed and said no. "I got lost once though and had to find a way to connect to the First Language.

"What do you mean?" asked Dorn, as all four sat on a log.

"I felt lost," she said, "and panicked. I felt alone because I thought that I would die soon. So I sat down on the ground and tried to ..."

"Why wasn't I here to protect you?" Dorn interrupted. "Where was I?"

"You were hunting with Huko," she replied.

"Shut up, Dorn, and let her finish," Burgo said. "Where was I?"

Leah laughed, "With Dorn, silly."

"Okay," said Burgo. "You may continue." Dorn lightly punched him.

Leah continued, "I sat down on the ground and shut my eyes and tried to relax. I opened my heart to connection and suddenly I could hear them sing."

"Who?" Pitra asked.

"Our brothers and sisters of the earth. The trees. The rocks. The grass. They sang. It was if they were set free. Then they talked to me. They said, 'Which way is the wind-breath?' 'Over there,' I said. 'Where are the moss and mushrooms on us?' they asked. Suddenly I knew where I was and how to return home. They then said, 'We are here for you and all your kind.' I wasn't scared anymore. I wasn't alone."

"I've known that," Pitra said. "I know what you're talking about!"

"I don't get it," Dorn said. "Where were you?"

"The moss and mushrooms grow on the other side of the trees than the wind-breath," laughed Leah. "I knew how to get home."

"Which way?"

"That way, silly!"

"But how did you know that way is home?" asked Dorn.

"Ugh!" sighed Leah. "Do you not know how the wind-breath blows when you're home?"

"Um."

"From that way," Burgo said, pointing. "Oh. I get it. You knew how to get home."

"Men!" Leah exclaimed.

"Hey, Dorn, she called you a man," teased Pitra. Dorn smiled.

"But how did you do that? I mean, hear the Earth?" asked Burgo.

"I opened up my heart," Leah replied.

"I think I understand," Dorn said.

Burgo looked at him. "You do?"

Suddenly serious, Dorn stood close to Leah and quietly asked her, "Leah, once my man hunt ends, will you mate with me?"

Burgo shoved him to the ground. "Not now, you idiot! You can't do that until after!!"

Leah laughed at both of them but said nothing.

Dorn heard a rustle in the forest but said nothing about it.

Dorn then shoved Burgo. "You all go on. I'll try to hunt a little for fresh meat."

Burgo hesitated, but they picked up the gathered firewood and walked back toward their camp.

Dorn watched as they disappeared out of sight. "What do you want, Rochek?"

Rochek stepped out of the shadows and faced Dorn. "I don't care who you are. I don't care who your birth Appa is. Leah is mine."

"She doesn't want you," Dorn countered.

"I will take her," growled Rochek. "Whether she wants me or not."

"That is not the way of the Earth."

"Who cares!"

Rochek swung at Dorn, hoping he'd contact and that's the end of it. But Dorn was very agile despite his size, and Rochek missed. They fought, each connecting, until finally Rochek got the upper hand. "She's mine," he gasped. "Say it."

"Never," Dorn gasped. Rochek got a hold of a rock and hit Dorn in the head, knocking him out. He then was in process of kicking him when out of nowhere Burgo attacked Rochek and rolled him away from Dorn. With atlatl in hand ready to strike, Burgo stood over Dorn and said, "Leave him alone." Defeated, Rochek moved back into the forest.

Burgo sat next to Dorn and looked at him for a long time. He then took some water and revived Dorn who looked at him and asked, "What happened?"

"You decided to go hunting," Burgo said. "Without weapons. Now sit up."

"Ugh. My head," Dorn complained.

"You should see Calla," Burgo said. "And then go to the elders."

Dorn sat up and thought a little. "No," he said. "Nobody can know what really happened here, Burgo."

"But he could have killed you."

Dorn paused. "I know. But there would be too much attention about it. I think that's what he wants. And then I think he'd lie and I'd end up being the attacker. Let's not give it to him."

"What if he tries to hurt you again?"

"I was stupid leaving my weapons at the camp."

"Me too. We'll have to remember to bring them from now on."

"Yeah. And not be alone. He won't touch me when people are around. Not until after the man hunt. Okay?"

Burgo paused. "Okay. Let's go home." At the camp, they joined Leah and Pitra and walked home.

When they got back home, people asked about Dorn's face. He told them he fell down a long hill and hit his head. Calla said nothing as she stitched his head, but Dorn knew that she knew the truth of it all. But she just smiled and nodded.

She also tended to Rochek's face. "Do you love her?" she asked. Rochek responded by suddenly grabbing her arm and stopping her from smearing healing lotion on his face.

"Did he tell you?"

"No." Rochek let her go.

"I want her," he stated.

Calla continued to paste the lotion on his wounds for a moment. Then she said, "How can you gain love when it's bought by hate?"

Rochek flared into anger and stood over Calla. "Your power will get you killed some day."

"I can help you, Rochek," she said quietly.

"You're just a woman." He then left her tipi.

The good news for Dorn is that Leah tended to him and said nothing to Rochek, even when he pointed his face out to her. Dorn knew that Rochek hated him even more for that.

The summer waned and the four, Leah, Dorn, Burgo, and Pitra spent as much time together as possible. Leah was quick to laugh and care about all of them. Eventually, Dorn discovered that his feelings for Leah had changed. He regarded Leah for who she is and one afternoon he realized that his caring for Leah was much deeper and more quiet than before. He sought out Kathe and stood face to face with his father. They stood in silence for a long time and Kathe did not know what was going on with his son. Neither did he ask.

"Leah," Dorn spoke finally and quietly. He then hugged Kathe. "Thank you Appa." Kathe finally knew how Dorn had changed but still remained silent. He simply smiled and slapped Dorn on the back.

Leah, Burgo, Dorn, and Pitra took packs and traveled to near the glacier one day. They stayed in the forest and Burgo hunted for food. Pitra walked to a stream to get water and then went hunting for wood to make a fire.

Leah and Dorn found themselves alone for the first time and tried to be silent and listen to the wind in the trees and the sounds of the earth. They gazed at the glacier and found themselves overwhelmed by the beauty of earth and of each other.

"You are more beautiful than the light dying," Dorn said quietly. "I wonder how that is."

"You just like my hair," Leah teased.

"No ... well, yes ... but ... Leah, I see you."

Leah hesitated and then looked deeply in his eyes. "I see you too Dorn. You are beautiful."

"We've been together for a long time now, and I just don't want to live my life without you," Dorn said. "You make me ... I can't ... I can't ..." He then made a circle motion.

"Dorn, I see you," Leah repeated.

Dorn then took her hand in his and marveled at its workmanship. "Leah, will you mate with me?" he asked quietly.

"Yes," she said simply. "Right now."

Dorn took her gently by the hair and caressed her head. She was beautifully black. Leah raised and took off her tunic, revealing her breasts to him. She then slowly lifted his tunic off of him, and layer-by-layer, both revealed themselves. Standing face to face they touched each other. She turned red with arousal. Naked, she discovered him fully aroused. They both explored, sinking into the earth. They both knew that sexuality was as natural as breath, but neither Dorn nor Leah knew the possibility of bonding until then.

Early humankind had no word for the romantic type of love. That came later in human history. To the tribe, love meant a deep and abiding caring and a profound sense of protecting. But the capability to love was as fierce in our early days as they are now. By the time Dorn and Leah mated, they both knew each other very well. By being together without touching, they matured in their relationship. It wasn't until later with a geographical section of the ancient Australian Aboriginal culture that it became custom for a couple to live in the wilderness together for a month without touching. This way, they could know the feelings they had for one another and relationships could be real. People created tribal rules to try to control sexuality for the sake of maintaining peace amongst people within the tribe.

Burgo came upon them, saw Pitra walking behind him, and they both turned away and walked to the edge of the moraines and talked for quite a while until Dorn and Leah found them. They built a fire and cooked the meat Burgo got for them.

From then on, the four were together, but Pitra was no longer between them. Both Dorn and Leah no longer needed to touch in public the way they did before. Their contact was heart to heart. Burgo said nothing whilst the four were together, but he and Dorn often talked about it and the wonder of it all. Pitra was happy for Leah. The four made trips to the glacier a few times, and every time Kathe made sure Rochek had a task to do.

Some time later, the four were down by the stream traveling to the lake to hunt for fish. They took their long spears and some line and bait. Suddenly, Leah slipped on a wet rock and fell, hitting her head. They were in water up to their knees and Leah went under. Without thinking, Dorn threw his gear onto the bank and lifted Leah out of the water. She was unconscious. With Burgo and Pitra's help, Dorn carried her up the bank, and then nearly ran with her toward the camp. Burgo ran ahead to get help. When people came near, Dorn realized that he was touching Leah and placed her on the ground. He grabbed a spear from Pitra and stood over Leah.

You will not kill her! You kill me first, if you can! Dorn motioned. He then let out a war roar that confused most of the tribe. Calla and Kathe knew Dorn's concern. Kathe stepped forward to Dorn.

"We will not kill Leah," Kathe said. "We never intended to hurt her."

"But I thought you said – I thought you meant –" Dorn stammered.

Calla bent down to Leah. "Let us have her son."

"You won't – ?" Dorn started.

"No," said Calla. "She needs us." At that, Dorn moved away and members of the tribe took Leah into the compound and into Calla's tent. Kathe stood near Dorn and Burgo and nodded. "It's time for your man hunt," he said. "You too, Burgo."

"Oh breath!" Burgo said quietly.

Dorn stopped Kathe and told him, "Leah and I have been together."

"I know."

"You know?"

"Everybody knows, Dorn."

"But … I thought …" Dorn stammered.

"No man would follow such a thing," Kathe said. He then slapped Dorn on the back and walked back to the compound. Dorn was dumbfounded.

Burgo, however, was excited. "But I haven't done anything with Cakana yet!"

"Wait … what?" Dorn exclaimed. "You like Cakana?" Burgo ran toward the compound. "You like Cakana?"

Dorn ran after him, leaving Pitra with her fish dangling. As she walked, she just watched them leave and quietly said, "Men!"

Chapter Four: The Man Hunt

Just as the sweat lodge is sacred space for women, so is the cathedral of trees in the forest for men. They chose the small clearing in the trees by how it felt. Their breath seemed close to the Breath of Life in this space and it was humbling to all of them. A sacred area was protection for them. Here, they belonged, not more than at home and other spaces, but different. They seemed to vibrate here, surrounded by tall, thin pine trees, as if Earth was speaking to them and they to Earth without words. They felt harmony. They knew that if they lived in harmony with the Earth, they would live a full life. They listened and heard the sound of the wind's breath through the trees and the melody of birds.

Nobody knows when or why the first time humankind thought it necessary to become. Men have no natural time when they become men except the slow change of voice and body. Somewhere along the timeline of early human, we thought it necessary to initiate men into society. It was probably a way to maintain peace within the community that we could not live without. We certainly cannot thrive without each other. And yet we cannot Become without change, and that means placing aside the obedience of childhood to become a separate individual both determining and living within the structure of the community or tribe.

Becoming means transformation. The point of the tribe's initiation rites was for a boy to leave the safety of home and return a man. For many indigenous people, that meant a literal scarring of the body to return

transformed. The Clovis people were no different and it
was now Dorn and Burgo's turn. In their sacred space
under a clear night with a full moon they called *chiskal*,
Kathe set out to scar Dorn's right pectoral. Dorn chose
the image of a pine tree in remembrance of Leah's gift.
Burgo chose the front view of a mammoth with large
tusks and Jefers scarred his right pectoral also. After
cutting, they packed black charcoal from the tribe's main
hearth into the wound that they brought with them. Dorn
and Burgo said nothing during this. Neither did they
flinch. Finally, they smeared a poultice made of herbs
and tallow over their wounds.

"You will know your earth be-ing and she will give
something to you so you can take her power," Kathe
directed quietly. "She may give her life, but if not, she
will give something else. You will find her. You will do
this only with a knife."

For the Clovis people, two individuals experiencing
their initiation rite together was ideal. The next trial
emphasized interdependence one human has with another
or the tribe. Some of the men beat a drum. As Kathe
and Jefers tied each wrist and threw the rope around a
branch of a tree, he said, "You will walk to the edge of
death and remember who you are. Say nothing until you
touch the ground." Some of the men pulled on the ropes,
lifting Dorn and Burgo off the ground. Their arms
stretched outward and upward. Dorn and Burgo faced
each other. They sweat with pain. While hanging, some
of the men forced them to drink a hallucinogenic tea.
They threw two knives on the ground beneath the two
friends.

Burgo was the first to realize what they needed to do.
He started to swing back and forth, back and forth. Dorn

did the same. Time became eternal to them both. Burgo then was able to wrap his legs around Dorn. Dorn gasped with pain in his wrists. Burgo lifted Dorn with his legs and he was able to reach Dorn's left hand with his right. Dorn passed out. He slowly untied Dorn's wrist and let his arm fall. Burgo then passed out, releasing Dorn. Dorn was then able to breathe again and woke up, drugged. He saw Burgo and did the same, releasing Burgo's arm so he could again breathe. Burgo then woke up. Burgo climbed the rope tied to his wrist and wrapped his legs around the branch of the tree. He was then able to release his other wrist and drop to the ground. But Dorn was too drugged to climb his rope so Burgo picked up a knife, climbed his own rope, and reached over and cut Dorn free. They both fell to the ground, too drugged to move further. If the two had not released themselves, men of the tribe would have cut them free. They would then continue with the initiation rite, but sometime in their lifetime they would need to try again.

The sound of the drum rocked Dorn and Burgo deeper and deeper into their dreams. Dorn could no longer tell dream from waking life. Perhaps there was no difference. Living his dream, he walked in a fog, unable to see his surroundings. The tribe walked into his sight. There was Leah. They then suddenly became afraid and ran. Leah stood still while people ran past, trying to get away from something. Fog overwhelmed his sight for a few moments. When it lifted slightly, Dorn then saw the tribe bound by their hands standing next to Leah. Leah walked away and the tribe left in the fog in the opposite direction.

He heard her first. Her blood-curdling sound cut the air and rushed into his mind. To his surprise, he was not afraid. Then the mountain lion appeared out of the fog next to him. She leaned in close to his face and asked, "What is your purpose?"

"To protect the tribe," Dorn replied.

"You are incomplete," she growled. Dorn smelled her breath. "What is your purpose?"

Dorn paused. "To protect everything."

She growled. "From what?"

Dorn paused again. "I don't know."

She quietly roared in his ear. "When you know, you will be Human." She then disappeared and Dorn woke.

He woke to early morning birdsong and the smell of earth. He found himself on a bed of ferns. Everyone was gone except Burgo who had not yet awakened. He felt different. More attuned to his surroundings and he still felt a connection to the mountain lion, as if he now inhabited her, or she him. He couldn't tell.

Burgo groaned, rolled over, and woke up. Still groggy, he looked at Dorn and asked, "When is it?"

"Light just begun," Dorn answered.

"I feel terrible," Burgo discovered.

"You don't look good," Dorn replied.

"Thanks."

Burgo sat on his bed of ferns and smelled the musk. The world seemed crystal clear with pure and vivid color. The sun warmed the cool air and he felt comforted by the cool wind and the gray/brown trees. This was where he belonged. Burgo stood and stretched.

"What's your earth be-ing?"

"Mountain lion."

"Oh great. That's just great. Oh yeah, that's fair," Burgo complained.

"Why? What's yours?" Dorn asked as he looked around for something to eat.

"Porcupine."

Dorn couldn't contain his laughter, although he tried.

"Yeah, yeah. Go ahead. Laugh." Burgo looked around for grubs. "Why do you always get the good stuff?"

"Hey," Dorn said, trying to be helpful. "Those four-leggeds are wicked, like you. And they can throw like you."

Burgo hugged a tree. "I have a sudden urge to climb a tree." Touching his chest, he said, "Oh breath, my chest hurts. What do we do now?"

"Well, we're not supposed to go back yet. I think we're supposed to find our earth be-ings so they can give us something. Then we can go back."

"Okay. First the mountain lion. These knives will keep us safe from a mountain lion," Burgo said sarcastically. "I'm hungry. Maybe these knives will help us kill a mammoth to eat. I'm sure that'll be fine."

Dorn looked at Burgo. "This is supposed to be serious."

"I'll bet there's not a man in the tribe who didn't think the same thing. And say the same thing."

"Yeah, yeah. Where's water? That's where we should look first," Dorn said.

"Yes, Dorn. I know that's where we should look first," growled Burgo.

"We got a plan, we got a plan," Dorn said.

Burgo climbed his rope again, reached over and cut Dorn's rope high near the branch, then cut his own and dropped to the ground. He then picked up Dorn's rope and wrapped it around his waist. He put his rope into his tunic. Dorn looked at him.

"What?" Burgo asked, annoyed.

Dorn just shook his head.

"I'm not facing a mountain lion with a knife."

"Maybe we're supposed to," Dorn said.

"So to become a man, you have to be stupid. Got it."

They both became still and quiet, feeling, hearing, and smelling their surroundings, especially for the smell and sound of water. Suddenly, Dorn threw his knife that embedded into a tree branch. "Oops," Dorn said.

"OH BREATH!" Burgo yelled. "No no no no no!"

"What?"

"He peed on me!" Burgo tried to wipe off his face. He was so agitated, he practically jumped around. "That squirrel you just tried to kill. He peed right in my face!" Burgo then heard the squirrel angrily voice his opinion on the matter. Burgo threw him a look that tried to burn into his mind. Then he said to the squirrel, "I didn't try to kill you! He did!" pointing at Dorn. "Why don't you pee on him?!"

Dorn climbed the tree to retrieve his knife whilst the squirrel scampered further into the forest. "I'm still hungry," he said.

"Why is it always me? Why can't you get peed on for a change?"

"Come on, let's go. Water's this way," Dorn said as he moved into the forest.

Burgo followed. "Right in my face."

"How ever did you live this long?"

"Shut up."

"I think there's something wrong with my knife," Dorn's voice drifted from the forest.

The two friends traveled toward the glacier, looking for streams and footprints. Eventually, they left the forest onto sparse vegetation. The moss felt soft beneath their feet. The hills had been sharply carved by the glacier as he inhaled. Soon, they were facing the glacier.

Later in the history of humankind, such a sight would prompt an overwhelming need to impose a godly characteristic onto the glacier. But during the earliest time of humankind, we were too closely connected to Earth to take that creative leap. Dorn and Burgo thought the glacier was just as alive as they were and just as much of the Earth as they were. They were nevertheless overwhelmed when confronting the glacier. He did not seem to threaten them, but they felt fear that was more akin to respect and the belief that he was an awesome manifestation of Earth than a fear leading to dubbing the glacier a god. Humankind had not yet conceived of an ultimate other having power to order and design beyond their perception. Indeed, humankind could not comprehend much of anything outside the tribe. They only knew that that they could not control, and they were used to that living condition.

The sun was mid-day, but the boys knew they needed to settle down and prepare for the possibility of danger. Dorn went back into the forest to gather enough wood to carry them through until morning. Burgo walked down into the rocky moraines and searched for stones suitable to make a couple of rough spearheads. Once he carried enough wood, Dorn said, "I'm going back in to try to find food."

"Don't miss," Burgo quipped.

"Yeah, yeah."

"Wanna use my knife?"

"Peuckle me," Dorn threw back as he entered the forest.

Burgo found two good-sized agate rocks in the moraines and a large hammer stone. He marveled at the patterns. Later, the rocks would be called Petoskey stones. Burgo did not know, but he was holding a fossilized ancient colony of coral that lived in the shallow sea millions of years ago. The glacier brought it to the Keweenaw and the sand and water somewhat polished it. It was a rare find, as today most are found in Lower Michigan, especially around Lake Michigan. He sat on the soft moss away from where they would sleep to shape the rocks. Many of the shards he knocked off could easily cut. The Petoskey stone was not ideal for shaping spearheads, but he could not find the obsidian rock his people traded from what is now known as Yellowstone. Nor could he find the flint that he was looking for in the short time that he had. Flint rock concentrated in Lower Michigan. But he thought the patterns and rather rough edges of the rock he found would help him shape it quickly.

Burgo spent the rest of the day and early evening striking and pressing the rocks into shape. Dorn came out of the forest with four raccoons. While in the forest, he had skinned, gutted, cut off the head and neck, and removed the scent glands. Knowing he could not use the entire animal, he left the remains in the forest for others to have. He also brought kindling, dry moss, and sticks to help make a fire.

"Wish I had my tools," he said, missing his flint to make fire. He placed the raccoons on top of the woodpile.

"Yeah. Me too," replied Burgo.

Dorn walked over to Burgo to see what he was doing. "Looks good, Burgo," he said.

"Yeah. Thanks. Looks like you did good, too," he said.

"I got lucky. Ran across a colony of raccoon," Dorn explained. "Got five, but one was taken by a four-legged before I could come back to get him."

"That's okay. Two will do me good. Thanks."

"Running and throwing a knife is not easy."

"How many times did you miss?" asked Burgo, laughing.

"As many times as it took to get five," laughed Dorn.

Dorn then went back to the woodpile, settled down with the materials and started to try to make a fire. Without flint, the task was tedious. Wood and friction catch whatever embers the friction created, with the dry moss to help. The sun was setting and the light off the glacier was beautiful. Dorn kept stopping to view the sky and glacier. Burgo noticed Dorn and said, "Stay with it, Dorn." Dorn finally concentrated and started a fire. Once started, he placed some of the wood onto the small but steady fire. While the wood was burning enough to make hot coals, he took the raccoons, separated the legs, the halves of the ribcage, and the spine into separate cuts. Dorn also removed the feet. He made sure to trim fat and any scent glands off the spine. Usually, he would not separate the meat, but he wanted to make sure all the scent glands were off. He then took the pieces down to the water's edge, making sure the glacier would not hurt him, and washed the pieces. He marveled at just how cold the water was, nearly too cold to drink. He then walked back to the fire, took fresh wood, placed the pieces onto it, and carefully placed it over the fire. This way, the meat would take longer to cook, but it would be more tender. Throughout history, humankind discovered ways to make living more enjoyable and easier, and the Clovis people were no different. Neither did they want to eat dirt or sand any more than we do.

Burgo finished shaping spearheads. He buried most of the shards. Some were very sharp and he wanted to keep them, but the only place to put them was in his hair. He kept two. He walked to the fire as Dorn was placing the meat onto a new piece of wood and into the fire.

"Smells good," Burgo said, sitting down by the fire. "Feels good too."

"Yeah. The cold should wake us up when the fire gets too low. So we can get it back up. Fire will keep us safe enough I think."

"Yeah. It's colder here than at home."

"Maybe he's doing that," Dorn said, indicating the glacier. "Maybe that's his purpose."

"I don't know."

"I don't know."

Suddenly, they saw a large four-legged who seemed to come out of the water and slowly move into the trees. What they saw was a glyptodont. This mammal was about nine feet long and five feet high, encased in a turtle-like shell full of scales, and sported an armored tail and skull. She weighed nearly a ton and was so cumbersome that Dorn and Burgo were not afraid of her. Soon becoming extinct, she was an herbivore and was related to the later armadillo. She ignored them as they watched her lumber along.

"Is that what we saw earlier before the first hunt here?" Dorn asked.

I don't know, Burgo motioned. "Maybe."

"What did the other one say?" Dorn pondered.

"I don't know. Michibeu I think," replied Burgo.

"This one didn't say anything," Dorn said.

"I know. I was here." Dorn picked up a rock and threw it at Burgo. Burgo looked at him and said, "Wow, you actually hit something this time. Maybe you should get closer from now on."

"Yeah yeah."

The moon was waxing and the sky clear of clouds, so light made the glacier glow. The two ate and gazed at the glacier in a kind of silence that stirred wonderment. "Did you see any footprints, Dorn?" asked Burgo.

"No I didn't," Dorn said. "I think we need to go deeper into the forest."

The two young men quietly ate together, pondering their task ahead. "I miss home," Dorn said.

"You mean you miss the tribe?"

"No," Dorn explained. "I miss everybody. I want to go home."

"Isn't this your home? I mean, isn't the tribe your home?"

"I don't know," Dorn said. "I don't understand why we left in the first place."

"Yes you do," Burgo replied quietly. "People were killing each other. You know that, Dorn. We were at war with each other. I don't understand it either really. I mean, why kill each other when we're supposed to protect each other and we're supposed to live in a tribe. I mean, Dorn, I lost my birth Appa and my birth Ema. Why … why did they die? You have yours here, but I don't. You have more home here than I ever will anymore."

"You stay with Jefers and Sofoa."

"Don't be stupid. You know what I mean," Burgo said without anger.

"I know. I'm sorry," Dorn said quietly. "I didn't understand what was going on at the tribal festival. People were very angry and shouting. I ran into the woods. Appa told me to run into the woods. Why did they kill each other?"

"Too many people wanting change, I guess," Burgo said. "I heard Huko say something about Fila and how weak she is and how other people have to take care of her. And that's the big problem."

"Her mate was killed and we're her tribe and so we're supposed to take care of her."

"I know," Burgo said. "I don't get it."

"Me neither."

"Takara killed him."

"He did?" asked Dorn.

"Yeah. I saw him."

"Did he kill your birth parents too?"

"I don't know," Burgo replied.

"Seems to me there's enough danger around that could kill us without us killing each other," Dorn said, thinking of his sister, Kale.

"It all started at the tribal festival, didn't it? A woman picked up a weapon and the leader from the Annuck tribe hit her and told her she should never touch a weapon. He knocked her down."

"Is that why the Annuck tribe and the Chao tribe started fighting?" Dorn asked.

"Yeah. She was from the Chao tribe. Then other women rebelled and picked up weapons."

"I still don't get it. Why fight at all?"

"Huko told me once while we were coming here," Burgo said.

"Why did he tell you?"

"He told a lot of people, I think trying to get them to see things his way."

"What did he say?" asked Dorn, impatiently.

"He said that the world is different now and in order to survive we have to change with it. We've been fooling ourselves that the four-leggeds are the same as us. We've been stupid to think women are the creators. They're weak and helpless without men, so men should make all the decisions and lead without women," Burgo explained.

"Kathe lead without Calla?"

"Yeah. But not just that. Men should tell women what to do and women shouldn't touch anything that belongs to a man like a weapon."

"That's strange. Did you believe him? I mean, will you follow Huko?" Dorn asked.

"Nah. It doesn't make any sense to me and we're supposed to protect. Didn't feel right." Burgo replied.

"I wonder why he didn't tell me."

"You're too close to Kathe," Burgo replied.

They sat in silence for a while. Then Dorn said, "I like to protect."

"Yeah. Me too."

Every five years or so several Clovis tribes in a region gathered together. It was a time to tell stories, catch up with old friends, a time to show off, and a time to find a mate outside their blood relations. They had strict cultural laws concerning who could mate with whom that basically said they could not mate with a blood relative, nor could they mate within a different generation. The Annuck tribe came with the agenda to rule, and it was the first festival in their memory when tribal people broke apart and gathered together in different groups for the sake of peace and survival. During the very early period of humankind, food and territory were not issues of contention, but conflicting ideologies concerning inner-tribal roles, relationship with Earth, and worth of persons broke the northernmost Clovis people.

Platock, the leader of the Annuck tribe, was a tall man with red hair who could physically crush nearly anyone who stood against him. Standing tall, he could capture people's attention and for several days loudly raged that humankind was meant to be great and above the rest of Earth beings. The purpose of humans was to dominate the four-leggeds and take what they need without the ridiculous ancestral stories and beliefs about Earth that made no sense.

He told the tribes that men were dominant over women because women need to be protected and they were weak. Without men, there would be no tribe, no people, and for this reason, men were the true creators, not women. Women were meant to serve men and that role was sacred. During his speeches, he often pointed out a woman who helped a man in an extraordinary way and praised her. For instance, Dokra nursed her mate, Nublo, back to health from an illness nobody understood. Platock praised Dokra and let people know that Nublo would not be alive without her. Dokra helping her mate was the woman all women should strive to be. To many people of the tribes, it felt good to be considered special, and they believed him. Others feared that his way led to walking away from their place as part of Earth, and believed that humankind would not survive without Earth connection.

Kathe tried to stand up against him and explain the pitfalls of such a belief, and Platock convinced many people that Kathe was weak, as weak as a woman. Platock mocked Kathe and everybody else who disagreed with him. He spread lies and rumors to the point that people did not know what was real and what was fake. Eventually, he convinced his followers to place bands on their heads and they called themselves Waynakok or Banders and everybody else they considered to be non-human. He labeled anyone not following him as Pocalo, meaning "masked illness." Pocalos should be killed because they spread the lies of the ancestors' beliefs and contaminate the true believers. He told them that the tribes in the region needed to be controlled by one man. And that man would be Platock.

Dorn and Burgo's tribe was named Vurago. The leader of Vurago was Takara, not Kathe. Takara fell to Platock's words and anger, and placed a band on his head. He vowed that his tribe will follow Platock, but many did not want to, which angered him even more. Then all the followers of Platock wore bands on their heads.

Then a woman from the Chao tribe picked up a weapon and Platock hit her. This enraged people of the Chao tribe and a fight was lit. Fila was also a member of the Chao tribe and she picked up a stone ax to give to her mate. Takara saw her and became very angry. He took the ax and hit her with it, shouting that no woman will touch a man's weapon. Her mate tried to protect her but was unable and Takara killed him. Within a full cycle of the moon, the tribal festival turned into war.

Kathe and many others escaped into the woods to run from the anger and hate. Calla took the sacred mandaka before she ran into the woods, but nobody following Platock cared. After several days, it was over. Those against Platock that the Waynakok could find were dead. Platock took his followers and returned to his territorial home.

The people who fled tried to help each other stay alive whilst in the forest. Several Waynakok entered the forest to find Pocalos and kill them, but the Pocalos climbed trees and could not be seen. Finally, the Waynakoks gave up, thinking that the Earth will kill them. Once the Waynakoks left, the Pocalos returned to a horrible sight of carnage. They could not take care of the dead according to their fashion, so they placed them side-by-side and tried to honor them. Many people gathered with Kathe and others with other leaders. The tribe Dorn and Burgo knew was without several friends and blood relatives and now included several people from other tribes, like Leah. They quickly fell into the way of living that they knew, with Kathe as leader and Calla as Woman Beside Leader.

Much of the equipment was burned, but not all. Most of the people had their knapsack on them when they fled, which helped them in the forest. They gathered what they needed – poles, covers, bedding, and the dried food they could find. Most of the dogs also fled into the forest. When they returned, they joined the people they knew. Kathe's group headed north whilst others went in other directions, just not the same direction as the Annuck tribe.

Dorn and Burgo talked well into the night, gazing at the fire. They remembered the friends they missed and the fear and horror they've witnessed during their young lives. Neither thought humankind was meant to kill each other, not like the followers of Platock did. But then there was the question that has plagued humans all during the history of humankind. They did not know it, but they discussed what would later be known as a "just war." Should we kill each other to prevent a graver killing? They had no more of a clear answer than anyone else. But they did agree that if protecting the tribe meant killing another human, they would. They had never known a human to kill another human until the tribal festival.

After a long pause, Burgo quietly said, "I wish my birth Ema still had breath."

"I wish so too. I wish we could make such things happen," Dorn replied.

"But we can't," Burgo said. "I wasn't even there when she lost breath. I couldn't sing for her. I couldn't make sure her breath traveled to the Breath of all. I couldn't protect her."

Dorn placed his hand on Burgo's shoulder. "Maybe that's why we try to protect. There's some things in this world we can't control. So we try to protect what we can. Maybe the important thing is we try."

"Yeah. Okay." The two fell silent and soon slept.

The next morning, both friends were refreshed and feeling good. They stood, stretched, and turned to enter the forest when a sound stopped them. They turned in time to see a portion of the glacier break with a loud crack. "Oh breath! Oh breath!" Several smaller portions broke from the glacier and avalanched into the water. Soon, the large portion broke with a boom and dove into the water, then rose hundreds of feet into the air. They stood mesmerized and ready to run as they witnessed glacier calving, the large portion breaking again, diving again, and slowly and loudly turning in the water. To Burgo and Dorn, it was a demonstration of just how alive the glacier was as well as his marvelous power. They felt fear to the brink of horror, but somehow knew they were safe at a distance. Huge waves of water crashed onto the shore. After the glacier came to rest, they stood for a while. Then they bowed to the glacier, turned, and entered the forest.

Once in the forest, they felt much safer. But they found they were both shaking uncontrollably. They decided to lie down on the leaves and fern and sleep for a while. Waking, they found themselves energized. They ran through the forest. They ran for pure joy. They ran because they were alive and vibrating, in tune with the life of Earth. They ran until they stopped at a creek and saw footprints in the mud.

Dorn looked at the footprints. "She's big."

Burgo was already down the creek. "She went this way."

They followed the footprints until they faded into the forest. Then they tracked the mountain lion, looking closely at misplaced fern, leaf, and twig. Not far from the creek, they came across a deer she had killed probably the night before. Leaves covered it, so they knew she'd return to eat more of the dead deer. Dorn and Burgo looked at each other, then Dorn grabbed a leg and Burgo cut a large portion of a hind leg, stripping the skin and only taking the meat. The two left the deer and returned to the creek, far enough away to not disturb the lion's return. They built a fire and cooked and ate the meat. Their goal was to wait for the mountain lion to come, so they decided to eat and sleep until nightfall. They made sure they were downwind of the deer carcass.

They woke when the night dew chilled them too much. They knew to not make a sound or move. Once dark, the boys heard a quiet rustling of foot on leaves. The moon cast eerie shadows of timber and fern and fallen trees that looked like an embrace of Earth amongst the stone. Here and there glowing rocks defined the cavities of the ground. Dorn and Burgo were wide awake, their hearts beating to the natural drum of Earth.

She came to eat. She settled into the Earth with her back to the boys. Thinking they were there to kill the mountain lion, Dorn and Burgo gripped both spear and knife. Slowly and quietly they followed the shadows to move closer. They stopped and crouched behind a large log. When ready, the two boys looked at each other, then suddenly stood from the log covering them and Dorn threw his spear to kill. He missed.

The rest was a blur. They heard a loud and deeply menacing growl behind them. At the same time, the lion reacted to Dorn's spear, stood and turned. Both Dorn and Burgo turned their backs to the lion to face a huge gray and black Dire Wolf. For a moment, they froze in fear.

Then the Dire Wolf sprang into action to attack the boys. But so did the lion. In a moment, she jumped onto the log then onto the Dire Wolf. But it wasn't just the log she caught, for Dorn was in her way and she launched off of him, too, leaving deep cuts in his upper back behind his left shoulder. Dorn collapsed in pain as the lion and wolf met in the air. Burgo also sprang into action as the lion and wolf fought to death. The first chance he had, he drove his spear deep into the wolf. By that time, Dorn was on his feet. Burgo's spear didn't end the fight, even though it slowed the wolf. Finally, the huge wolf threw off the lion and Dorn jumped onto his back and plunged his knife into the wolf. The Dire Wolf raised up, his front claws fighting the air and Dorn unintentionally slid off of his back. Burgo centered himself on the ground and beneath the wolf struck his knife into the wolf's heart. He barely was able to step aside as the wolf crashed to the Earth, dead.

Dorn used the wolf's tail to stabilize himself. Then the boys noticed the mountain lion. She stood and panted in front of the boys but was quiet and made no move against them. With just his knife, Dorn took a step toward her.

"No Dorn," Burgo quietly said.

"No?"

"No. She's your earth be-ing and gave you her token."

Dorn stepped back and looked at Burgo. "My life," he said. "She gave me my life." Dorn turned to the mountain lion and bowed. "Thank you, sister." With a quiet growl, the mountain lion turned and ran off into the woods.

After she was gone, Burgo said, "Well, I was thinking about your cuts, but your life will do."

"How does it look?" Dorn asked, turning his back to Burgo.

Burgo examined the four rather deep cuts on Dorn's upper back. "Looks pretty good. Gonna scar really good." He then slapped Dorn on his wound. "Yep. It'll do."

"Oh breath!" Dorn exclaimed in pain. "Will you stop?"

"Oh look. I have blood on my hand." Burgo then wiped his hand on the back of Dorn's tunic.

"What are you doing? Stop it!"

"You already have blood on it. What difference does it make?"

Dorn growled and started to look for his spear. Burgo gently moved the Dire Wolf a couple of times with his foot. "Now why couldn't he be my earth be-ing? That would have been raching. You suppose I could SAY this wolf was my earth be-ing?"

"Oh breath!" Dorn exclaimed. "Burgo, come look at this!"

"I can't go back telling the tribe my earth be-ing is a porcupine. I'll tell them it's a giant wolf."

"Look at this!"

"I did kill him. So maybe he really is my ..."

"Nobody'd believe you," Dorn interrupted. Burgo stopped and pouted. Dorn looked at him, made a face, and said, "Get over here." Burgo walked to Dorn and stopped. "Look what my spear did!"

Burgo was dumbfounded. "Is that ...? Is that ...?"

"I don't know," Dorn said.

Near a small creek, lay what is now known as the Ontonagon Boulder. Weighing around 3700 pounds, it was a solid piece of copper. The outside skin was mostly green, oxidized copper called patina, and Dorn's spear had scarred it, showing the bright orange-red copper underneath. It was located near the West Branch of the Ontonagon River. At that time, the ancient Lake Duluth's main outlets were west of the Ontonagon River now known as St. Croix and Brule Rivers. Today, Lake

Superior drains into Lake Huron by way of the St. Marys River. The large Ontonagon River feeds into Lake Superior, but during Dorn and Burgo's life, the Ontonagon River was a shallow river and the West Branch was a creek.

Dorn's spear had hit the boulder, leaving exposed a scar of copper underneath. The boys looked at the scar closely. The morning sun made the copper sparkle. "Is this his Breath?" asked Burgo. "Did we kill him?"

"I don't think I killed him," Dorn said. "But if this is his Breath, it's beautiful."

"We should help him heal," Burgo said.

Dorn kneeled next to the boulder and placed his hand over the scar. Burgo followed and did the same. "I'm sorry I hurt you," he said quietly. The boys then quietly opened themselves up to touch the essence of the boulder and his surroundings. Silently, they felt in their hearts their connection with the boulder. The beauty of the scar and their harm that they perceived helped them mature in their connection with the earth. Burgo then went to the creek and brought back a handful of mud. Giving some to Dorn, they covered the scar with mud.

"I wish Calla was here. She'd use her medicine," Burgo said.

"Yeah," Dorn replied. "Maybe that's something we should learn better about."

"Yeah."

Dorn and Burgo were the first humans to see the large copper boulder of the Keweenaw. The Ontonagon Boulder became a legend for the indigenous people of the area. The PaleoIndian people learnt that it was a metal and discovered float copper that they could pick up off the ground as well as discovering how to mine in a primitive fashion. But the Clovis people did not know its worth in terms of human economy. And yet, Dorn and Burgo, thinking they had harmed the Boulder and released some of its Breath, saw perhaps a greater worth of Earth.

The early morning breeze reminded the boys of the Dire Wolf. *I'm hungry*, Burgo motioned.

Me too.

The boys felt a need to move on and searched for a little time for grubs to eat instead of returning to the dead deer and make a fire. They drank deeply from the creek by the boulder and continued their adventure. But Burgo noticed that Dorn's cuts were still bleeding.

"Maybe we should go back home," Burgo suggested.

"Why?"

"Calla should take care of your cuts."

Dorn reached behind his left shoulder and discovered blood on his hand. "I'll be okay. We gotta find your earth-being." Then he wiped his hand on Burgo's tunic.

Burgo jumped back. "Look what you did, you slug!" holding out his tunic.

"Don't be an infant," Dorn replied, laughing. "You can say it's the blood of the giant wolf."

Burgo stopped and thought about that. "Yeah. That would be rega."

The boys followed the creek a little, knowing that animals would not walk near the Dire Wolf except those of whom dead four-leggeds meant food. They traveled toward home, knowing instinctively which way was the way to home. To early humankind, the earth was a place so diverse in its topography, they were aware of their surroundings without thinking about it. It was a matter of survival and the boys were at ease in their surroundings. They especially knew where the glacier was standing. They could smell the musk of earth as glacier water affected the soil, much like the smell of rivers except stronger.

Early humans developed the sense of smell called Petrichor so we could find water. What we smell is Geosmin that is a chemical released by dead soil bacteria when water disturbs it. Humankind is even today very sensitive to it, and the olfactory system can detect at a concentration of five parts per trillion. The smell associated with rain is different. When detecting a thunderstorm, the electric discharges from lightning strikes can split diatomic oxygen in the air into individual oxygen. Combined with other diatomic molecules, the phenomenon creates ozone. The ozone travels downward and downwind. This way, we can smell when a rainstorm is coming.

The boys traveled quite a while and thought a place with a grouping of pine trees will reveal a porcupine at night. They looked around near a creek and found tracks distinctly porcupine with the claws and tail drag visible in the mud. They knew that one was there recently. Burgo and Dorn settled down a ways from the trees. Burgo went to a birch tree and started carving and peeling bark.

"What are you doing?" asked Dorn.

"I'm not gonna face a porcupine without something!" Burgo declared. He carved several large pieces and flattened them as much as possible. He then took the rope he saved and with Dorn's help attached them to the outside front of his tunic as tightly as possible, wrapping the rope around his chest and abdomen. When satisfied, the boys settled down and quietly waited. They drifted off to sleep.

They awakened to the sound of teeth clicking and moving about. The dark was illuminated by a waning moon and clear, starry sky. They looked up and saw a porcupine slowing climbing the tree directly above them. Burgo motioned that he would climb the tree and Dorn stepped away from the tree, keeping trees between himself and the porcupine.

Slowly and quietly, Burgo climbed the tree until he was above the porcupine. He tried to ready his spear to strike, but branches were in his way. He quietly placed his spear onto a set of branches and took out his knife, but needed to be closer, so he quietly moved closer to the porcupine. Ready to strike, the porcupine suddenly moved, Burgo yelled and fell out of the tree.

Dorn ran to him and laughed for quite a while. The porcupine struck Burgo in the upper leg and he had several quills sticking up. Burgo, in pain, was crying and Dorn was laughing when the porcupine came down from the tree, sniffed Burgo, and then waddled off into the trees. This set off another round of laughter from Dorn.

"Get these things out of me!" Burgo roared.

"Okay, okay." Dorn then sat down to pull the quills out of Burgo's leg. "Looks like you got your token tonight! Does it hurt?" as he pulled another quill from Burgo's leg.

"Oh breath!"

"You want me to go slow or fast?"

"Shut ... Up!"

Burgo tried to set his mind against the pain. He held a needle and looked closely. "Look at this," he said.

"What?"

"Ow. When I feel the tip here, it's sticky. I think it helps keep it in me. Ow."

"Quit feeling the tip."

"Well, I'm feeling bumps, but they can't be just bumps."

"I'm almost done. Who cares about bumps?" Burgo discovered that the porcupine quill had barbs, but he did not know it at the time. He thought about a different shape of spearhead that would stay better in the four-legged when they hunted for food.

"No wonder women cut off this end... We gotta go see Calla. We gotta get back home," Burgo mused.

"Yeah," Dorn replied. "She's gotta look at my back. I can feel it bleeding."

At that moment, they heard a rustling nearby and soon a whimper. A dog, Traco, came into view, and Dorn and Burgo suddenly became alarmed.

"Come here, Traco! Come boy," Dorn said. The dog came to them and they saw blood on him.

They examined the dog. "It's not his blood," Burgo said.

"We gotta go. Traco, come along."

Chapter Five: Mipeashu

Dorn and Burgo ran during the night until they could no longer run. The sky clouded and, unable to see very well, they tripped over logs and rocks. They decided to sleep for a while until light, and Traco, happy to be with his tribe, curled up with them.

The next day, they found home. About half of their homes were burnt and items strewn on the ground. Smoke, blood, and the smell of death were still in the air. Some people were dead, but most were just gone. They found Joga, Lio, and Dabra dead inside the compound. Fila and her baby were also dead outside the compound. Next to them was Pitra. Three of the dogs were also dead. Traco lay down beside one with grief.

"What happened here? Where is everybody?" Dorn asked the wind. Dorn then went into his home and picked up his knapsack and atlatl. He found some short spears around the camp. Burgo sat next to Pitra. Near the gate, Dorn said, "Come on, Burgo." But Burgo didn't say anything or move. Dorn went into Jefers' home and got Burgo's knapsack and atlatl, then went and dropped them near Burgo along with some short spears. "Come on, Burgo."

"They took all the food," Burgo quietly said, looking at Pitra.

"What?"

"They took all the food. Look around you. They took all the food." All the pits had been dug up and all the food for the winter taken. "They came back for the food."

"Okay, they took the food."

"We have to bury them," Burgo said.

"No, we have to find them."

"We have to bury them. Before the four-leggeds take them."

"We have to find them! Look, there's walking here and they're not us," Dorn said, scanning the ground. "Their prints are bigger than ours, and there's blood here." But Burgo didn't move. "Come on! COME ON!" Dorn then started toward the eastern trees. "We have to find her!"

That got Burgo's attention. Dorn hesitated. "You don't care about me," Burgo said quietly.

"What?"

"You don't care about me," Burgo repeated, standing. "You don't care about anybody except yourself … and Leah!"

"Leah's out there!"

"Pitra was our friend, Dorn. Pitra was our friend and you don't care. We have to bury her. Look what they did to her. She took five spears to kill her. She was trying to protect Fila and her baby. She was a warrior."

Dorn did not look at Pitra but moved toward the trees. "Fine. Bury her."

"You selfish shokab!" Burgo yelled.

Angry, Dorn ran back to Burgo with a short spear in his hand threatening to strike. Burgo stood his ground. Face to face, Dorn stood threatening and Burgo stood with his hands down. Soon, Dorn stepped back. "Peuckle me." This time he meant it. Dorn then ran to follow the trail and left.

Burgo stayed with Pitra for a long time and cried. The smoke, the smell, the death reminded him of his friends, his birth Ema and Appa, all that he had lost. And now this. He felt despair. Finally, he got up and found an empty pit he could bury them in. He took Pitra by the arms and dragged her to the pit and as gently as he could, he placed her in. Then he placed Fila and her baby.

While dragging Lio, Dorn came and quietly took his feet. He was surprised at how cold they were. But that is death, when breath is gone and cold has touched them. Together, they placed Dabra and Joga in the pit also, without speaking. Dorn went into Calla's home and found a bag of red ochre. Meantime, Burgo got the three dead dogs and placed them in the pit also.

Red ochre is iron oxide and highly prized by the tribe. The symbol for its use was beyond Dorn and Burgo's memory. They just knew that it was essential to help those no longer breathing to join the Breath of all.

"We have to find their stuff," Burgo said.

Yes, motioned Dorn.

The two friends scoured their homes and found what was needed to see their tribal family members happy in death. They found a bone needle for Dabra who could make clothing very well. For Joga, they placed a knife. He was skilled in making traps. For Fila, they placed flowers next to her as she loved the colors. For her baby, they placed a rattle made of rawhide, teeth, and a wood stick. For Lio, they placed his spear that was covered in blood. They knew he felled the enemy before he died. And for Pitra, they found a necklace of beads made from bones that were colored. The two friends then stood together at the edge of the pit and quietly sang the song of death. Burgo softly drummed the echo of life and death. Traco stood next to them and, seeking comfort, leaned against Dorn's leg.

Breath

No longer breath
No longer to be what might have been
No longer to be made
No longer to become
You've left the sacred dream
And you're going home
I'll walk with you as you find a brand new home
I'll walk with you as you cross the muddy river
I'll walk with you as you journey through the mist
I'll walk with you past brother tree and sister stone
I'll walk with you as you see behind the light
I'll walk with you as you find a brand new home
For you belong
You still belong to us
You belong to Earth
You belong to Breath
You stand with us
Together, never apart
Together
I'll walk with you as you find a brand new home
I'll walk with you as you cross the muddy river
I'll walk with you as you journey through the mist
I'll walk with you past brother tree and sister stone
I'll walk with you as you see behind the light
I'll walk with you as you find a brand new home
Oh Breath
Help us see and hear
Help us never to forget
Their breath is our breath
Always

Early humankind vibrated to the teachings and
patterns of sunrise and sunset, the passing of time, and
the ages of becoming. Past, present, and future wove

together in a myriad of shapes and sounds. They knew that the breath of their tribal family continued on, and they knew that they continued because their people came to them in their dreams that they knew were not dreams but visions. They knew that people before them helped guide them because the sound of their breath could still be heard, even during waking life. They knew that the breath of their people did not end but became one with the Breath of all.

Dorn then quietly stood beside Burgo and gave him the bag. Burgo sprinkled red ochre over the bodies. Then the two friends pushed dirt and rock on top of them. After a while, Burgo finally turned to go.

"I'm sorry," Dorn said quietly. "I'm sorry Burgo. You were right and I'm sorry."

"I know, Dorn. Come on." Burgo picked up his things that Dorn had dropped near him.

"What do we do now?"

"We find them," Burgo said. "It's too late to start now, but we can in the beginning light. Let's try to find something to eat. Come Traco."

Traco trotted over to Burgo and Dorn, happy to have the closeness, as much as did the two young men. They went into Calla's home so Dorn could return the red ochre bag and they found some dried meat. The mandaka was there also. Burgo wrapped it in a piece of soft leather and set it away from the door. Eventually, the two friends and Traco curled together and slept. They said nothing, but each knew comfort from the other. And both were worried whether they would find their tribe with breath or not.

At the next light, Dorn and Burgo found more dried meat to take with them and set off with Traco who knew how to fend for himself in these times of need. They followed tracks going east and south until midday when they lost their way.

"I don't see anything," Burgo said. "How can they just disappear like that? Look, there's blood here, but now nothing."

"Let's ask Earth," Dorn said.

"What?"

"Do you remember when Leah tried to teach us the way?"

"No."

"You were probably sleeping as usual."

"Fine," Burgo smiled. "What's the way?"

"I think it's like finding water. We stay quiet and smell the Earth. Except we open our hearts and listen. Come on."

Dorn then sat down on the ground and Burgo sat next to him. They closed their eyes and quieted their minds. "What if their breath is gone?" Burgo asked.

"Don't think anything Burgo. That's what Leah said."

"Easy for you to do."

Dorn gave Burgo a look and closed his eyes again. "Oh yeah. Leah said to breathe. I mean, to know you breathe." They sat together and felt their minds quiet to the point that they could listen to Earth. They felt their heart beating. After a while, there came a time when the boys could feel the vibration of Earth and just begin to hear the whisper of Breath that was more a deep feeling than words. Images entered their minds and both could not help but open their eyes and look up at the trees.

"Do you know?" Dorn said at last.

"I think so," Burgo replied. "I think they went this way."

"That's what I heard too. Let's go."

They turned south and traveled through the trees until they came upon a clearing. Traco was waiting for them. "Lots of damage here. It could have been a deer herd," Burgo said.

"Hey Traco. You know where they are?" Dorn asked. Traco indicated that he did by becoming more excited. "Humm. Maybe we should just listen to Traco."

"Yup," Burgo agreed, rubbing Traco. "I guess becoming man doesn't mean we stop being idiots."

"Calla always said that the Earth will help humans who ask for help. We just gotta be more aware about how that help comes."

"Do you think they still have breath?"

"I think I feel them," Dorn answered. "Come on, Traco." *Find them.*

Traco then set off southeast back into the trees and the boys followed. By nightfall, they were hungry and tired. They stopped for the night, but did not light a fire despite the danger. They were in a small clearing but it soon became dark. They ate some dried meat and settled down for the night. Traco curled up with them.

The two gazed up through the trees at the stars. "I wish I knew what that is," Dorn mused.

"Calla says they're the breath of our ancestors," Burgo replied. "I wonder if my birth Ema is there."

"I thought our breath went into the Breath of all," Dorn said.

"It does. Maybe there too though Dorn. Maybe that's where Breath of all lives. I don't know. Maybe they are memories and when we become aware, we connect to those lights up there and that's why we remember so well sometimes."

"I think your birth Ema is there Burgo."

"Maybe that's why I feel close to her now."

The two friends fell silent for a while, each in their own thoughts. Dorn continued to gaze at the stars. "I don't want Leah to lose Breath, Burgo."

"I don't either. But to me, she's just a friend, Dorn. I wouldn't mind her as a mate though." Dorn sat up. "Nah, I know I know. You seem different about her."

Dorn settled back down. "I do, Burgo. There's something about her I can't explain."

"Her hair, her lips, her …"

"No, it's more than that," Dorn cut in. "She's more beautiful than the dying light before night. She takes my breath away and when she's not near me, I feel like I end a little, like my cold has come. When she's gone out of sight, a part of me is gone too. She'll be more than my mate, Burgo. She's me, so what happens to her, happens to me. I look at hearth fire and I see her, her warmth, and all I want to do is to be better. To be a man. I want to do more than protect her, Burgo. I want to give her … me."

"I think I get it. I look at the lights and it's like I'm there with them. But I'm here too and I belong with the trees and grass and water. That makes me who I am. You belong with Leah. That makes you who you are."

"Thanks Burgo."

"Thanks Dorn."

The young men drifted off to sleep and slept well. Right before light, Traco got up and softly growled. The two were awake immediately and grabbed their weapons. They said nothing whilst trying to see what was out there.

"Don't."

"Who is it?" Dorn asked.

"Huko." Finally, Huko stepped close enough for them to see.

"Are you alone?" asked Dorn.

"Yes," Huko replied. "Do you have any food?" he asked as he sat down, rubbing Traco.

Burgo searched his knapsack and drew out dried meat. "Here," he said.

They sat together while Huko ate. "Where is everybody?" Dorn asked.

"Over there a ways. They can't hear us if we're quiet."

Dorn waited a little while before he said, "You gonna tell us what happened or do I have to beat it out of you?"

This got Huko's attention. "You think you can?" he asked.

"I can," Dorn replied.

Huko just looked at the two. "Maybe. But I'll tell you." He settled in. "It wasn't me. It was my birth-son. It was Rochek."

Come on Rochek motioned to Garath. While Burgo and Dorn were seeking their earth-beings, Rochek tried to give Leah a knife but she refused. She told him that she will not mate with him. She will mate with Dorn after his man hunt.

"What," Garath murmured.

"We need to find a place to bury Dorn."

"Why, is he dead?"

"Not yet, stupid. We're gonna kill him. Go get your stuff."

"Oh," Garath said. "Okay."

Garath hurried into his tipi and got his knapsack, atlatl, and short spears, as well as his knife and came back to Rochek. Rochek walked over to Huko who was sitting on the ground trying to fix a point for a short spear. "What are you doing, Appa?" Rochek asked.

"What's it look like?" Huko replied. The two stood watching him work. "What do you want? I'm busy."

"Oh. Me and Garath are going on a hunt."

"When you coming back?" asked Huko.

"I don't know," answered Rochek. "We might be away a few days."

"You'll miss Dorn and Burgo's man hunt rite in a couple of days," Huko reminded him.

"I don't care."

"Okay. Tell Apia," Huko replied.

"Why?" asked Rochek. "I'm a man. I don't answer to her." Apia was Rochek's birth Ema and Huko's mate.

Huko stood and faced Rochek. "You sure you want to face me?"

"No, Appa. I'll tell her." Huko sat back down. *Come on*, Rochek motioned to Garath.

They looked over and Apia was helping Fila lift a large leather piece onto her tipi. Fila had just fixed the hole that mice had chewed through and with sinew sewn on a patch. Rochek and Garath looked on and smirked. As they moved closer, they could hear the two women.

"Thank you, Apia," Fila said. "Here, I've got something for you." She went into her tipi for a moment and came out with a necklace of shells. She gave it to Apia.

"What are these?" asked Apia.

"I don't know," Fila said. I found them near the water. Well, they were pretty high up in dirt by a small creek me and Dabra found when we were trying to find mushrooms to eat. We saw some sorrel by a little cliff and that's when I saw these." During the Early

Proterozoic about 2.3 billion years ago, the land was flat and a large shallow sea covered much of the upper North American plate. The glacier pushed the shells embedded in sedimentary rock and erosion revealed the sea shells. Fila bored a hole in each shell to make the necklace.

Rochek took the necklace out of Apia's hands and examined the shells.

"Give it back, Rochek," Apia said.

"Looks stupid," Rochek said, as he handed back the necklace. Anything Rochek did not understand, he labeled as stupid.

"What can we do for you?" asked Apia.

"Nothing," Rochek replied. He turned to Fila. "Especially not from you." He then turned back to Apia. "We're going hunting. Don't know when we'll be back."

Surprised, Apia said, "Thanks for telling me."

Without another word, Rochek turned and walked into the forest with Garath. They went out quite a distance to explore the area far outside the camp, hoping to find a place where they could place Dorn and nobody would know.

"Are you really going to kill Dorn?" asked Garath.

"Sure. Why not?" countered Rochek. It was night and they had killed a deer. They took the leg and left the rest for the four-leggeds and moved quite a ways upwind from the carcass. Rochek made a fire whilst Garath set up a lean-to shelter of small branches, fern, moss, rocks, and leaves. Like the rest of the tribe, the two were at home in the forest.

While they were eating, Garath said, "I don't think you should."

"Why not?"

"What do you want to kill Dorn for anyway?"

"So Leah won't mate with him."

"She won't mate with you though. Even if he's dead."

Rochek suddenly hit Garath who landed face up on the ground and Rochek stood over him. "Then she won't mate with anybody." He stood over Garath while Garath rubbed his face, and finally stepped away. "Got it?"

Standing, Garath said, "Yeah. I got it."

The next morning, the two continued looking for a small cave. They came upon a group of people they had never seen before. They were taller than Clovis with different colored hair. Some had blond, most had red, and some light brown. They were pale in skin, and Rochek first thought they were ghosts. The Clovis all had dark brown hair and dark skin. They may have been related to Denisovans who were close cousins of Neanderthals. Whilst there's evidence of some kind of humanoid besides Clovis, there's no evidence of them being Denisovans in North or South America. The evidence shows that Denisovans lived in Siberia's Denisova Cave from about 128,000 BCE to 44,000 BCE. Their red hair especially linked them to the Neanderthal. They seemed like giants to Rochek and Garath.

Nearly all of them wore finished copper ornaments. Rochek and Garath had never seen such ornaments before. They hid in the forest to see what they were doing.

When Rochek and Garath found them, they were cracking a large boulder apart by heating the base with fire, and breaking off chunks of rock with imbedded copper that Rochek called fire rock. They did not have the same language, but their motion language was similar, so the two could understand them. Rochek discovered that the fire rock could be melted. They also found fire rock on the ground. Today, we know that what they found on the ground was copper float rock that the glacier deposited.

"Look at that," Rochek said.

"What is it?"

"I don't know." But Rochek knew that he wanted it. They abandoned their search for a cave and followed them at the end of the day to the Other's camp. The two men climbed trees to hide and see the Others. It was a large clearing in the heart of the forest, not a meadow. Their homes were a combination of rock and timber and were rectangular structures. They filled the cracks of the roofs and sides with moss. Set aside was another area for a fire. This is where they smelted the copper out of the rock. Like the Clovis, they had a center hearth that was always burning. Near the forest was a large fenced-in area with one young woman as captive. There were few women there, and their tasks were to cook and find food. The women hunted while the men worked the mines. Rochek and Garath discovered several rectangular dig sites near the camp where they had extracted copper. The place was not a tribal home, but was a temporary setup for mining. They came from the east and made their home in the eastern south. They traveled to the copper during the spring and returned in the fall.

The next day, Rochek and Garath saw them pile up stones about as high as their chest. Then they piled firewood on top. Rochek thought that maybe that was a special hearth fire. The two men followed the Others again to the mine and watched them work. That night, things were different. They took their drums and sang and danced around their hearth fire. And they focused on the young girl in the fenced area. They gave her something to drink that nobody else drank and she seemed to see beyond the others. They took her and put her up on top of the wood. Then the drums stopped and they killed her with a knife. The moon was full, so they could see during night. Then the drums started again and they sang and danced while they burned her.

The two young men panicked and made too much noise descending the trees. Garath fell to the ground in pain, clutching his ankle. Alerted, the Others quickly found them and brought them to their hearth.

What are you? What are you doing here?

"Clovis. We're people," Rochek tried to tell them. The two were only tall enough to reach the Others' heart. *Don't kill us!*

Why not?

Thinking as fast as he could, Rochek replied, *We're useful. We can help you.*

Slaves, said an Other. They dragged Rochek and Garath into the fenced area and gathered around the hearth. The Others spoke amongst themselves in their own language far into the night. Some wanted their death as sacrifice. Others, tired of mining copper, wanted them to be slaves and do the work for them. Someone said that there must be others of their kind and they should go get them as slaves for their tribe. Pockets of their kind came to the area from spring until fall to mine copper. It was time to go back soon, and if they had slaves, then the slaves could carry the copper and bedding. They finally agreed to this course of action.

The next day, Garath's ankle was better and not broken. But he still could not walk very well. Some of the Others went to the smelting area with the rocks they had gathered. They had dug holes in the ground and placed a long tube out of each hole. A couple of Others crushed the rock into as fine a powder as they could on a large stone with an indentation on the top to keep the powder in place. Others started a fire in the holes with twigs and the fire from their hearth. Once the fire in the hole was well-lit, they placed charcoal from their hearth into the holes. They then sprinkled the powder on top and added more charcoal. They topped each hole with grassy top-earth. For a couple of hours, the Others took turns blowing into the tube, causing the heat in the hole to rise. They then removed the turf top and placed the charcoal into a container with water. The copper bonded together, they took it out and let it cool. Any residue fragments they took also. After cooled, they put the copper into a bag to take back home.

The more Rochek watched them, the more he wanted the fire-rock. He did not know at the time that unchecked want can lead to injustice, but that was for humankind to create and experience later. One of the Others brought to their hearth the men's short spears but not their atlatls. The Other just saw the atlatls as sticks on the ground. He examined the spear points and wondered how they made them. Trying to be friendly, Rochek mimed how they made the spear points, but the Other did not understand. He only knew his way, and he could not imagine beyond his own knowledge.

That evening, it was clear to Rochek that they wanted to eat one of them and Rochek quickly tried to communicate to them. Rochek told them there's a lot of food where his home is as well as people who will be slaves. One of the Others got close enough to Rochek for him to notice that the Other had two sets of teeth and that frightened him even more.

Suddenly, Huko ran to the Others from the trees. Running, he threw a short spear and killed one but the Others were too many for him to kill. One of the Others caught him in the legs and tripped him. Several pinned him down and tied his hands and feet. Huko thought he was dead that day. But Rochek yelled and told him that they want slaves. So Huko told them he'll take them to where he lives.

The next day, they started off, but Garath could not travel well enough to go with them, and the Others kept Rochek in the pen. Most of the Others left with Huko who was half-dragged with a rope tied to his wrists. They made him point the way home, but eventually one of the Others knew he was lying and hit Huko hard enough to knock him out. The Others then stoned him until they thought he was dead.

I've seen it, the Other said. *From here, I know where to go.* The Others looked at Huko and the leader said, *Leave it. We'll pick it up later.*

Huko woke and hoped he was not too late. He managed to get the rope off of his wrists and knew he had to get to the tribe before the Others did. He ran a different, shorter way to home but he was too late. The Others had killed people. Huko saw them kill Lio and subdue Kathe who was fighting like a mountain lion. They herded the rest of the tribe to their compound. Huko had never felt so helpless in his life.

"Their home is near here," Huko told them. "Over there. They have a fence and our people are there."

"Have they killed anybody?" asked Dorn.

"No. Not yet. Except for those at home."

"Oh breath!" exclaimed Burgo quietly.

Burgo asked why they didn't kill Rochek and Huko said it was because he showed them his weapons. They were especially interested in his spear points. But they were also hungry and their tribe needed food. "Rochek told them that we have food and he'll show him where it is if they don't kill them. So the Others kept Garath in the fenced area and told Rochek to show them where we are. But Rochek tried to show them the other way and hoped Garath could get away," he lied. "But one of them knew. They knew where home is. They stoned Rochek thinking they killed him, but they didn't. They all left him and he got to the tribe before they did."

By the time Huko finished, it was light and Traco had disappeared into the forest, probably in search for food. "How did you get away?" asked Burgo.

"Rochek got me away. He came right before they came and told me to leave alone. I left Apia. It wasn't until later that Rochek told me everything. I didn't know what would happen until it happened. By then there was nothing I could do to protect."

"You coward!" Dorn said. "Rochek knew they were coming and said nothing to the tribe except you? You knew they were coming and you ran?"

"You don't understand," replied Huko. "They're not human. Rochek was afraid and I've never seen him afraid. They're not people! Kathe and the others tried to fight but had no time to prepare. You just don't understand! They're big and our people were so afraid that they could do nothing. These things had spears and I saw them kill Lio!"

"They killed Pitra too, did you know that?" Burgo asked quietly and angrily. "It took five of their spears to kill Pitra. She tried to protect. You ran."

"I didn't know. I'm sorry."

Suddenly, Dorn attacked Huko. "You did this!" Dorn got a punch away to Huko's face but then Huko overwhelmed him and Dorn found himself lying on the ground with Huko on top of him. Burgo sat on a log to watch. "I don't believe you! I don't believe anything you say."

"Shut up Dorn! You're too loud. They'll hear you!"

"I don't care!"

"You're a man now! Act like it!"

That calmed Dorn down, but it was a deadly calm. Huko let him up and Dorn looked at him with fire in his eyes and said, "Don't you ever tell me what to do again," he said quietly. "You don't have the right to say that to me. Not anymore. You're supposed to protect the tribe, but you ran instead."

"I didn't know they would take and kill our people. When I got back, they were forcing our people to go with them. They had our spears."

"This was in my home!" Burgo said, showing his atlatl. "Why didn't they take this?"

"I don't know," replied Huko. "I don't think they know what it is."

"Where's Rochek?" asked Dorn.

"He's there with them. They gave him fire rock and he's just there with them. Everybody else is in the pen."

"Why did they do that?" wondered Burgo. Neither answered him.

The three quietly moved to within eyesight of the Other's camp. Some of them were packing up bedding and food into packs that they carry. Others were smelting the last of the copper. Rochek was looking through the bag at the copper near the edge of the camp.

"Oh Breath!" murmured Burgo. The three backed away and took off their tunics so they could have a freer range of motion. They also took mud and streaked their bodies and face as camouflage.

"We herd them like mammoth," Huko said quietly.

"They're big like mammoth," said Burgo.

"No," Dorn replied. "There's not enough of us. We need to get our people out of there. Burgo, you go around and get the gate. Huko, get as many spears as you can so our people can fight. But don't until they see us. I'll try to get their attention away from the fence if I have to. I'll wait until you're ready Burgo."

"Look! They're roped," Burgo replied, as he saw that their hands were bound to their legs.

"Okay," Dorn said. "I'll wait until you go in back and cut their ropes. Here's my knife."

"Don't need it," Burgo replied. "Wait until you see me at the gate."

"Okay," Dorn said, replacing his knife. "Take my weapons and give it to Kathe then."

"Okay," Burgo replied. He took Dorn's atlatl and short spears, and left to circle around to the fence.

Huko started to move right. "Where are you going?" asked Dorn.

"To get closer to their spears," replied Huko. "What do you think?"

Huko moved as close to Rochek as possible without being seen. He then threw small rocks at Rochek to get his attention. Eventually, Rochek saw him, looked toward the Others, and started to walk into the forest. An Other named Lalkpo who was packing saw him. *Where are you going?* he motioned impatiently.

To relieve myself, Rochek motioned back. The Other turned back to what he was doing with a grunt. Rochek quietly walked to Huko and they moved away from the camp.

"What are you doing here?" Rochek asked. "They'll kill you."

"What are you talking about?" Huko shot back. "They can't kill me."

"They ate Chikel last night! That's what I'm talking about!"

"Oh Breath."

"Go home Appa. That's all you can do."

"We're here to get our people, Rochek."

"Who's here?" asked Rochek.

"Dorn and Burgo."

"They'll get us all killed then!" Rochek said, nearly panicked.

"Shut up and listen to me Rochek. When the time comes, you help me get their spears so we can fight. Okay?"

Rochek thought for a moment.

"Okay?" Huko asked again.

"Yeah. Yeah sure. I gotta get back," Rochek replied.

"Wait!" Huko said. "I told Dorn and Burgo that it was you who showed them where home was."

Rochek looked at him and quietly said, "I should have taken your breath a long time ago. I'd be warrior now and not you. And I could have Leah easy."

"I'm sorry," Huko said. "I panicked. They're not like hunting a mammoth. It's too different."

"You shokab." Rochek quietly entered the compound. The Other named Lalkpo saw him and Rochek just smiled and nodded, picked up the copper bag and set it near the smelters.

Burgo quietly moved to the far outside part of the fence when Calla saw him. *Quiet!* motioned Burgo. *Stay still.* Calla got Kathe and the two slowly and quietly moved to where Burgo was crouching. The other tribal members saw what was going on and quietly moved to shield them from the Others' sight.

"What's going on?" asked Kathe quietly.

"We're getting you out of here." Burgo took his knife and cut Kathe's rope. All were bound by their wrists and their legs. The ropes were tied together by a single rope so it was difficult to move. "Here." He then pulled the two sharp shards out of his hair and gave them to Kathe who cut Calla's ropes and she then cut and gave to Cakana and Dirk. They all held their ropes, pretending to still be tied. This took a long time to move slowly and quietly until nearly everyone was freed of the ropes. "I'll open the gate and you all get out of here." Burgo then gave the weapons to Kathe. "Here."

"Good," Kathe replied. "This is good. Thanks."

While they were waiting, Kathe asked while facing away, "Where's Dorn?"

"Waiting for me to show at the gate. Then he'll try to distract them," Burgo replied.

"Did you finish your man hunt?"

Burgo smiled at that. "Yes Appa. We both did and we both need Calla."

"Good. Good," Kathe smiled.

"Huko's here too."

"I thought they killed him."

"Nope."

After speaking with Huko, Rochek quietly returned to the compound. Lalkpo came out of his shelter and saw him. *What are you doing?* he asked.

Going to get water, Rochek replied. Lalkpo then turned to reenter his shelter but turned back to Rochek. "Va chakkar par ka dra hiem kigjen. Da kil bara mine chakkan. Da kil bratta des untre af ditt slac ar ta med oss."

What? Rochek motioned. *I don't understand.*

The group of Others stopped their smelting job and walked toward a shelter. When Rochek's attention turned to them, Lalkpo became angry. He threw a pack at him. "Da kil bara mine chakkan! Lig dis du sulken." He threw another at Rochek. "Lig dis du sulken!"

"Okay! Okay!" Rochek smiled and bowed to him, picked up the packs, and stood there.

Lalkpo angrily stormed to Rochek and grabbed the packs from him and threw them on the ground. He pointed to the fence. "Lig dis du sulken!" *I will kill you!*

Rochek became afraid and bowed to Lalkpo. He picked up the packs thinking to put them by the fence and began to carry them to the fence. Lalkpo grabbed them again and threw them near a travois. "Pachaleo!" he snarled. Lalkpo then hit Rochek to the ground, and Rochek quickly moved toward the travois. That calmed Lalkpo down and watched Rochek hurry toward the travois. Lalkpo then entered his shelter.

The Others watched Lalkpo and Rochek throughout all of this, then continued on. Rochek noticed that they put today's copper into the larger copper bag that was already on a travois and then entered their shelter. Rochek bowed and smiled and placed the bags on the travois and started to place skins on another travois in case they were watching. Once he thought they were gone, he quickly and quietly moved to the fence gate. At the gate, Rochek confronted Jefers who was not yet unbound.

"What's going on?" Jefers asked. "Why aren't you in here?"

"I don't know," Rochek replied. "I think they're packing up and want you all to be their slaves." Rochek then opened the gate. Dorn was quite alarmed because he did not yet see Burgo, but kept quiet.

Jefers was also alarmed. "What are you doing?" he asked.

"Back away Jefers." Rochek replied. When Jefers could not move fast enough, Rochek shoved him to the ground. "I said move!" Rochek then grabbed Leah who was also still bound and forced her out the gate. He then tried to tie the gate, but Leah struggled.

What happened next was a blur. Leah fell to the ground, Rochek could not tie the gate closed, and reached for Leah. The tribe members were desperately cutting ties inside the fence, and Kathe and Burgo moved to the gate as fast as possible. Rochek forced Leah to her feet and Huko yelled, "Rochek no!"

That's when things exploded. Lalkpo came out of the shelter and Leah screamed. The Others came out also yelling and reached for their spears. But Huko had gotten to them first and carried them to the fence. Garath was not yet healed and continued to help free his tribe from the ropes. Huko was cutting Jefers free when Dorn yelled, "Let her go, Rochek!"

"She's mine, Dorn!" Rochek yelled back. Lalkpo grabbed Leah by her hair and jerked her away from Rochek. He pulled her close and put a knife to her throat.   Dorn ran into the compound and everyone seemed to stop.

Dorn faced Lalkpo with knife in hand and said, "Rochek, get her away from him."

Rochek just snorted and said, "If I can't have her, nobody can." He slowly moved away from the center of the scene.

Huko muttered, "Oh breath! What have I done?"

Dorn then addressed Lalkpo. *Let her go,* he motioned.

Lalkpo looked at Dorn and smiled. *Sacrifice.* He then cut her throat. Dorn ran as fast as he could to Lalkpo, avoided Lalkpo's knife as Leah fell to the ground, jumped high, and plunged his knife into the back of Lalkpo's neck, killing him. Because they surprised the tribe at their home and easily captured them, the Others underestimated the tribe at war.

Kathe yelled at Calla to get the women and children into the woods. Cakana ran to Leah but she was dead, and Calla lifted her up and told her to help the women and children. Calla tried to stay at a safe distance. Kathe used his atlatl as well as did Burgo and killed the Others as long as they had short spears. Dorn killed one after another, moving faster than Burgo has ever seen him move. Kathe and Burgo then used their knives. Huko killed as many as he could with his knife. Jefers, Dirk, Bulak, Kobo, Sham, and Garath killed the Others with their own spears until the cache of spears was depleted.

The Others tried to fight, but the men were too short and quick to be killed, although several were wounded. The Others drew out short spears from their dead and tried to use them, but were not used to throwing them.

Traco came with other dogs who entered the war. They saved many lives, including Calla who was seeing to Leah after she pulled off Cakana. An Other was about to strike her down when Necan jumped and grabbed his throat. Sham finished the kill.

Throughout all this action, Rochek quietly moved out of the way and made his way to the bag of copper. He quickly filled his knapsack with pieces of copper, pulled a short spear from one of the Others and disappeared unnoticed into the forest. He was never seen by the tribe again.

It seemed like a lifetime, but the war ended. All of the Others were dead. Dorn ran to Leah and held her. Calla helped him. Burgo entered Lalkpo's shelter. Hanging on a wall was a long tunic made of scales that reminded Burgo of the glyptodont they saw by the glacier. The tunic sported a mountain lion's head and a tail with copper. Disgusted, Burgo left the shelter and went to Dorn.

Dorn held Leah and rocked back and forth in shock. Calla tried to lift up Dorn from Leah but could not. Calla kept saying, "Her breath is gone, Dorn. Come with me." But Dorn could not hear and all he could see was Leah. Sham, Jefers, and Kathe tried to help Dorn also but Dorn seemed to have the strength of a mountain lion and would not let go of Leah. Burgo was more invasive with Dorn and lifted him up. Leah came with them, but Dorn could not keep her and she fell to the ground. This made Dorn frantic and tried to get Burgo to let go of him, but Burgo held tightly.

"Dorn, her breath is gone! She's gone!" Burgo pleaded. In a moment of strength, Dorn pushed Burgo backward and broke his grasp. When Burgo tried to grab hold of him again, Dorn hit him hard. Burgo fell back and hit his head on a travois. Finally aware, Dorn ran to

Burgo.   "What have I done?   Burgo!   What have I done?!"

Kathe and Calla ran to Burgo and Dorn stood, but he could no longer see. His mind was black. All he knew to do was to run. "I killed him!" he yelled as he ran into the woods. Kathe looked at Burgo and cried out, "He still has breath! Dorn! Dorn!" But Dorn was unable to hear. All he could do was run. His guilt and loss and grief were too much for him and his mind was dark. He entered into the darkness every human faces at least once in a lifetime. All light within his mind was gone and he hated. He hated Leah for leaving him. He hated Burgo for leaving him. He hated the earth, the tribe, and every four-legged. He hated his breath be-ing, the mountain lion. He hated his life and all life. He entered the shadow world and hated himself most of all. Hating himself, he saw no reason not to hate, not to hurt, not to kill everything and anything. He saw himself as a warrior against the earth and knew he could take the breath of anything without regret. He hated the beliefs of sacrifice of the earth and hated everything he was taught. He found himself beyond time. That's when he tripped and fell. He lay still and smelled the earth.

Dorn was more calm when he moved a few moments later, but the blackness did not subside. His hatred did not abate. The calm he felt was of despair and utter loneliness and absolute, blinding pain. It seemed to be like entering an empty cave having no light. He saw himself enter the darkness of the cave and he didn't care. Suddenly on the walls of the cave he saw images. He was there but not there. He did not understand what he saw, a different world. He saw men kill four-leggeds and did not eat the meat. He saw people hurt dogs and kill mindlessly. He saw the earth shake and groan as rivers became full of pollution. He saw images of the sky turning a sickly brown. He saw cloud spirals come down from the sky and destroy. He saw humans covering the face of Earth and then too many becoming sick and dying of something they could not see. He saw great structures being built, choking the world and covering the earth with liquid that hardened into stone. He saw a vast body of water full of items that killed living creatures he could not understand. Images. He saw birds and animals eating the items and dying. He saw trees burn and plants crying and dying. And through it all, he saw humankind doing it all without regard or care. He saw humankind so disconnected from earth that they did not know what they were doing.

Then everything turned black again. His mountain lion appeared from the black and screamed in his face. Dorn was without care and was not afraid. He was ready to die. The mountain lion nearly touched Dorn's face when he growled. "What is your purpose?"

"To protect the tribe," Dorn automatically replied.

"You are incomplete," she growled. Dorn smelled her breath. "What is your purpose?"

Dorn paused. "To protect everything."

She growled. "From what?"

Dorn broke down to dust and a small, faint light entered his mind and vibrated with life. He paused, shocked by what he suddenly knew.

"From me."

"Then live, human." And the mountain lion disappeared. Immediately, Dorn found himself traveling through a spiral. He saw the earth heal. He saw humankind reconnect to the earth, and he knew that what we do to the earth we do to ourselves. He passed the lights in the sky and the earth became smaller and smaller. His grief did not diminish, but his hatred did. He slept.

Chapter Six: Return Home

Calla examined Burgo for blood and gently told him to wake. When he did, his head hurt. He opened his eyes and saw Calla, Jefers, and Kathe looking down at him with care in their eyes. He looked around as he sat up. "Where's Dorn?"

"He ran," Kathe answered. "Dirk and Kobo are trying to find him now."

Burgo stood. "You stay still for a while," Calla ordered.

"Ugh. Okay." And Burgo walked over and sat against a structure. Traco came and curled up on him, giving Burgo the comfort he needed at Leah's death.

All of the tribe except Dorn, Dirk, and Kobo were in the compound. Huko and others were gathering weapons, the Others' as well as their own. They took a cache of knives, the Others' long spears, their short and long spears, and their atlatls. They also took any food and skins from the Others, knowing they needed to repair their home. Much of the Others' belongings were already packed up for their journey east and south.

Cakana tended to Leah and cleaned her. She brushed her hair as much as possible. Kathe and Bulak readied a travois and placed Leah on it, covering her with a leather skin from the Others. They carried the dead Others and placed them into the fenced area to let nature take her course. Their grief was too keen for them to talk very much. Their grief was not only for Leah, but for Fila, her baby, Pitra, Dabra, Joga, Lio, and the child, Chikel, they knew they lost.

Calla tended to wounds as much as possible without her materials. Apia found some things that looked like Calla could use. When she gave them to Calla, Calla grabbed her hand, looked at her, smiled, and squeezed a little. Apia smiled back with appreciation. Apia stayed to help Calla, interrupting the wounded in their tasks to help them heal. Calla cooked a tea for people to help them feel better and gave some to Burgo.

Huko walked up to Kathe. "I think we should stay here until light begins again," Huko told him. It will be dark soon and it's safer here."

"You're right, Huko. Maybe Dorn will come back in time."

"I'll hunt. Take Sham with me," Huko said. Kathe nodded. They took their weapons and disappeared into the woods.

"Sariah," called Kathe. When she came, he told her they'll stay the night. She got Sofoa to help her clean one of the structures for the night. It was large enough to hold everyone to sleep.

Cakana and Bulak took the children, gathered wood, and prepared a hearth fire. Jefers became interested in the tools the Others used to mine and smelt copper. He gathered them together, found a bag, and placed them on a travois. He also took the bag of copper Rochek left behind.

Dirk and Kobo came back empty-handed. Kathe looked at them. "We couldn't find him," Dirk said. "It's like he just disappeared. No trail. Nothing."

Burgo stood and walked over to Kathe. "I'll find him."

"No," Calla said.

"I'll find him," Burgo repeated as he picked up his atlatl and short spears.

Kathe realized that Burgo was no longer a boy and nodded his head. "Take Jefers with you," Kathe told him.

"No. I'll go alone."

"Here. Eat something," Calla said as she gave him some dried meat.

"Thanks Calla." Burgo then walked into the forest. Jefers started to walk with him, but Kathe motioned for him to stay. Somehow, he knew that it was Burgo's task alone.

Once in the forest, Burgo found signs of Dorn passing through and he followed them until all signs were gone. It was like Dorn disappeared. By that time, it was dark in the forest and raining. The ground was wet and smelled musty. Burgo did not know what to do, but he remembered Leah's lessons about connecting, and wondered if he could connect to Dorn to find him. He sat on a wet log with his back to a tree and closed his eyes. He concentrated on his own breathing and after a while realized that his own breath was connected to the Breath of all. He felt space fall upon him and coming closer and closer. Then he heard the click and rustle of a porcupine and opened his eyes.

In the trees, Burgo saw Pitra. Standing, he called out to her, but Pitra said nothing. Then without a sound Pitra moved deeper into the forest. Burgo took a few steps toward Pitra, and when he saw her again, Pitra was standing the same distance away from Burgo as before. Pitra moved again and again Burgo followed. The night was dark and Burgo felt he was in a dream. Pitra kept moving and Burgo slowly followed throughout the night.

Then suddenly, Pitra, standing a distance away but in full sight of Burgo, disappeared. He again heard the sound of a porcupine and when he looked toward the sound, he saw Dorn lying on the ground.

Burgo quickly ran to Dorn and tried to wake him. "Dorn. Dorn. What's going on?" Finally, Dorn opened his eyes and saw Burgo and panicked. He stood quickly and backed away.

"Your breath is gone!" Dorn gasped.

"No. I'm still here."

Dorn then grabbed Burgo's face to make sure he was real. He then remembered Leah and collapsed back to the ground with grief, the darkness of his mind beginning to return. "Burgo, I can't … I can't…"

Burgo put his hand on Dorn's shoulder and said, "We're not supposed to do it alone."

The darkness lifted from Dorn. He looked at Burgo and said, "What am I to do without her?"

"Live," Burgo replied.

At that, Dorn began to cry, but this was a healing cry. Burgo sat down with him, grabbed him, and cried with him. They believed that a strong man cries. The weak man holds back. In the privacy of a dark night, the two friends held each other and helped each other heal for a long time. They both needed the close friendship they had for each other, and together they cried from that of a boy to the sorrow of a man. Suddenly, they heard a rustle in the forest and both rose quickly on their feet. Burgo readied his atlatl.

"Traco!" Dorn exclaimed. Traco happily came to them and offered them company for the rest of the night. They tried to make a fire, but the wood was too wet to be of much use. So they made a lean-to and tried to sleep until light, but sleep eluded them. They both looked at the sky through the opening in the lean-to.

After a long silence, Dorn said, "I wish I could see the lights."

"She's there," Burgo replied.

There comes a time when humans have to accept what they cannot control, even in the midst of grief. Dorn summed it up simply when he said, "Okay."

Silence again, and then Traco lightened the mood by snoring, making them both smile. "I'm alone," Burgo said.

"Thanks."

"No, really. I'm serious. When I woke up, I sat there and watched our people take care of things, including Leah."

"What did they do with Leah?" Dorn interrupted.

"They're taking her home, Dorn," Burgo replied. "But I sat there and watched them and all I could think of was the smell. It was the smell of death and blood and it reminded me of seeing my birth Ema and birth Appa lying together without breath. It was like I was there in that world and not here. I understand the need to eat, but I don't understand killing. Not our own kind. Not like the Others. I understand the need to protect. But I don't understand war with each other. Maybe you do. You think more than I do." Dorn shook his head no.

"But, then, I continued to watch them," Burgo continued. "And I wanted to protect them, even to the end of my own breath. But it was like I was not with them. I was alone. Then they came back without you, and something lit up inside of me and I had to find you. So I followed your trail and it's like you disappeared. I don't know what happened. You were as gone as Leah and Pitra. So I sat and asked the earth to tell me where you are. And the earth took me. I felt myself falling into the earth, but I wasn't moving. I wasn't afraid or anything. I felt I belonged and I wasn't alone anymore. I could speak the first language. I *was* speaking the first language. And there was Pitra standing there."

"Pitra?" Dorn interrupted.

"Yeah. She told me to follow her so I did and found you."

"Oh breath!" exclaimed Dorn quietly.

"So now I feel alone again."

Silence. Then Dorn spoke up. "Maybe when we aren't so connected to the earth, we're supposed to see each other. And seeing each other makes us not alone."

Burgo paused. "Yeah. I think you're right... Bye Leah. Bye Pitra."

Dorn echoed Burgo. "Bye Leah. Bye Pitra."

Soon, the two friends drifted off to sleep.

By the time Dorn, Burgo, and Traco got home, most of the tribe was there. Most were rebuilding their *waginos*, using the materials they brought back from the Others as well as cutting new poles. Traco trotted over to greet Necan and the other dogs. Cakana was the first to see them and ran up to them, greeting Burgo.

"When did you get back?" asked Burgo.

"The light was there," replied Cakana, pointing straight up and a little south.

Calla, Kathe, Jeffers, and Sofoa walked up to them. "Let's see to you two now," Calla said.

"No," replied Dorn. "Where's Leah?"

Jefers pointed to a new grave. "She's there, Dorn. We'll sing with her tomorrow when the light comes again."

"You haven't yet?" asked Dorn.

"No. We wait for you... both," Jefers replied.

"Enough of this," Calla said firmly. "You two come with me now."

Dorn and Burgo looked at each other, then at Kathe.

"I would do what she says," Kathe said.

"I'm a man now!" Burgo protested.

"Man, boy. What difference does it make?" Calla said. She then grabbed them and led them into her tipi so she could see to their wounds. Jefers turned and saw Sofoa smiling, then with great intent, walked away. "Cakana, bring water. These two stink!" Calla called.

By the time Calla was finished with them, Dorn and Burgo were refreshed. Sariah and Sofoa supplied them with clean clothes, Calla made sure all of the quill pieces were removed from Burgo and stitched up Dorn's wounds where needed, and both sported poultices to help them heal.

Huko, Dirk, and Bulak came toward the compound with two deer and two rabbits. They hung them from a tree branch, and Gala and Apia worked to process them to eat that night, with Dirk's help. Dorn saw Huko and quickly walked up to him. At the first movement Huko made, Dorn hit him and knocked him to the ground. He stayed down as Kathe and the others ran to them.

"What is this?" Kathe demanded.

"Why was Rochek outside the fence, Huko?" Dorn asked. Huko remained silent. "Huko hurt the tribe."

"That's not true," Huko said, heating up. "Rochek claimed Leah and you didn't like it. That's all."

Kathe thought a few minutes, "There's something here that needs to be known." He then directed the tribe to move into the compound and sit in a circle with Huko standing in the center. For serious crimes, the tribe needed to determine the most truth they could. All the elders, men and women, were allowed to speak if they wanted. It was a very strong custom for all parties to not lie, and Huko was very much aware of that expectation. Furthermore, everyone was expected to remain calm.

Kathe spoke. "We will know," he said. "Dorn, what do you know?"

Dorn stood, but did not enter the center of the circle. "I know he pushed me down when I saw Rochek take Leah. I heard him say that she belongs to Rochek."

"Did you say that Leah belongs to Rochek?" asked Kathe.

After a pause, Huko replied, "Yes. Rochek wanted her and he took her. I think that at the time she belonged to him. But I was trying to keep Dorn from alerting the Others that we were there. Everyone knows Dorn doesn't keep control of himself very well."

"This is true," Kobo said.

Jefers then confronted Dorn, "What makes you think Huko hurt anybody of the tribe?"

Dorn paused as he had to confront himself. "I don't know."

"Then sit down and be quiet," Kobo said. Dorn sat down. Kobo then addressed Kathe. "This is wrong. Huko did nothing wrong and Dorn was wrong to hit him. We should go eat."

"Why was Rochek outside the fence, Huko?" Kathe asked.

"I don't know," Huko said angrily.

Garath interrupted, "But I do. And I know that you know, Huko."

"How do you know, Garath?" Kathe asked.

"I was there," Garath replied.

"Tell us what you know," Kathe said.

"Rochek and I were taken by the Others," Garath began. "We were in a tree when they saw us watching them, and I fell and twisted my ankle. We saw them kill a girl and burn her and I was sure they were going to do that with us. But Rochek. He ... I mean we watched them for a couple of days and they dug in the earth and got this fire rock. Rochek wanted it. He wanted the fire rock. But they were too big for us. Giants. They put us in the fence. You know. And I think they were out to kill us or something, like the girl. But Huko. He saw it all. I ... didn't know he was there. So when they put us in the fence, he killed one. Then some of them tried to kill him, but they couldn't so they stopped and Huko stopped. Huko is ... a ... great warrior. So they talked and Huko made a trade. He gets Rochek. And they get the rest of us. They wanted slaves I think. So Rochek stayed in the fence and I was in the fence and Huko brought them here I guess. I don't know about that part. But Huko left with them. When you got there, they let Rochek out. That's all I know." Garath sat down.

Everyone was stunned that Huko would betray them so severely. Kathe sat for a while and looked at Huko. "Is this true?" he asked quietly.

Huko looked at Kathe and the rest of the tribe, wondering how he could handle this. He could barely keep his anger under control and wanted to kill Garath. Finally, he simply said, "Yes."

"Why?"

Huko wondered how he could deceive the others looking at him and thought that surely they could see his anger. "Rochek is my birth son," Huko said simply. "I did not know the giants would kill. I did not think they would. They wanted slaves, and I thought I could free you when the time came. So I protected Rochek."

"You gave no thought to Garath?"

The question hit Huko hard. He knew his purpose was to protect everyone, and he realized that he did not do that. "No. I was without seeing."

Kathe also had to control and try to hide his anger against Huko. "Then you will stand and let the spear speak," Kathe declared. "Do the elders agree?" They all solemnly indicated yes.

Early humankind had to find a way to keep peace within the tribe, and that meant forming a justice system to satisfy all members of the tribe. It was the custom to exile those members whose crimes were grievous, and to the tribe, that was a sure death sentence. But Huko had not run and when it came down to the wire, he admitted the truth. So he was to face the spear. The person throwing the spear was bound to try to kill, but that was not always attained. The person facing justice stood without moving. Whatever the spear would do was just, whether it killed or injured. It was the way to have justice and also to have an end to it.

The tribe stood and moved to each side of Huko. Jefers gave Kathe one of their long spears and Kathe moved a ways off to strike Huko down. Calla then brought the mandaka and called on the Breath of All to help know. She then faced Huko.

"Huko, you are a great warrior and you have protected us many times," she said, quietly. "Do you know why you face the spear now?"

Huko stood up straight and said, "Yes."

"Will you tell us why?" she asked.

Huko looked at Calla, then moved to face the rest of the tribe, walking in a circle. "I have tried to protect, but I did not because all I saw was my birth-son. I thought that everybody would be okay and I can free you later. I am sorry for this. I have the same feelings about those who no longer have breath as you do. But there's no excuse that I can give." He then moved to his place in the center. Calla walked to the tribe.

"Does anyone have anything to say?" Kathe demanded loudly.

"I do," said Kobo. "Huko is our best warrior and knows how to kill four-leggeds so we all can live. He has proven his skill over and over. I say if his breath remains, he remains standing among us as warrior."

"What do the elders say?" Kathe asked. The elders talked amongst themselves and then indicated that they agree. "Then I will have a say," Kathe said. He walked closer to Huko to face him, his anger barely contained. "You taught Rochek your ways, and your ways are not the ways of the human. Your ways are poison to us." Kathe turned to the tribe. "I say if his breath remains, he will no longer hold his ways." Kathe then walked up to Huko, close to his face. "Do you agree?"

"Rochek could not see. He only knew what he wanted," Huko replied. "He wanted Leah and was out to take the breath of Dorn. He wanted the fire rock. And now he's left us. I did this. I agree."

"All right then," Kathe said as he moved back to throw the spear. A couple of people beat the drums while Huko walked outside the compound gate.

Suddenly, Dorn spoke up. "I speak," he said. The drums stopped. "I say that I hold the spear."

Kathe was surprised and hesitated. "What do the elders say?" Kathe asked. Everyone knew Dorn's love for Leah and thought it right for him to take the throw. But they also knew that Dorn did not throw very well. They thought it was justice for both Dorn and Huko.

Dorn walked up to Kathe and said privately, "Your anger is not justice."

Facing himself, Kathe's anger disappeared and he nodded. "Dorn takes the spear," Kathe said, giving Dorn the spear.

As Dorn was taking Kathe's place, Burgo went to Dorn and talked privately with him. "You know you can't hit a mammoth if he was sleeping at your side."

"I know," said Dorn.

"Then why? He killed Leah."

Dorn hesitated, then said, "I think everyone walks the path in the dark at some time. And not everyone has Pitra to show them the way. I think Huko has walked in the dark long enough."

Kathe cut into their conversation and reminded them that justice needs to happen. "Will you do your best to take his breath?" asked Kathe.

"I will," Dorn declared. The drums started again.

Dorn then hauled back and when the drums stopped, he threw the spear as best he could. It caught Huko in the right side of his chest and scraped the outside of his ribs. Huko went down in pain, but it was not life-threatening. A couple of people beat the drums again and Huko stood and entered the compound.

As was their custom, the tribe immediately surrounded Huko, patted him on the back and welcomed him back to the tribe. They all said something positive about him, mostly how much he protected the tribe and his skill as a warrior. Huko found his anger dissipate when experiencing this kind of reconciliation and he was determined to protect them. For a long time without it, now that he experienced it, he discovered happiness and belonging with the tribe. Everyone was happy that Huko still had his breath, including Dorn who walked up to Huko and clasped his arm. Huko said, "Well done, brother!" The others laughed because of Dorn's lack of skill. "Next time I'll put you in front of the mammoth!"

"Last time you did!" laughed Dorn.

"Well, you run well," countered Huko.

Burgo and Dorn moved away from the crowd and Burgo marveled at Dorn's skill at killing the Others. "What happened?" Burgo asked.

"I think I got mad," Dorn said.

"Next time we get attacked by a wolf, get mad then!" They both laughed.

Calla took Huko's tunic and pulled him into her *wagino* to stitch his wound. When he returned, the tribe was back to normal life. He went to Apia.

"Will Rochek ever come back?" she asked.

"I don't know," Huko replied. He then bent down and felt the trodden grass in the compound. "I guess I give him to the earth and hope he finds his way."

The next day, it was time to sing to Leah. The entire tribe was saddened by all that they had lost. But Burgo and Dorn had sung to the people buried and it sufficed for them to know that their breath was with the Breath of All. Now, it was Leah's turn and people gathered at her burial site. Calla had already given the red ochre when they buried her. The drums sounded. Calla carried the mandaka and led the song.

Breath
No longer breath
No longer to be what might have been
No longer to be made
No longer to become
You've left the sacred dream
And you're going home
I'll walk with you as you find a brand new home
I'll walk with you as you cross the muddy river
I'll walk with you as you journey through the mist
I'll walk with you past brother tree and sister stone
I'll walk with you as you see behind the light
I'll walk with you as you find a brand new home
For you belong
You still belong to us
You belong to Earth
You belong to Breath
You stand with us
Together, never apart
Together
I'll walk with you as you find a brand new home
I'll walk with you as you cross the muddy river
I'll walk with you as you journey through the mist
I'll walk with you past brother tree and sister stone
I'll walk with you as you see behind the light
I'll walk with you as you find a brand new home
Oh Breath
Help us see and hear

Help us never to forget
Their breath is our breath
Always

Dorn felt as if a mountain lion had opened his chest and shredded his heart. Burgo stayed with him for the rest of the day, saying nothing. He was just present for Dorn. The tribe returned to the compound. The two friends walked in the meadow a little ways from the compound and settled down near a tree. Burgo sat with his back resting on the tree trunk and Dorn lay on the ground. The smell of earth was comforting to him as well as the quiet presence of Burgo. After a time, Dorn listened to his own breathing and felt himself embraced by the earth. It felt as if the earth covered him with a blanket. He dropped into half-sleep, half-awake and entered the realm of the sacred dream. He saw Leah walking toward him and a mountain lion joined her. Her earth-being, a raven, swooped down and landed on her shoulder. They walked side by side for a while, then the raven flew over to the mountain lion and landed on his back. Leah then turned to her right and walked away out of sight. The mountain lion stopped. He said nothing. Then Dorn woke fully and discovered that his grief was manageable. He felt as if Leah was with him and somehow he knew that she would not leave. He stood and said, "Let's go."

"Good. I'm hungry," Burgo said, rising and walking with his friend.

"You're always complaining about something," Dorn replied.

They saw Kathe and Calla standing and talking together. Huko walked up to them and spoke with them. Kathe shook his head no, *Wait*, and saw Dorn and Burgo coming into the compound. Kathe then called the tribe to council. Everyone sat in a circle around the center hearth. Cakana sat next to Burgo.

Calla stood before them with the mandaka and made a sign of passing the mandaka over them by walking around the center hearth. "We should all be together," she said, "support each other, even those who have wronged us and we have forgiven. That is what brings the circle together. Our circle together."

They were much fewer in number than a few days before. Everyone could feel the soft heat of the fire and smell of the smoke. The smoke danced around, giving everyone a breath in turn with the slight wind. Kathe explained the problem and the decision to be made. They could either stay or travel to a better place. While Kathe spoke of their home and the dangers of being a small group, Calla walked the outside of the circle and touched each person with the mandaka.

Bulak stood. "I will speak," he said. Kathe nodded. "The Others know this place. If they bring more of them, we will all die. I say we leave." He sat down.

"The Others are our greatest threat. We lived here for quite a while before that threat came to being," Kathe said without standing. "But it's a threat."

"I will speak," Garath said as he stood gingerly on one foot. Kathe nodded. "I don't think the Others live here like we do. Rochek told me that they live that way," he said pointing southeast. "They were getting ready to leave. If we killed them all here, maybe there will be no threat." Garath sat down.

"Why were they in the forest away from their home then?" Sham asked without rising.

Jefers stood. "I will speak. But let me get something." Everyone waited while Jefers entered his tipi and exited with the bag of copper. "They were taking this from earth," he said. He then reached into the bag and pulled out several pieces of copper. People marveled at the fire rock.

"Is it breath from earth?" asked Apia without standing.

Calla then said, "No. Breath is in everything. Breath is unseen. This is a kind of rock."

"But the Others prize it," Jefers said, still standing. "I say we learn this task. And if the Others come again, we have something to trade so we can live in peace. These are some tools they used." He showed them the tools he found at the Others' site. Jefers then sat down and passed the tools and copper so everyone could see them.

Kathe nodded and said, "This rock is pretty but it means nothing to us and something to them. I don't know how they took it from earth."

Garath rose again. "I know how they did it. Rochek and I watched them." He sat down.

Kathe rose. "All right. We can try to trade with the Others if they return. But the question still remains. Do we stay or go?"

After a few moments, Dirk rose. "I will speak. We are too few to stay. We need to find another tribe and join with them. We need to live." He sat back down.

Huko stood. "I will speak. We are too few to walk. Staying here, we know the land. Mammoths have not traveled far since we came here. There is food for mammoth and our four-legged brothers and sisters. There is food here enough for us."

"But what about the cold season? It's coming and we have too little food saved," Sariah asked without standing.

"We will hunt through the cold season," Huko said. "I will protect the tribe." Both Dirk and Kobo echoed Huko, "I will protect the tribe." Huko sat down.

"Dirk," Kathe said without standing. "Do you stand with Huko now?"

"Yes. If Huko says we can live, I'm with him."

Huko stood again. "I will speak again. I name Burgo to be after me. I will teach him how to lead the hunt and to lead attack." Dorn and Burgo looked at each other wide-eyed.

Kathe said, "Burgo, stand." He does. "Do you accept that kind of responsibility to protect the tribe?"

Burgo stammered. "It … it is an honor. Yes." Huko sat back down.

Kathe smiled. "You can sit down again, Burgo." He does.

Calla stood. "I will speak. I name Cakana to be after me. I will teach her the ways of healing and of Breath."

"Cakana, stand," Kathe said. She does. "Do you accept that kind of responsibility to protect the tribe?"

"Yes, oh yes, thank you!" Cakana said and sat down. Calla sat down.

The tribe paused and Kathe let it happen. Such decisions needed to be slow. The tribe was used to such ways and tried to trust each other. Finally, Kathe asked, "Is there anyone else who needs to speak?"

Sham stood. "I will speak. Our numbers are too few now. I need a mate and I can't find one here. We need to go toward the dying sun and find another home. We need to do it now before the cold comes." He sat down.

Sofoa rose. "I will speak. There is much to do to rebuild our home here and we would need to hunt. But we would still need to hunt if we leave, and it's better to be ready here." She sat down.

Kathe allowed another long pause. Then he asked again, "Is there anyone else who needs to speak?" Nobody answered, and after another pause, Kathe stood.

"Do you accept Burgo and Cakana's new protection for you?" People nodded, so Kathe continued. Then I will speak. After a long pause, he said, "We will stay as long as we need to be stronger. We know the danger. We know our need for food and we know that here is a good place to live until the four-leggeds move. When we are able and stronger after the cold, we will move toward the dying sun. Do you accept?"

The tribe nodded and said yes.

"There's one other thing," Kathe said. "I name Dorn to be after me. I will teach him how to listen. Is there anyone who wants to speak?" Nobody said anything, so Kathe continued. "Dorn, stand." He does. "Do you accept this responsibility to protect the tribe?"

Dorn stood silent and tall, thinking. He then said, "No. I am not able. I am not good." He looked squarely at Kathe. "I am not you."

Kathe paused and said, "You must be you, not me. We will work on it. Meantime, if anything happens to me, I name Jefers to be after me. What does the tribe say?"

Huko stood. "Jefers is as old and slow as you!" Members of the tribe laughed at that and some slapped Jefers on the back. "But I say yes and wait to see Dorn's becoming." He sat back down.

"Does anyone have anything more to say?" Kathe asked. Nobody indicated anything more to say. Then Kathe declared, "Then it is said. Now let it be done."

The council was finished and people went back to their work rebuilding their home. Huko took Burgo, Dorn, and Kobo to hunt as quickly as possible before the light died.

On the way out of the compound to go into the forest, Dorn turned to Burgo. "You ready for this?"

"Of course I'm not ready. Nobody's ready to do something they've never done before," Burgo replied.

"Oh. I didn't think of that," Dorn said.

"Of course you didn't!"

"Oh shut up," Dorn said, hitting Burgo on the back.

"No, you shut up." Burgo then hit Dorn on his back where he was hurt.

"Ow! Breath!" They entered the forest.

Dorn wondered why Huko selected him to hunt with the other two, but then realized that he and Burgo were a team. And nothing is done very well without each other.

Part II

Woodland
5000 BCE

Part II Dramatis Personae

Belia .... A young woman

Inda .... Woman of the Wikangatra tribe

Maelys .... A girl of the Wikangatra tribe

Wandago .... Inda's grown son

Kandra .... Inda's grown daughter

Danica, Avah, Allotar .....Women of the Wikangatra

Cree, Kapono ... Men of the Wikangatra tribe

Broch .... Belia's mate, Woodland tribe

Kace .... Broch's best friend

Tac'kana .... Woodland tribe Healer

Jokan .... Woodland tribe Leader beside Healer

Shoria .... Jokan's mate, Tac'kana's daughter

Narsa................ Kace's mate

Haol, Lena .... Women of the Woodland tribe

Luko, Danuku .. Men of the Woodland tribe

Dosh, Flep .... Men of the Woodland tribe

Chapter Seven: Summer

She awoke, opened her eyes, gazed at the clouds wandering in the deep blue sky, and wondered why she was alive. It was still day but the moon was out. Belia took great comfort in the moon. She didn't know why. Perhaps it was because the moon was alive and she knew that life always changes. Maybe it was because the moon was almost always there. Maybe it was because the moon gave light when she needed light the most.

Maybe it was because the moon never hurt her.

Belia wished she belonged. Lying on the grassy ground felt cool. She wasn't sure, but she could almost hear the earth tell her that she belonged to her, the earth. But the louder voice within her, the voice she didn't like, always convinced her to not listen. She was worthless. She was an object, nothing more. She certainly wasn't a human. She was nothing, belonged nowhere, wanted by no one.

To Belia, she was experiencing her Summer, one of many she will have in her lifetime. At that moment, she knew who she was. But her Summer came from her Spring, and so her thinking was affected by Life itself. It was not unlike the Clovis understanding of Becoming, but within a human's Becoming at this stage of humankind were circles of Spring, Summer, Fall, and Winter. Human circles did not match the seasons of nature. All human circles formed a spiral of life, an experience of breaking and transformation.

Standing, she checked herself. No broken bones, just bruised and sore. Lucky. Her face hurt. She couldn't remember why they beat her this time. Sometimes they just do it. Wandago seems to be angry all the time.

Nobody was around. Mid-spring still carried snow in the air and on the hills were scattered patches of snow. A mere five thousand years ago, the glacier finally gave up the last of his icy essence and Lake Superior was at rest. But the glacier made his mark. The Keweenaw Peninsula was too hard for the glacier to affect her much because of the basalt rock within her, but the glacier's breathing created hills and mountain ranges along Lake Superior's border. Both the Huron Mountain Range and the South Range mountains stood in their prime and taller than today. The glacier's inhaling and exhaling left remnants of moraines scattered near the peninsula, in Wisconsin, and lower Michigan. Sometimes we can see the moraine area as rocky hills that are higher than the surrounding area. The west side of the Keweenaw has end moraines. Nearly everywhere, we can see large rocks gouged and scarred by the passing of the glacier. A notable glacial groove can be seen near the school in Calumet. When he receded one last time, the glacier left sediment, float rock, and a taste of copper within surface rock. Ancient humans found copper under the surface of the earth. Thousands of years later, humans would find an amazing abundance of copper deeper underneath the surface of the Keweenaw.

Where was Maelys? Belia had to find Maelys. Belia was fifteen years old, but Maelys was only twelve and Belia doubted she could protect her much longer. Despite her age, nobody wanted Belia as a mate because of her dark red hair.

When the glacier receded north, the earth exposed different outlets that drained Lake Superior. Lake Duluth was engulfed by Lake Superior and his boundaries shrank to where they are today. The Ontonagon River widened from the stream that Dorn and Burgo knew. The Ontonagon River now has a drainage system with about 1,400 square miles and is Michigan's largest of the tributaries entering into Lake Superior. More than 200 square miles of the Keweenaw Peninsula drains into Portage Lake. The lake and its outlet are at the level of Lake Superior, as are also Torch Lake and an inlet to Portage Lake. The inlet travels southeastward across the peninsula past Hancock and Houghton. A ship canal now connects the head of this inlet with Lake Superior by a cut about thirty feet deep across a gravel bar of Nipissing age. St. Marys River at the far east is Lake Superior's main outlet. The ancient Lake Algonquin south and east of the Keweenaw Peninsula slowly drained with new outlets exposed and formed Lake Michigan and Lake Huron. During Belia's life, Lake Superior's water level was not quite finished and would not completely level until 5000 years later. Without the glacier, the jet stream had no barrier and the continental climate was similar to today.

The environment had changed since the Clovis people walked the Upper Peninsula. Gone were the mammoth, dire wolf, the glyptodont, and other species not found today. The forest still teemed with four-leggeds though, but the people's environment was nearly the same as today. The earth developed a boreal forest, but the gradual warming after 9500 BCE brought more southern flora and fauna onto the Keweenaw. The glacier deposited mostly till plain on the surface of the Keweenaw Peninsula, and we walk on top of the same till plain as did Belia at 5000 BCE. Glaciers form till plains when a sheet of ice breaks from the glacier and melts, thereby depositing sediment caught in the ice. The glacier also deposited float copper in the forms of boulders, rocks, and sheets that prehistoric peoples discovered and found to be an amazing venture. Besides searching for and picking up float copper, prehistoric people also learnt to extract the metal from rock that demonstrates both a technological and creative mind.

Belia picked up her basket and placed in the roots and herbs scattered around that she had found. She walked near the cliffs on the Keweenaw. By chance, she found a small cave behind some brush. It was too shallow for bats but kept out the rain. Belia liked it. It was dry and cool. She felt safe there and suddenly fell asleep. When she awoke, it was mid-afternoon and she knew she had to get back to the compound.

By the time she found the compound, it was late afternoon. Today, their home would have been north and east of Phoenix on the Keweenaw spine near the Delaware Mine. Camp was in a large clearing, and, much like that of the Clovis tribe, surrounded by a log fence for protection from bear and wolf. Scattered about were drying racks, a pit for refuge, and another pit for storage. Their homes were more permanent than Clovis and were made of logs and bark. They placed poles in holes in the ground, bent and tied them together at the top, and laid sheets of bark as sheathing. The sheathing left a hole at the top for smoke to exit. Depending on the size of the family, each home structure was different in size and shape. Some were round whilst others were oblong shaped. Belia lived with Inda, Maelys, and Inda's two nearly-grown children, Wandago and Kandra. A bear killed Inda's mate three seasons ago. Their hut was of medium size and oblong, and stood near the compound's fence. In the middle of the interior was a hearth fire. The floor was dirt and bearskins.

Belia found Maelys sitting outside the hut and leaning her back on the side of the hut. She was watching Pula playing with her baby. Belia sat next to Maelys and Maelys pulled her close so she could speak softly. "Are you okay?" she asked with concern.

"Yes," Belia replied and kissed her hair. The two young women relaxed against the hut.

"I'm watching Pula's baby," Maelys said. "I like babies. Do you think I'll have one some day?"

"Of course," Belia replied. "Your hair's not red like mine." They watched as Pula tickled and kissed her baby. "Look at her," Belia mused. "Look at her. Stretching her feet up in the air. Up. Up. Her legs growing, her toes drumming the air. Up. Up. We have to feel the sky before we can plant our feet on the ground. There is no ground without sky."

Inda stepped out from the corner of the hut, snatched Belia's basket, and scoffed. "That's a stupid thing to say. Get up and get to work. Kandra's bringing fish." Inda then returned to the hut.

Belia moved to rise, but Maelys pulled her back down. "I like it when you talk like that," she whispered.

Belia smiled and placed her hand on top of Maelys' head. "Come on Maelys. I'll help you get the fire going." Belia then walked to the hut opening and called in. "I'm going with Maelys to get wood." She expected no answer and got none. Both then walked into the trees to gather wood. But Maelys was pensive.

"Why do you stay?" she asked.

Belia stopped picking up wood and turned to her. "What?"

"Why do you let them do that to you? Why do you stay?"

Belia stood still for a while and then sat on a downed log. She hugged the wood she'd picked up. "I think I would die without the tribe," she said. "Where would I go?"

"You have your sling. I've seen you use it."

"You can't tell anyone. Please," said Belia with alarm.

"I don't want to tell anybody, Belia. But I just don't understand." The tribe thought Belia to have evil reside within her and did not want her to touch weapons.

"All right. Sit down." Maelys sat on the log next to her. "Listen, Maelys, everybody has a role in the tribe. So I'm the nothing so they can feel good."

"They like hitting you?" Maelys asked.

"Of course they do. And I deserve it."

"Because you have red hair?"

"Partly I guess. But I make them do it too. I fight against them so I deserve whatever they do to me. I guess maybe I even keep the tribe safe. They've got somebody to hit so they don't hit themselves."

"That's not right," objected Maelys. "That's crazy talk." Belia just sat there staring at the ground for a while. Finally, Maelys broke the silence. "Are you okay?"

Still staring at the leaves on the ground, Belia quietly said, "Sometimes I wonder why. Sometimes I wonder what it would be like to live somewhere and people don't hurt me or tell me I'm nothing. I don't think I would even understand it. But I think maybe there's a different world that I would like to be a part of."

"You mean a different tribe?"

"I don't know," Belia replied. "This can't be right though. I think Grandmother Earth would want something different for us. For you, too."

"Do you think Grandmother Earth is real?"

Belia looked up at the tree canopy and something vibrated within her. "Yes. Yes I do."

Maelys suddenly took Belia's arm. "Belia, I know you can do it. You can go on your own and find another tribe. You're strong. I just know you can.

"They'll find me, Maelys. They don't want to lose their slave."

"You have to try! You just have to!"

"I don't know that I can. You say I'm strong. But I think I'm supposed to live like this. I don't know."

"I do, Belia. I think you could get away and be happy."

This idea struck Belia deeply. "But what about you? I wouldn't be able to see you any more."

"I'll be okay. When I can, I'll come and find you. Then we can be together."

"I'd like that," Belia said.

After another pause, Maelys said, "I love you, Belia."

At that, Belia looked at Maelys and realized that she wasn't a child anymore. Maelys was a woman. "Thank you Maelys. Thank you for being my friend. I love you too.... But we better get going before Inda gets impatient."

"Okay."

They returned to the hut and the evening was without incident. Kandra brought in fish that Inda cooked. Belia waited in her space until everyone was finished before she took any food. Maelys cleaned the cooking space and by the time she finished, Inda, Wandago, and Kandra were all sleeping. Inda did not allow Maelys to sleep in Belia's space, but she was next to it, and that close distance made Belia feel good, just to have somebody not be afraid to be near her.

The next day, after Belia returned from washing, she walked to the hut. Inda was outside airing her bearskin. Inda looked at her and said, "You better get going with it today. Ganta wants her bag soon."

"Okay," Belia acknowledged, and went to continue to make Ganta's bag. A tapestry bag was rare during this age. A simple leather bag was far easier to make. Early humankind discovered that the worth of an object was partly determined by its complexity and the skill of the artisan. And Belia was a very skilled artisan of tapestry. Throughout history, humankind also implemented impressive creativity to make tools. Such is the human bent.

Belia entered the hut and brought out the objects she needed to make Ganta's bag. She had a simple loom rectangular in shape that she built some time ago, its length about the same as her arm. The loom was made of scraped and polished wood. The top and bottom pieces were smoothed sticks. They were secured with rawhide upon two side sticks with a forked tip at each bottom and then the rawhide dried to make the loom strong and secure. The top of the loom was the same but without the forked tip. The top rested on natural knobs and secured with rawhide she placed when wet and then let dry. It took a long time to find two side sticks to evenly hold the top and bottom. She tied the long weft fibers to the bottom of the loom and stretched it taut to the top and continued to wrap the weft around the top and bottom sticks until she got the width she wanted. She had already prepared the textile fibers. The inside bark of plants and shrubs were good for the project – especially basswood, dogbane, and milkweed. Belia carefully twisted the fibers. She made the weft fibers as dense as possible so they would not stretch. The horizontal warp fibers were less dense and more flexible. She carefully spaced the weft evenly across the top and bottom. Bclia used the strong fibers and laced them under and over the weft three rows, carefully using a comb to tuck them to the bottom of the loom. This secured the weft and she can then make the tapestry with the more flexible warp fibers. She placed in a shed stick, or weaving sword, to separate the weft. Working from left to right, she could use the shed stick twisting it onto its side to separate the weft to easily place the warp. But from right to left, she had to flatten the shed stick and draw the warp fibers over and under by hand. She left rather long tails on both sides of the warp. This helped her fold the tapestry and tie the sides of the bag as well as for decoration.

Meanwhile, she had dyed fibers at her side to make patterns in the bag. She used roots that looked like carrots, except carrots were first known in Persia and Asia Minor hundreds of years later. Belia searched for roots with color. For brown, she used dandelion roots, oak bark, and walnut hulls. For pink, she searched for berries and red and pink flowers. And for blue, she found blueberries that were prolific in late summer in her area.

When making her bag, once in a while, she replaced part of a row with a porcupine quill for decoration. It was Maelys' job to cut the quills at Belia's instruction. It was also Maelys' job to drill or punch a hole in very small pieces of copper. Belia would loop the warp once in a while and using a fine long piece of copper as a tool, thread the warp fibers through at the loop. The more pieces of copper indicated a higher sacred object for Ganta. Inda expected a fine bearskin for the bag. It was a long and tedious project, but Belia liked it. She sat facing the camp with the loom resting on the side of a drying rack. This way, she could work and witness the life of people.

Turning to Maelys, Belia said, "Look. There's Cason and Jaxe working copper now."

"Rega!" Maelys replied. "I always like seeing what they do with it."

Over at Cason and Jaxe's area, various items made of copper were placed here and there. Fishhooks, awls, knives, punch flakers, beads, and chisels. The tribe traded raw copper, but the made items were more valuable. The best of the made copper items were for trade, but the rest found their way into everyday life of the tribe. The tribe adapted to their awareness of copper and its use, but copper was not essential to the economics of the tribe; they could live without it. That was left to later humankind who learned to care about symbolic artifacts and a way to gain economic and social status. At this time in the Keweenaw, people's awareness was copper's beauty and usefulness, mainly for utility within their own lifestyle and trade value amongst tribes. They placed a value on copper that was sacred based on their view of the cosmos, but not enough to place copper on a symbolic pedestal. Because of their cosmological point of view, copper was precious because of its ties to power in nature and in trade. Copper was useful to their way of life but did not define their way of life. Trading copper in the Keweenaw wove tribe to tribe, from ancient time to European discovery of the Keweenaw, despite the development of changing indigenous cultures.

The two men were heating up the copper much like the Others did hundreds of years ago during the Clovis period. They would then beat the copper to the shape they wanted. Depending on the size of the copper, they'd fold it to the thickness they wanted the tool to be. Beating the copper hardened it.

"I don't see why people don't like your hair," pondered Maelys. "In the sun, it's the same color as copper."

"They think that the color of my hair tells them who I am," Belia replied. "You know that."

"Yeah. I know," Maelys admitted.

It did not take long for humankind to find prejudice by the appearance of differences. Whether born of fear or a need for self-worth, an abhorrence and curiosity of physical traits straying from the norm grew in a heart sickened by a disconnection from the self. Perhaps the encounter between Clovis and the Others struck fear in humankind along the string of this story. And that encounter grabbed hold of fear morphing into an exclusion of any human passing on its ancient memory with physical traits. Or perhaps it was the influence of Rochek and his greed and distain for women handed down from generation to generation. But however it happened, Belia knew the consequences of prejudice within her own tribe, and she constantly fought those consequences to the point of desperately trying to regain her own sense of self to be determined by who she wanted to be rather by who others thought her to be.

Belia watched as Danica and Avah walked to Allotar's hut. The three sat outside with their looms and materials.

Belia took a deep breath and stood. Maelys suddenly became frightened. "Don't! You'll just get hurt again." She pulled on Belia's tunic to try to get her to sit back down. But Belia gently took Maelys' hand in her own.

"I have to try," she said. Belia walked over to the three women, taking her loom but not the rest of her materials. Danica noticed Belia and alerted the others.

"She's not so bad," Avah whispered. "I want to know how she loops."

Humankind needs community beyond the need to survive. Humankind also has an emotional need to belong that helps people advance toward self-being. And as community progressed to be more complex, groups within community developed. In Belia's tribe, called Wikangatra meaning People Who Live Above, groups formed according to distinct interests like tapestry and copper-shaping. Cason and Jaxe often worked together shaping copper whilst others worked the rock to extract the metal. Danica, Avah, and Allotar formed a different group interested in making tapestries. This way, interests and competence helped mold self-identity and connected the person to the larger community by offering a very real role in living together and meeting wants and needs. From this humble beginning, humankind eventually formed trade guilds that were often connected to a patron god or goddess. Later, guilds offered protection in an ever-developing world and, at its Western peak during the medieval era in Europe, determined the time a person worked as well as the price of items. The medieval community sought the best quality and quality determined economic status. In the early Oriental world, workers of distinct trades banded together to achieve an assembly line to build. Often, they would erect a large building this way, each guild contributing their work when the timing was right. In the West's modern history, unions formed to protect the worker.

But it all happened from a small group of people having similar interests to play a role in their community. Today, people continue this basic human need. We see it when a group of mostly women get together to have a quilting session or mostly men engaged in fantasy football. The problem came when people chose to exclude a person from the group due to prejudice or oversight or downright pettiness. Avah wanted Belia to enter the group, but Danica was more susceptible to the tribe's belief about appearances.

"What do you want?" demanded Danica as Belia moved close to the group.

"It's okay," Avah said, addressing Danica. "She's really good with this."

"She's bad luck!" Danica exclaimed as she stood to face and stop Belia.

Avah also stood to face Danica. Allotar looked disgusted. "Really? We're gonna do this again?" she said without standing.

Avah looked at Allotar. "I want her to tell me how to loop like that."

Inda exited from the hut and saw what was going on. Maelys tried to take Inda's attention away from the group. "Hey look, Inda!" Maelys showed her a large copper piece. "Do you think I should drill two holes in this? It might make it nice, don't you think?"

Annoyed, Inda hit Maelys in the face, knocking her down. "I don't care what you do."

Avah pulled Belia down to sit with them and Danica gave up and decided to leave the group. But Inda grabbed a hold of Belia's arm, preventing her from sitting down with Avah and Allotar. "What do you want with Belia?" asked Inda. "She has work to do."

Avah said, "She knows how to make loops in her bag. They're really good." Belia found herself on the other side of Inda.

"Oh, she learned all that from me, you know," said Inda. "She isn't really very good at doing anything. I have to take it apart and do it all again. But she just takes all the credit." Inda laughed a little.

"Really?" Avah asked.

"Don't be stupid," Allotar said under her breath to Avah.

"Of course! I taught her everything she knows. She just isn't smart enough to do it right, that's all. But, anyway, we need to get back to work. Lots to do."

Inda took Belia by the arm and led her back to her hut. "Well, okay," Avah said. The women returned to their tasks.

Once back, Inda very quietly told Belia to pick up her things, which she did. Inda then pushed her into the hut. Once inside, she pushed Belia so hard that she fell onto Wandago. "Get off of me!" he said, kicking her.

"I'm sorry. I didn't mean –" Belia said. She quickly crawled into the corner of the hut where she sleeps. But Inda grabbed her by her hair and forced her to stand. Belia dropped her items that scattered around the corner of the hut.

Forcing Belia to look at her, Inda demanded, "Why can't you do what your told? Why do you always have to make trouble?"

"I just wanted to join them, that's all," Belia stuttered.

"They didn't want you there. You were pushing yourself onto those girls and nobody wanted you there. You even made Danica leave."

"No, Avah wanted me to show –"

"Don't lie to me! I saw it!" She let Belia go and cower in her corner. But Inda wasn't finished. She stood over Belia.

"Isn't it enough that I have to feed you? And clothe you? What have I done to deserve this from you? Day after day I let you stay here –"

"The elders said you have to –" Belia interrupted.

"Nobody says I have to do anything!" Inda shoved her hard enough for Belia to fall onto her bedding. Inda became quietly and dangerously angry. "I take you in. I let you stay here. I take care of you. And all you do is embarrass me in front of the tribe. All you ever do is spit on me."

"I'm sorry. I'm sorry."

"Want me to beat her again?" asked Wandago.

Inda stepped back and turned to Wandago. "No. She's had enough for one day."

"But she doesn't listen and she doesn't learn," Wandago insisted.

Inda turned on him in anger and slapped him. "You like it too much! Too much! Why do you think you can't get a mate?"

"I'm a warrior!" Wandago countered.

Inda laughed. "Sure you are. Sure you are. Now go out and either hunt with the men – "

Wandago interrupted, "They're already back from hunting."

Inda stepped up to his face. "Either be with the men or dry meat with the women. Come back with food. Do I have to tell you twice?"

Wandago stepped back. "No mother." He left the hut to seek out the men to help them process their cache.

Inda turned to Belia. "I'll never understand how you can show yourself to people. You're a freak... Go outside and continue making Ganta's bag. Make sure people know that all is well here.... Comb your hair." Inda threw a fish-bone comb at her. She then left the hut. She turned the corner of the hut and saw Maelys in the same place, working with copper beads. "Go get a fire ready," she said. Maelys gathered her items and tried to place them near the hut's opening before looking for wood for a hearth fire within the hut. But Inda pushed her and bits of copper scattered. Maelys did not wait to pick up her things, but left to gather wood. Thousands of years later, someone with a metal detector would find a small piece of copper with a strange hole in its middle. Inda then reentered the hut and abruptly came face to face with Belia who stared at her. "What are you doing?" asked Inda.

Belia continued to look at Inda. Then she said, "You have forgotten the voice of Grandmother Earth." This stunned Inda for a few seconds, enough time for Belia to push past her and exit the hut. She ran into Wandago who pushed her aside and entered the hut.

Once inside, Wandago grabbed Inda's arm and pulled her to him. "Mother," he said through clenched teeth. "I am a warrior whether you agree or not. People here see me as a great warrior! I'm a man!"

"Yes, yes," Inda stammered. "I feel so sick. Please stay with me Wandago. Don't leave me here like this."

"Like what?" asked Wandago, releasing her arm.

"Nothing. Nothing. I'm all right. I'll be all right."

"Belia do something to you?"

"Yes. Well no. No. She can't help it, son. She is what she is, that's all. She didn't do anything. Not really."

Wandago looked at her for a while. "Go smoke. It'll make you feel better." The tribe smoked several plants, none of which were addictive.

"Get it for me, please. Help your old mother. Please."

"Get it yourself," Wandago said, quietly.

"Not you too? Doesn't anybody care about me? I'll go out this winter to die. I'm useless now."

With a sigh, Wandago said "Fine." He fossicked through her things and pulled out a pipe and a leather pouch of dried plant. She held out her hand and he helped her sit down on her bearskins and gave her the pipe and pouch.

"Thank you, Wandago. Thank you! You're a good boy."

Wandago stepped back. "Shok!"

"To your mother, I mean! That's how I meant it. You're a man, a man, a great warrior," Inda said quickly. Wandago left the hut and Inda proceeded to happily lie back and prepare her smokes.

Wandago saw Belia working her loom and said, simply, "I know who she is." He then left to be with friends across the compound.

Belia thought that was odd since Wandago rarely said anything that did not demean her.

Everyone was gone and Belia wasn't being watched. She had her knife, so maybe she could get away. Very quietly, she placed her loom in back of the hut. The hut was near the fence, so she stealthily moved down the fence to the compound opening. She got out of the compound, but Wandago saw her go. "Shok!" he exclaimed. And he ran after her.

Belia did not know where she was going, but she knew she had to leave. She ran as fast as she could, not knowing Wandago was running after her. To Belia, leaving was a matter of survival and she grieved her loss of Maelys. She knew she took a chance of dying being on her own, but Maelys' words spurred her on.

She stopped to take a breath, and Wandago tackled her from the side. She struggled. "Get off of me!" she cried. She kicked him hard and he lost his balance. She stood and said, "Don't touch me!"

"You really think you could leave?" he laughed. "You are to stay with Inda and the rest of us."

"Why?" asked Belia. "Why do you want me around?"

"We don't want you around. You're a tool, that's all. And Inda uses you."

Belia started to take off again, but Wandago grabbed her. He drew her to him and caressed her hair and became aroused.

"No! No!" yelled Belia. But Wandago was stronger than her. They struggled and at a time when Belia nearly broke loose, she said, "Now I know why YOU want me around, Wandago. You're pathetic!"

This angered him and he forced her on the ground. He forced her to kiss him and struggled with her, trying to dominate, hitting her in his attempts to subdue her. To his surprise, Belia suddenly became calm. She had her knife at his neck. She looked closely at him as he breathed heavily and said, "Go ahead. The moment you do this, you'll have my evil inside of you. You'll live with evil in you all the rest of your life."

This shocked Wandago and he thought she was telling a truth. He knocked the knife away from her and said, "You'll never use a knife again." He then stood, reached down, and took Belia by the front of her tunic and lifted her up. He then hit her over and over with his fist, still holding onto her. When he stopped, she fell to the ground, and he then kicked her several times. Bloody, Belia was barely conscious.

Wandago looked at her, picked her up, and carried her over his shoulder back to the compound. Once there, people stopped and stared. He looked back at them with anger. "She fell," he said. They said nothing.

The tribe's prejudice of appearance different than theirs and their fear of Wandago kept them silent about Belia. Most saw her as bad luck for the tribe and so they felt justified not standing up to the injustice of her life. Belia was outside their protection. Looking at Belia made them afraid, so they thought she deserved oppression. Looking at Belia also made them feel superior, and some felt good about that. Some, however, saw the hurt and slavery of Belia, thought it was wrong, but did nothing. Nobody wanted to deal with Wandago, Inda, or their own views, so they did everything possible to keep the status quo.

When he entered the hut, Wandago dumped Belia onto her bedding. "What is going on?" asked Inda. "You beat her again?"

"She tried to run away," he replied.

"Oh. She deserved it then."

"She always deserves it," he snarled.

Maelys held Belia and cried. "I'm sorry I'm sorry," she said softly to Belia.

Maelys took care of her for four days. Belia was dangerously depressed. Once she was able, she worked again on Ganta's bag, and that helped her mental and physical health. People noticed her wounds but said nothing. She liked the fresh air.

After a good smoke, Inda decided to confront Belia and went outside and told her to come inside. When Belia entered the hut, Inda slapped her across the face. Belia did not expect it, but maintained her control and did not fall. "Why did you try to run? Why can't you give back to this family? What is wrong with you?" demanded Inda.

Belia stood before Inda and with quiet anger said, "I know what it's like with our people. I know what it's supposed to be like. I know what everybody else's life is like except mine. Nobody keeps people out of their hut but people don't walk in because they respect people's hut. If anybody needs something, somebody gives it to him ... or her. But you keep me from everything, everything."

Nearly white with anger, Inda interrupted. "I've given you everything. You eat. You have a place to sleep ..."

"Not unless I pay for it!"

"Shok! You pay nothing. You do nothing unless I make you. You have a bearskin to sleep on, you have ..."

"Nothing that's mine. You make sure it's not mine."

"You haven't earned anything!"

"I'm a slave to you! Why? Because I have red hair! What difference, real difference, does it make that I have red hair?"

"You're bad luck. Always. But that doesn't matter. You're here, you've always been here, and it's one battle after another with you."

"You think the tribe doesn't know how you treat me?"

"I LOVE YOU!! I give you a place to sleep because I love you!"

"You can't say you love me and then hit me."

"I hit you because I love you! I'm trying to teach you something. But you never learn … never! This is all your fault, Belia. You hate me. I give you everything and you hate me for it. You do nothing around here."

Belia looked at her and reveled in the silence. Finally, she said, "I need to go out and work on Ganta's bag. So you can have a new bearskin." At that, Belia exited the hut and sat back down to work on her loom. To keep from crying, she focused on the activities of people within her view. Cree was painting the bark sheathing on his hut. His painting was of a pregnant woman. Nearby was a hut painting of a mother and child. Despite their prejudice, born mostly of fear, the tribe saw an equality of women with men. Both were valued and had equal status in the tribal structure. Their survival depended on both hunting and gathering. Their perception of the creative within woman bent them toward seeing woman within nature.

To the tribe, creation centered on fertility they saw in nature and their painting images of that fertility drew them closer to a healthy relationship with the earth. They saw the four-leggeds bear and birth their own kind and saw beauty in it all, a beauty of survival. When studying our prehistoric selves, we tend to relegate anything we don't understand about what they did as an expression of religion. We see the cave paintings in the Lascaux caves and imagine a religious act. But perhaps such paintings were expressions of celebration or a way to connect to Mother Earth within her womb, the metaphor womb of the caves. Our creative bent is a characteristic of our species, and art connects us to something beyond and greater than ourselves. Belia's tribe and the people who painted in the Lascaux caves knew what they were doing.

Women were considered to be the creators of humankind. The tribe did not know the science of reproduction, but they did know the male's role and see a woman bear a child, and they relied on that observation to connect to the cycle of life itself. Our perception of women changed when we developed from a hunter-gatherer people to an agricultural people able to settle down and domesticate both plant and animal. Domestication meant an attempt to control nature, and, according to Gerda Lerner in *The Creation of Patriarchy*, this created a shift to patriarchy. Eventually, men wanted to control women's reproductive capacity for economic reasons. Children were assets who could work the fields and care for the animals. According to Susan R. Martin's *Wonderful Power*, this did not happen during the PaleoIndian era of the Keweenaw. Belia's tribe and the other tribes wandering the Keweenaw around 5000 BCE lived in relative peace with one another. Water and food were plentiful. They could stay in one place for quite a while and have enough to thrive.

The first form of religious expression may have been the mother-goddess, but during this time of humankind, thinking was not yet ready for religion. The tribe believed life breathed within everything much like the Clovis people believed. But somewhere along the way between Clovis and Woodland peoples, humankind saw a design in the world that they could neither control nor understand. They saw this life design by perceiving patterns in the broader sense and felt the movings of what they called Grandmother Earth. Later, it was Grandfather and the Great Spirit, but at this time in humankind, the great designer of human as well as nature was Grandmother Earth. Such a perception kept people closely connected to the earth. An early form of the mother-goddess, Grandmother Earth was comforting to people. Much like The Dreaming's relationship with, and the formation of, the ancient Australian Aborigine's culture as Law, Grandmother Earth also gave them a sense of a need to live in peace and taught them a morality and ethics. Grandmother Earth was very real to them and communication was desirable. This is what they believed at this time, and by the time of Belia's living, that morality and ethics was known on a deeper, ancestral, level. Their beliefs of living were passed down as an oral tradition for generations.

But for Belia, people of her tribe thought her to be different and outside the boundaries of belief and morals. They mostly ignored Belia, but to Inda, her presence was a constant shame.

Chapter Eight: Fall

Kandra entered the hut with a flourish. "Kapono and Cree are back. Come on. COME ON!"

Inda was stunned for a moment while Wandago and Maelys exited the hut. "Wh ... ? What?" She then turned to Belia who moved to see what was going on and said, "You stay here and work on Ganta's bag."

"But I'm almost finished."

"Then finish it!" Inda exited the hut. Belia peered out the door to see people walking quickly to the center hearth, including Inda. She then picked up her bag-making items and grabbed food left on the hearth and ate as fast as possible as much as possible. She was used to taking advantage of these opportunities. Holding her items, she quietly moved toward the center hearth. She hid near a hut, but close enough to hear.

Kapono and Cree came back with two deer that they laid down on the ground near the place where they processed the meat. They told the tribe that they encountered a sight that frightened them significantly. On their way back to the compound, they ran across a different tribe's compound and everyone they saw was dead. People were shocked and afraid, and talked amongst themselves. The leader told them to quiet down.

"Was it war?"

"I don't think so," Cree replied. "There weren't any marks on them and nobody had used weapons. We found almost all of them inside a hut and lying there like they were sleeping. But they were dead."

"It was *maji*, evil," Kapono said. "It smelled."

"It was death," Cree said.

"We need to see for ourselves," Kandra said. "Can you take us?"

"I'm not going back," Kapono said.

"I'll take you," said Cree.

"All right then," Wandago said. He turned to the tribe's leader. "We'll go tomorrow and try to know what happened."

The leader motioned for them to go. The tribe talked amongst themselves around the main hearth. Some moved to process the deer. Belia quickly returned and sat down outside the hut. She was working on the bag when Inda returned. Inda looked at her harshly. "If there's *majimanidoog,* evil spirits, around, you better leave." Belia was shocked hearing that from Inda. Her words were actually kind. They both knew that if anything hurtful happens that cannot be explained, they recognize it as evil, and, since Belia was the tribe's scapegoat, they would blame her. Inda was worried that if they blamed Belia, she would also be blamed.

That evening, Kandra and Wandago huddled together with Inda. Both Belia and Maelys were as far from them as possible and still be in the hut. "Something evil is killing people," Kandra told Inda. "They got there and everybody was dead. Everybody. And Kapono came back here sick."

"Where? What tribe?" Inda asked.

"Cree told me the Huxinin tribe," Wandago answered. The Huxinin tribe's compound was near what is now Deer Lake. Thousands of years later, archeologists would find projectile points made of Hixton material, scrapers, and other tools near Deer Lake shoreline, as well as evidence of human cremation. So prolific were items that archeologists found items mostly from the Late Archaic period, but also items from Belia's time. Items made of Hixton material typically came from Wisconsin.

Motioning to Belia, Kandra said, "We better keep her inside here for a while until the evil passes. If they blame her, they'll blame us too, I'm sure of it."

Wandago looked at Belia. "You stay inside here," he told her. "If you're seen outside, you stay outside."

"But I need to take care of myself," protested Belia.

"I'm not staying inside with her doing her business," Inda said.

Wandago rose and approached Belia. "Then do it in the dark and that's all."

Belia shrank against the wall of the hut. "Okay. Okay."

"If you're seen," he continued, "you'll stay outside. Right now, people have forgotten you."

"That's good, that's good," said Inda.

Wandago retreated before getting very close to Belia. "Right now, we leave her alone. If we do nothing to her, they'll continue to forget."

"Yes," agreed Inda.

"How sick is Kapono?" Wandago asked Kandra.

"He's gotten worse," replied Kandra. "Since this morning."

"I finished Ganta's bag," Belia said hopefully.

"Give it to me," demanded Inda. Belia rose to take it to her but Wandago cut her off with his spear.

"Stay away," he said. "I don't want you to make me sick." Wandago was not thinking of contagion, but was worried that Belia would make him sick because he thought the evil he perceived within her could kill him and others. In his perspective, the evil was strong negative energy, or spirit. Wandago's prejudiced beliefs turned to fear and thus came back to hurt him. Belia tossed the bag to Inda who admired it but said nothing.

The next day, Wandago, Cree, and Kandra left to try to understand the mysterious deaths. For the next several days, Belia went out only at night. She enjoyed the night air and the darkness surrounding her like a blanket. During the day, she stayed in her corner of the hut. Maelys tended to stay in the hut also during the day. Inda gave the bag to Ganta and received a new bearskin. She was happy about that.

Neither Belia nor Inda knew that it would happen so fast. Cree, Kandra, and Wandago returned in ten days. By then, Kapono had sickened and died. Danica and Avah were ill as well as others and the Healer was kept busy using both plants and rites to try to dispel the evil she saw had invaded the tribe. To try to combat the disease, the Healer used several smudging tools. She burnt a combination of herbs like pine needles and lavender in small bowls to try to purify the air and environment of the ill person. The smoke would attach to negative energy that caused the illness. The smoke would then disperse into the outside air and release the negative energy so it would change to positive energy. The act is rooted in a oneness with Earth. The Healer would also use healing amulets earnestly made by people of the tribe. They made them of sinew, feathers, bone, and copper pieces, and the Healer placed them on the sick person's chest, stomach, and forehead to draw out the negative energy.

The virus seemed to methodically create an epidemic amongst people, but humankind at that time did not know what it was or how our immune system fights against disease. They saw it as an unseen, evil, alien negative energy or spirit that invaded them and they struggled to conquer it. In this respect, we now know that the tribe was close to being correct. A virus is an unseen alien that invades us, and if we are unable to fight it or keep it from spreading, we may die. Throughout the history of humankind, we sought ways to destroy such illnesses. In ancient Egypt, they perceived illness to be associated with demons, and doctors would place a poultice of lead, leather, soot, semen, cow bile and excrement on an ill person. They believed that the demon would be so disgusted as to leave and find a better host. The person tended to die. Today, science has made amazing strides to help our immune system combat a new, unknown, virus.

Every day more tribal members became ill and the leader decided to house in the main hut everybody who was sick. Many people were more than concerned and several entered and exited the main hut to try to help the Healer. But neither plant nor rite would keep the virus at bay. Wandago and Kandra hunted for the tribe so were mostly away from the illness. Danica, Avah, Cason, Jaxe, and Cree died, amongst many others. Men were busy burying the dead. At last, the illness reached Belia's hut and Kandra became ill. After moving her into the main hut, Wandago stormed into their hut, grabbed Belia by the hair, and threw her out. That awakened the tribe's fear and anger against Belia.

"You did this! You did this!" yelled Wandago. "Get out! Get away from us!"

"I didn't do anything! I didn't do anything!" cried Belia as she picked herself off of the ground.

"If I could kill you, I would," Wandago said angrily. "You've killed my sister! My sister! She is my blood!"

Inda followed them outside and had mixed feelings about what was going to happen. Belia would be exiled, which usually meant death. That would get Belia out of her hair, but it also meant she wouldn't have Belia to work for her anymore. Maelys was just frightened. She'd been concentrating on keeping away from people, but she did not believe that anything was Belia's fault.

Several tribal members came to see what was going on. Wandago shoved Belia toward the compound opening with the blunt end of a spear, then stood back. "She brought this on us! She is bad luck and we're finally paying the price. She is evil!" Wandago roared. The tribe, afraid and angry, shouted at Belia to get out. Meantime, Belia cried and begged them to let her stay. She was afraid that being without a tribe meant her death. But she was more afraid that Wandago would use this as an excuse to beat her again, perhaps to death. Wandago then pointed at Inda and said, "What do you say, Inda? What do you say?" The crowd became quiet.

Inda paused to think for a split moment. She decided to save herself above all. "She's been nothing but trouble ever since she came here. She doesn't belong here. She brought evil here."

The crowd was mob angry and someone grabbed a spear. Wandago stopped him, however, saying, "Don't kill her. The evil will come out of her completely if you do and we'll all die." Belia thought for sure that

Wandago wanted to kill her himself. Maelys also cried and tried to convince them that Belia is harmless. But the crowd did not notice her and began to stone Belia to drive her away. They threw stones to drive her away, not to kill her, so they avoided her head. The stones bruised her as she begged to let her stay. Maelys ran into the hut, then came and ran to Belia as the stones were being thrown. Wandago and Inda tried to stop her from facing Belia, but Maelys was strong and fast. Soon, she stood in front of Belia and gave her the sling out of sight of the crowd. The crowd stopped throwing stones.

"Here," said Maelys quietly. "Stay alive, Belia. Please. Stay alive." She kissed Belia quickly, and grabbed her in a hug. Maelys then turned to return to the hut, but Wandago said, "No! You can't come back, Maelys! You have to go too now!" But Maelys either didn't hear him or didn't care, but moved toward the crowd. In an instant, Wandago grabbed the spear and threw it, hitting Maelys in the chest. She dropped, fatally wounded. Belia ran and caught her as she fell to the ground. Wandago pulled the spear from her chest and told Belia to stay away, to go. But Belia's grief was too much. She begged Maelys to not die, but Maelys said one thing to Belia as Belia bent down close to her. "I see the sky," she said. "There is no ground without sky." Maelys then died, and Belia wailed and found a strength within herself to stand and face the crowd who had quieted.

"Why did you kill her? She was a child. She was innocent!" Belia cried.

"You did this," said Inda. "You killed her."

Tears running down her face, Belia quietly looked at the only people she knew. "You have forgotten the voice of Grandmother Earth," she said. She then turned and ran out of the compound.

Once Belia was gone, the crowd's blood lust was satisfied and they returned to taking care of the sick as well as daily needs. Grieving, Inda squatted next to Maelys and nearly took her hand. But Wandago grabbed her arm and forced her up and away from Maelys. "Don't touch her," he said. "She accepted the evil when she touched Belia."

Inda stood up to Wandago and slapped him. "You killed your own sister."

"She wasn't my sister."

"Your father was her father."

"You lie."

"Her mother died giving birth to her. Your father brought Maelys to me."

"You LIE! Maelys was NOT my sister!"

"It's the truth."

"You're telling me now? NOW?!"

"I'm telling you now."

Wandago picked up Inda and, in a rage, threw her into a curious crowd. Several people fell to the ground as well as Inda. Wandago then stood over her with quiet, dangerous, anger. "One day, you will regret you did not tell me. You're to blame that I committed this act."

"Why do you think she lived with us?" countered Inda.

"Get out of my sight." Wandago then left to see to Kandra and make sure the Healer would take good care of her.

Inda entered her hut, and for the first time she found herself alone. Looking around, she saw the hearth and beyond that, Belia's shadowy place to sleep. Loneliness descended upon her like fog and she felt the grief of her loss. But she didn't want to feel. She didn't want to feel at all. So she lay down and slept, hoping sleep will rid her of her sense of loss.

After a while, Wandago returned, picked up Maelys, and took her to Kapono's hut and placed her in with others who had died. Kapono and his family lived in a large hut in a corner of the compound, and since they all died and the epidemic continued unchecked, the tribal leaders decided to use his hut as an ossuary. Wandago did nothing to see that Maelys would have a good journey. There was too much death for anything proper. The Healer made sure Wandago was cleansed with her smoke.

Placing people in mass graves was not unprecedented. When a person died, the tribal members wrapped him or her in deerskins or bearskins. Usually the dead was kept by the family until it was time to place in an ossuary with other kin or friends. But the epidemic was so severe that people simply placed the dead in Kapono's hut.

Belia had no way of knowing, but her exile saved her life. Blinded by tears, she ran through the woods as best as she could, tightly holding the only thing that could keep her alive. She had nothing else. No covering, no knife, just the sling and her grief and fear. She eventually found herself looking up at the cliff and remembered the cave she found not long ago. It was nearly dark when she found the cave, still empty and dry. She had no flint but she knew how to make a fire, so she did. The night was very long to her as she gazed at the shadows dancing on the walls. To her surprise, she felt safe, and finally she fell asleep.

For the next several days, Belia tried to find something to eat. She mostly ate grubs. Occasionally, she would happen across a partly eaten four-legged to cook and eat. She took what she could, and every day felt herself dying. Within her circle of life, she entered the Fall. Each day, she tried to be aware of Grandmother Earth but she found it difficult to hear. Nevertheless, she discovered that her attempts to connect consoled her to a degree. Her grief of Maelys' death overwhelmed her many times whilst in the shallow cave.

Belia eventually knew that to live, she would have to return to the tribe. She was not equipped to survive. She left the cave and stealthily found her way back to the compound. She climbed a tree outside the fence both for protection and to see inside the compound better. Smoke wafted up from Kapono's hut. They had burned it along with the dead. Her hut was nearby. Peering from the tree, she saw only five people.

Everyone had bundles and it was obvious that they were moving. Their packs were constructed like those of the Clovis. Wandago exited Inda's hut. Belia heard someone ask, "Is she still alive?"

"Yes," replied Wandago.

"What do we do with her?"

Wandago paused, looked back at the hut, and then said, "Leave it." He picked up his bundle and left with the others. The tribal leader was not amongst the people. Neither was the Healer. Belia realized that Wandago was the leader now. Something told her to wait and stay quiet. She did not move from the tree for at least an hour. Her heart pounding, she climbed down and quietly entered the compound.

The compound was eerie in its abandoned state. Without life, there was no smoke coming from the center hearth or from the huts. No children. No laughter. Just silence as impenetrable as a wall. It looked like all but the five people died from the virus that had run its course. Belia concentrated on trying to find the things she needed. She first entered the Healer's hut and found a small bag of herbs, smudge pots, and amulets. In other huts were weapons left behind. Belia was grateful to find a good bow, a quiver, and a lot of arrows lying around. In one hut was a cache of dried meat that she took. In another was a knapsack so she could carry what she needed. In yet another was a knife and sheathe that Belia then wore. She found flint. These were treasures to her. She found Ganta's bag that she had made and took it.

Inda's was the last hut she entered. She put down her knapsack and weapons before she entered the hut. To her surprise and dismay, she found Inda lying on a bearskin still alive. Inda was no longer contagious, but Belia did not know that. She knew nothing of contagion and disease. The tribe's ignorance killed them. But Inda was very sick. Belia quickly left the hut. She didn't know what to do. She tried to listen to Grandmother Earth but felt nothing. It was as if when seeing Inda, Belia found herself completely cut off from her hope. It was up to her then.

Belia sat outside until nearly dark. She felt numb when she found wood around the compound and carried it into the hut. She exited the hut again and placed her knapsack in a different hut and brought flint into Inda's hut and made a fire. Inda's fever was fierce, and Belia made sure she was as warm and comfortable as possible. She left to get water and close the compound's gate when she returned. Inda drank a little water, and Belia washed her as best she could. That cooled her a little. She did not know the medicine needed to help her, but she tried to help her as much as she could. She found a couple of large soft leather sheets and put one under Inda to catch her waste, what little there was.

The next day, Belia cleaned Inda and found clean clothes for her. She also placed a sheet under her. She went to the stream and washed Inda's clothes and the leather sheet, then placed them on the hut to dry. After checking in on Inda, she went hunting. All members of the tribe knew how to hunt and how to use a bow and arrow. Inda, Wandago, and Kandra tried to keep Belia from learning how to use weapons, but throughout her years, she learnt in secret. They thought she would use the weapons against them. Now she spent hours in the forest trying to feel Grandmother Earth and felt nothing. Eventually, she shot a goose.

Standing over the dead goose, she raised her hands, faced toward the sun, and said, "Thank you! Thank you! Thank you!" She then picked up the bird and cradled her and continued, "You will travel to the other world and return and live again." She picked up the goose and walked back to the compound. Once in a while she would stand in the midst of trees and try to feel the wind that was quivering tree leaves. She could not. She saw the wind but could not feel her breath. Belia was separated from her own body. She had difficulty knowing how she physically felt. She also felt no hunger, but she knew she had to eat to survive.

Once back at the compound, Belia checked on Inda and gave her as much water to drink as she could. Seeing she was comfortable, Belia sat outside the hut and pulled the feathers off of the goose. Usually, she would keep the feathers, but the situation was different now. She was grateful that nothing happened during her exile and return to put her in danger. She did not need to use the sling to defend herself, and now except to find food, she did not have to use her bow and arrow. She gutted the goose and set to cook it. But to help Inda, she tried to make broth. She found a deep copper pot in one of the huts to do that and cut up some of the meat into very small pieces to boil, along with dandelion roots that she also cut up. She also placed in the pot some birch bark to simmer as part of the broth to try to ease some of Inda's aches and pains. She pulled out the bark before giving the broth to Inda. That night, Inda was able to sit up.

Inda acted grateful for the broth and needed no help to consume it. For the first time, she spoke to Belia. She looked at Belia for a long time and then asked, "Why are you being kind to me?"

Without looking at Inda, Belia tended to the rest of the goose cooking over the fire and replied, "What kind of human would I be if I didn't?" Truth be told, Belia didn't know why she was helping Inda. She could not feel. She could not know herself. But something inside of her prompted the response. Perhaps that was the person Belia wanted to become.

Several days passed as Belia continued to help Inda, clean her clothes and person, hunt, and cook. Inda could then stand and, with help, take care of herself and her needs. The stronger Inda became, the more her character renewed. She shoved Belia when she tried to help her up. "I don't need your help," she said.

"Really? This is how you are with me?" Belia asked quietly.

"What has changed?" Inda replied.

Belia was dumbfounded. "Look around you," she said. "Everything's changed."

Inda found her smokes and settled down again. "We need to find a tribe. We can't stay here."

"I know. You ready to take that on?"

"Yes." Belia then looked at her for a long time. Inda felt the accusation and her hatred grew toward Belia for forcing a truth from her. "No. Not yet," she admitted. She thought it an admission of weakness. They ate in silence. Afterward, Inda complained that all she ate was meat and wanted berries too.

"I haven't had the time to do anything except hunt for meat, dry what I can, and take care of you," Belia said. Belia looked up from cleaning and Inda hit her hard enough to make her fall to the ground.

"Don't talk back to me," Inda said. Her anger was thick as her smoke.

Belia remained silent for a while until the chores were done. Finally, she quietly said, "You want to come with me tomorrow?"

"Why should I?"

"Might make you stronger so we can go try to find another tribe."

Inda continued to smoke for a while. Belia listened to the night sounds that always comforted her more than frightened her. Finally, Inda quietly said, "I can't believe how stupid you are." Inda then put out her pipe and settled down to sleep. Belia just looked at her and wondered what shaped her to be so unkind. She fell asleep.

The next day, Belia was surprised to see Inda up and about. They said nothing to each other. After a bite to eat and tending to her person, Belia picked up her weapons to go out to hunt. Inda threw a basket at her. Belia had to drop everything to catch it. "You carry this," Inda demanded.

Belia threw the basket back at her and said, "Carry it yourself. I'm not your slave anymore."

Inda picked up the basket and murmured, "You never were."

"What?"

"Nothing."

Belia retrieved her weapons and went outside. Inda followed. "You coming then?" asked Belia.

"What's it look like."

Belia took the lead, hoping for a deer so she could dry the meat for traveling to try to find another tribe who would let them in. There is not much evidence that serious conflict happened between tribes during this time. Around 1300 to 400 BCE, population increased as well as tribal hostilities. By the turn of the first millennium, the great Nations of the Americas were forming. Ojibwa peopled the Keweenaw, and they were brothers and sisters of the Cherokee. Trading happened between the northern tribes in the Keweenaw and the southern tribes. Archeological findings tell us that later people interacted more frequently, as items from outside the Keweenaw found themselves more prevalent in the Keweenaw. But 5000 BCE found only the whisper of the formation of the great tribal Nations. During Belia's time, people were more amenable to outsiders needing a tribe when disaster rendered them homeless or alone. It was more a recognition of a need for survival than compassion.

The wind was mild and the sun warm as Belia and Inda quietly moved through the forest. Often, Inda would find a root or plant she wanted, and she and Belia moved apart, but Inda caught up. They were about a half-day hike south and east of the compound when Inda caught up with Belia once again, her basket holding a few herbs and roots. "You're going too fast," complained Inda. "I smell water over there. Let's take a rest." Rivers change course, width, and depth over time, but Inda and Belia were near what is now known as the Montreal River.

"We go any further and we won't make it back." Belia glanced toward Inda, but she had disappeared toward the stream. Belia followed until she could see Inda picking her way toward the water. "Inda, you make too much noise. I can't get food this way."

"You blaming me? It's not my fault you never learned how to hunt."

"Actually, it is," replied Belia. "You never let me go out."

"Here it is," Inda declared. She stopped at the entry of a deer trail down to the river and waited for Belia. Once Belia caught up, Inda hit her in the face, knocking her down. "Don't talk back to me," she growled.

But Belia rose and faced her. "Don't ever hit me again."

Inda sat down. "Or what?" she asked grinning. Belia looked at her silently, then moved away. "I thought so."

Across the shallow river, a young buck appeared. Excited, Belia quietly and slowly gathered her bow and arrows and took aim. Just as she let loose, Inda coughed, the deer took notice, and bolted. Angry, Belia asked, "Why did you do that?"

Feigning ignorance and innocence, Inda replied, "Why did I do what?"

"You made me miss."

"No I didn't. You're not good enough." Suddenly, a murder of crows came out of the trees and attacked Inda who got to her feet and tried to swat them away from her. She tripped and nearly fell into the water. She ended up face down in the mud and tried to protect her head and neck with her arms and hands. Belia watched with amusement. The birds finally stopped, flew up into the trees, and Inda sat up furious. "Why didn't you help me?" she roared.

"Looks like Nanabozho doesn't like you. He sent his birds to tell you so," Belia replied, amused.

"What do you know?" growled Inda, who moved to the water's edge to clean her face. "Look what they did to me! They cut me all over! Come here and wash me."

Belia was silent for a moment and sat down. She picked up an arrow and straightened out its fletching. "No, I don't think so." She then took her knife and worked the arrow to straighten it as much as possible.

Inda continued to wash herself and intended to take a stick and beat Belia. But neither Wandago nor Kandra were with her. Sitting down in the shade, she pondered the river water and thought about Mishi Bizi, the underwater mountain lion beneath earth and, as a manitou, resided in the water beneath. A manitou was an entity to tribal members and affected particular realms and aspects of nature. Beneath Earth was the water realm where people placed a negative force. Above Earth was the sky realm where people placed a positive force. The tribes of these ancient people knew the manitous to involve their relationship with each other, and they seemed to have similar characteristics as do people. Mishi Bizi was known to come out of Gichagumma, now known as Lake Superior, with the head of a mountain lion, a body with scales, and a copper tipped tail. He would roar with rain, thunder, and lightning and reminded people that he was a manitou who owned the copper. Today, we know the legend as Mishipeshu, the dragon of Lake Superior. Mishi Bizi's nemesis was Nanabozho. Nanabozho was a positive manitou residing in the sky and people believed the sky manitous protected the fortunate people. The main icon of a sky manitous was a large bird, and the thunderbird was a common icon. Inda hoped that Mishi Bizi would support her efforts to put Belia in her rightful place. She wanted the power over Belia she thought she lost.

To the ancient people of the Keweenaw, sky above and water below Earth with manitous living related to observable good and evil. During the thousands of years between Clovis and the initial Woodland people, humankind made the creative leap from seeing life within and through all things to seeing design in the actions of various aspects of living. We need to try to control and understand. A perception of good and evil requires judgment, and good was overall a judgment of something that benefits us whilst evil was a judgment of something that hurts us or blocks what we want. Because judgment was grounded in a person's perception, allowing a negative force to determine human thought and action led to a corruption of our judgment of good and evil societal norms. Underlying the adoption of a negative force is fear, and due to recent life and death experiences, fear was palpable to Belia and Inda. Inda wanted the negative power of Mishi Bizi to support her to get the power she craved so she could maintain her love of self that depended on superiority over others.

Ancient people saw Grandmother Earth neither as good nor evil but as a relationship that sought balance and health and, connected to earth, was more immediate and ongoing than manitous residing above or below Earth showing up once in a while. Our own actions determined our relationship with Grandmother Earth. Part of the relationship with Grandmother Earth meant we have an obligation to protect the earth and everything residing within her. If we break that balance, we could and probably would die. Ancient humankind created rites and amulets to help maintain that intimate balance.

After a while, Inda thought she knew how to hurt Belia. "It's too bad," she said, "that when we find another tribe, you won't be coming."

Belia knew that Inda was thinking about something, but to hear a pleasant voice surprised her. She stopped working the arrow and put it down. "What do you mean?" she asked.

Inda moved to sit down and lean her back against a tree. "The evil within you, of course. No tribe will want you."

"I'm not evil," Belia countered. "Not everybody thinks I am."

"You've been with me all your life, Belia. You're bad luck to any tribe and you never really belonged anywhere."

"Yeah, but I'll go where you go."

"Do you think so? What makes you think I want you?" Belia was on the verge of tears. Inda felt a power within herself that she hadn't felt since the illness came to her tribe. She stood and walked toward Belia. "Nobody wants you, Belia. Nobody has ever wanted you. I didn't."

Belia stood and wanted to run but her feet were rooted to the ground. Inda's words cut her to the bone, mainly because she knew that Inda's words were true.

"Why?" cried Belia softly. "Why?"

"Look at you!" Inda said with malice as she stepped closer to Belia. "Everybody can see the evil within you. Your red hair, your skin, your eyes."

"I have done nothing except do whatever you and Wandago and Kandra told me to do. I've been a slave to you all my life. What made you so mean, Inda? What?"

Inda was shocked by the question. She couldn't stop herself from speaking. "You don't know anything about me. You deserve nothing from me. Nothing. You deserve to be beaten every day of your life."

"And you did! You or Wandago beat me nearly every day. What did I do that was so wrong? What? WHAT?"

"Did you ever wonder why I had to take care of you? Why the tribe made me put up with you?" Inda stood face to face with Belia.

"No. I just thought they told you to."

"I was shackled to you every day, every single day. And I hated it."

"Why? What did I do?"

"You came from me! THAT's WHY!! You're my daughter, Belia." Inda backed off from Belia as her memory overwhelmed her. "I was gathering herbs when a man stole me. He stole me and he raped me. And I had to give birth to you. When I saw you, I should have killed you right then and there."

Belia reached out to Inda. Crying she said, "You're my mother? Why didn't you tell me? I'm so sorry Inda. Nobody should rape a woman. You're my mother?"

But Inda slapped her across the face. "Don't you dare call me mother. I have paid a terrible price because of you. Every woman deserves to say what is to be done to her. Every woman has a right to her own body. Every woman has a right to say no. Every woman! But he put his hands on me. Then he put evil inside of me. I struggled. I screamed. And now, every time I look at you, I see that evil." She stepped up close to Belia. "I'll find a tribe and you won't be coming with me. You are evil. You don't deserve it. They will never accept you. I don't want you. I never wanted you. You're a freak! You're worthless!"

Belia's knife struck upward into Inda who gasped. Soon, Inda fell dead into the river. At that moment, Belia discovered that her own hatred outweighed her compassion.

Chapter Nine: Winter

Belia ran. Her mind darkened and she could see nearly nothing. She ran and could not stop until she faced Lake Superior. She ran down the steep decline of the Keweenaw to the place that is now known as Bete Grise Bay. The sand stretched out to the depths of Lake Superior, and the cold water caused her to stop in her tracks. Her guilt was more than she could bear. Facing Lake Superior, toward the south-east, she saw herself as ugly in her nothingness and that contrasted so starkly with the beauty of the lake. The coming night quickened her spirit as it transformed the dark blue beauty of the lake into a more subdued beauty. Should she end herself? That was the question. What was her life if nothing? Why was she here? She sat on the sandy beach for hours wondering why and no answer came to her. She felt an empty hole within her and she felt her overwhelming need. What that need was, she did not know. To belong perhaps. To feel loved perhaps. She had no concept of either.

The half-moon rose and Belia discovered that she was comforted once again. The night was free of clouds and she could see the mystery of the night sky and tried to feel her ancestors and tried to think that they were close. But she couldn't. There was no one to protect her. There was no one to care about her. She did not build a fire on the sand. She hated herself for what she had done. And she discovered that she'd been hating herself all of her life for what she had done. What had she done before today? Belia did not know. She only knew that she was alive, so she hated herself for being alive. She wasn't supposed to be alive, so she did not care if a four-legged came during the night and killed her. She welcomed it. Eventually she fell asleep.

As the sun came up, she woke, and all the grief, nothingness, and self-hatred once again flooded her being. Her guilt spoke of evil within her. Her tribe was right; she was evil. Inda was right. Her grief made her awake in a sacred way. She not only grieved Maelys' death, although that was in the front of her awareness, but she also grieved her own lack of living. Even though she lived her life with people who oppressed her and hurt her, now she felt completely alone. She knew, without a doubt, that there was not one person in the world who cared about her. Her rebellion was over. She could no longer stand up for herself to anyone. She did not know who she was and realized she never knew her own identity. She thought herself as an object for so long that once those ties were cut with Inda and the rest of the tribe, she realized that she was not even an object. She was truly nothing. She found herself without protection; nothing was left to defend. Belia's awareness was far more on a felt level than an intellectual level. She did not understand it and could not voice it. She felt it and that is all. She also felt dead. *Death, then Transformation.*

Belia turned and saw the forest line. It seemed to be an alien place not welcoming to humankind. Looking into the trees, she saw a young woman step toward her. "Maelys! Maelys! You're alive!" She began to run to her, but the image of Maelys put up her hand and Belia felt a push backward. She fell.

"No," Maelys said. "No. But I am here Belia. I'm here with you."

"Why?" asked Belia, standing.

"To tell you ..."

"No," Belia cut her off. "I'm not worth anything."

"You don't know how wonderful you are, Belia. You are such a rega good woman. You are strong."

Belia began to cry. "You're not real," she countered. "You lie. Go away." Belia then collapsed on the sand and cried. She did not know it at the time, but it was healing for her to cry. When she looked up, Maelys was gone.

She stood and turned back to the water and wanted Mishi Bizi to come out of the water and kill her. She would gladly be sacrificed. So she sang. She sang all day and nothing happened to her. Giving up, she finally knew that she needed to let go of her past and she realized that future was an illusion. Belia lived in the present and discovered that there's both wisdom and wholeness of presence. She tried to embrace the present, but she was not yet ready to do that on a conscious level. All she could do at that time was to acknowledge that her loss was more profound than she could understand.

The next day she woke up feeling clean and she realized she was not yet dead. She did not understand it. She faced and prayed to the four directions and still nothing happened. She saw the life within her from the outside. Since all of her masking layers were stripped off of her, she was more aware of her surroundings than she'd yet experienced. She'd known that life was in all things and through all things, but now she became aware of just how sacred life is, except for her own. She saw life within herself, but could not feel life. She felt herself standing on the outside of life looking in.

Where was Grandmother Earth? Silence. But Belia decided to believe. She hoped that she trusted Grandmother Earth and grabbed hold of that hope. Belia then spent several days trying to listen to Grandmother Earth. Then her hope became realized. Grandmother Earth held her and Belia found herself standing on the edge of the spirit world.

Her awareness extended life as sacred to life as spirit. An essence of spirit raised her awareness to something more. Spirit vibrated life to be more than it is. Spirit vibrated and quickened life to its potential. No, she told herself. Not her. Not her. She rejected these feelings for herself because she thought herself to be too evil for that. Life as spirit was connected to Grandmother Earth in such a way that Grandmother Earth was more real to her now, for Grandmother Earth was the great weaver of life with life. The only thread she could hold onto was Grandmother Earth and her awareness gave her hope that she thought she did not deserve. She only knew that the hurt and oppression were gone and so there was nothing in her.

Inda was gone. Belia had spent several days on the beach trying to die. In the middle of her last night on the beach, she watched the Aurora borealis dance in the night sky. She followed the path of the sky manitou and danced with him. The beauty of white, green, and red helped weave her back into the dance of life and living.

Finally, she knew that Grandmother Earth wasn't going to let her die, so she left the beach and traveled up the peninsula to the spine. After two days, Belia found the compound that seemed ghost-like in her memories. She found her pack that she kept away from Inda. Then with the things she needed to survive, she found her way back to the shallow cave. Entering the cave felt like entering her own emptiness. She made a fire and ate a little dried meat and could do nothing but dimly think. Every day, in a fog, she went to hunt, gather, or process the food given to her in order to eat and then sleep and that is all for an eternity of time outside her awareness.

Belia did not know that she was going through something profound. Like a caterpillar in her chrysalis, Belia could not see the world or herself clearly. She was cut off for weeks. She did not know that the struggle and pain and inner chaos were necessary for her to become who she was meant to be. Holding onto Grandmother Earth, she gradually broke through and struggled to live. She gained a small sense that perhaps she was a person. She did not know it. She did not understand it. She just did it.

The weather began to change and Belia knew that fall, then winter, would come too soon. The day was warm and partly cloudy. Belia wanted strawberries, so she took a basket made of grass and went searching. She left her bow and arrows in the cave and took her sling. The summer beauty of the Keweenaw helped mend her heart and as long as she focused on searching for berries, she felt better. The soil turned somewhat sandy in a clearing and she found quite a lot of strawberry plants.

Nearby, she was startled when she heard people screaming. Leaving her basket, she ran toward the sound and saw a pack of wolves running toward her. One had a small child. The wolves did not notice her, but she stood her ground with her sling and waited. She hoped she was out of sight of the wolves. She hid behind a bush and got her sling ready. Within distance, the wolf carrying the child got close enough to Belia that she threw a stone and caught the wolf on the nose. Startled, the wolf dropped the child who screamed. By that time, Belia could see people running toward her. So did the wolf pack. Belia threw another stone and hit the alpha again, slightly fracturing his nose and driving off the pack. Seeing the wolves gone, she ran to the child to try and calm him down. Upon inspection, she saw a few puncture wounds, but otherwise the child was unhurt except for shock.

Seeing the tribe running toward her, she ran. She was afraid that they would see the evil within her and kill her. All but Broch stopped to see to the child. He ran after Belia.

"Stop! Stop!" he yelled. But Belia did not hear him. Finally, Broch gave up and returned to the group.

"Did you see where she went?" Kace asked.

"No. She ran into the forest," replied Broch. "How is he?"

"He'll be all right I think," replied Haol. "We need to get back home as soon as we can."

"Okay," said Broch. "I want to find the woman though."

"Why?" asked Haol.

Broch just looked at her and said, "I don't know."

Kace slapped him on the back and laughed. "I'll go with you. Narsa, will you be okay going without me?"

"Sure," Narsa answered.

Kace continued, "Let's camp here for the night and tomorrow we can go on. Broch and I will catch up with you."

Haol tended to the child while Narsa and Kace went back for their packs. Broch and two other men started to set up camp by preparing a fire.

Belia found her way back to the cave without her basket. She waited in the shadow of the cave for a while to see if anybody followed her. Saving the child helped her heal, although she did not realize that she was getting better. Finally, she decided that nobody was looking for her and she relaxed a little. She ate some meat that she had dried a few days ago and decided to try to protect herself by honoring the Thunderbird. She took some charcoal ash from her hearth and took out the small copper bowl she found in the compound. She put the ash aside and put water in the bowl. She had a rabbit hide from yesterday's hunt that she had intended to use as a patch, so the hair was removed. She made a fire, cut the hide into pieces, put the hide in the water, and heated it up. The water did not boil. She poked and stirred with a stick until the stick was covered in glue. She did not need a lot of water. Once she had glue water, she removed the hide and stirred in the ash to make a dark gray paint.

She exited the cave and found a green stick she could use as a brush. She took her knife and sliced one end into thin strips. Back in the cave, she smoothed over the portion of wall in back of the cave she intended to paint. She then carefully painted the outline of a large thunderbird. The painting was a front view with wings stretched out, and the bird's head looking toward the cave opening. She painted the detail of the wings and head. On the chest area, she painted a crooked line that reminded her of lightning. Below the crooked line, she painted five dots in a vertical row with her finger. Then she paralleled another five dots, making sure all the dots were inside the thunderbird. To Belia, the thunderbird represented the sky manitou who carried positive energy and captured that energy by way of lightning. The dots allowed the positive energy to be released from the manitou into the world – in this case, into the cave. Seeing the wolf with the child reminded her that she was vulnerable. She did not know what to do, so she honored the thunderbird as a hope for guidance and good luck.

To show her sacrifice to the sky manitou, she took the most beautiful thing she had with copper in it, Ganta's tapestry bag, and buried it beneath the thunderbird. She had no drum or instrument of any kind, so she sang to the thunderbird. Unlike the Clovis who sang with words, Belia sang vocables that are syllables that do not have referential meaning. No words, just sound with vocables that often were repeated. Throughout the years, vocables were a unifying agent to the growth of more and larger differing tribes of North America. Thousands of years later, somebody would find the tapestry bag and it helped archeologists understand prehistoric people living in the Keweenaw.

Humankind in the Keweenaw during Belia's living saw manitous as having cosmological power and played a role in people's lives. To the PaleoIndian, they had the same kind of characteristics and motivations as people, but were more powerful than people. They were seen only by way of consequence and nature's workings, not in physical forms. The Aurora borealis was not a sky manitou's physical form, but the remnant of the path of his dance and was a great honor to witness. Humankind developed symbolization in imagery to the point of helping them gain a sense of security to live. Nearly the entire world was still unknown, and whilst people had begun to see the possibility of domestication of both plant and animal, they had very little control over the circumstance of living. Believing sky above earth and water beneath earth helped them explain what happens in life. Positive energy and negative energy was a natural development of a perception of human-like opposites in a world beyond our control that turned into good and evil, right and wrong, and eventually the God and Satan of Europe's medieval age. Throughout human history, we perceived the perception of opposites, from the balancing of an oscillation of alternating opposites within the ancient Greek worldview, to the judgment of a soul after death with the ostrich feather in ancient Egypt. The Keweenaw ancient people thought of these opposites as kin to oriental thinking of Yin and Yang. They desired the Upper and Lower powers to be in balance and saw a relationship between the two opposing energies.

Within the path of this story, Grandmother Earth connects the Breath of the Clovis to the Great Spirit of Native Americans' later awareness. To Belia, Grandmother Earth was an unseen but not unknown guide and comforter, and because Grandmother Earth connected to humans having relationships with each other and the earth, their awareness was more focused on Grandmother Earth than the manitous. Grandmother Earth was more powerful than the manitous, but Grandmother Earth rarely interceded when manitous acted for or against humankind.

Belia knew that she needed to find a tribe that will take her before winter. She thought of the people she encountered, but her fear at the time, her adrenaline kicking in, and the suddenness of their arrival caused her to not think at the time about her need for a tribe. She left the cave to get water.

Broch and Kace had tracked Belia and saw her exit her cave. "There she is!" Brock said quietly. "Come on. Let's get her."

"Hold on Broch! Where's the rest of her tribe?" asked Kace.

Broch paused. "I don't see anybody. Let's go."

"Wait a minute!" Kace said. "Why is she alone?"

Broch turned to him. "Kace, standing here and wondering won't answer any questions."

"Oh. Okay. You can go."

Broch rolled his eyes. "Thanks…. Wait. You coming?"

"Oh. Okay."

Broch and Kace quietly moved closer to Belia, but the terrain was difficult. The harsh winters stunted the growth of some trees and brush was dense between the trees. Soon, Belia noticed them and once again dropped her things and bolted as a reaction of the fear that they would see her as evil and kill her. Both Broch and Kace dropped their packs and ran after her, trying to tell her that they would not hurt her. Finally, Broch tackled Belia and ended up sitting on her stomach with his hands pinning her arms. He looked down at her and said, "Hi beautiful."

"Get off of me!! Don't touch me!!"

"Okay, but we're not going to hurt you," replied Broch. He stood and stepped aside. Belia lay there for a moment, so Broch took her arm to lift her up.

Before Broch could let go of her, Belia yelled, "I told you – don't touch me!" She then hauled off and hit him in the eye. "OW!" she cried in pain, clutching her hand. Then she regained her composure.

By that time, Broch was bent over holding his eye making all sorts of noises, and Kace was laughing. The scene told Belia that they were true to their word and wouldn't hurt her. She just stood still and examined her hand.

Broch walked over to her and reassured her that he would not touch her. "I'm Broch and this is Kace." Belia did not offer her name and the two men stood there, paused. "You're alone," he said.

"I'm alone," she replied. "I'd think that was obvious." Kace laughed.

"Where's your tribe?" Kace asked.

Belia just shrugged and said, "Dead."

"I understand," Kace said. "The illness hit us too. We're going back now."

There was an awkward pause before Broch asked, "You want to come with us? Winter is coming."

"Well, not quite yet," said Kace.

"Soon enough," Broch said, annoyed.

Belia looked up at something moving in the trees. It was an owl flying by and landed on a branch nearby.

"I'm not sure your tribe will want me," Belia said simply. The owl flew straight at Belia and touched her hair with his wing before landing on another branch. Broch and Kace were surprised at the owl as well as Belia but they said nothing. Belia felt a communication with the owl and perhaps they would not see her as evil. She felt as if she was entering a spiral.

Kace interrupted her thoughts. "I can't speak for the tribe or our leader, but I think you'll be okay."

Belia looked at the owl and decided. "I'll go with you. Where's the rest of the people I saw?"

"They went on. We'll catch up with them," Kace replied.

After hesitating again, Belia said, "Let's go where I stay and start out in the morning. I have food."

"Good plan," Broch said, and started walking north.

"It's this way," Belia said, walking west. Kace laughed and slapped Broch on the back as he passed him.

Belia walked back and picked up her water pouch and they walked in silence to a stream. All of them replenished their water pouches. They went back and picked up the men's packs. Then in silence, Belia led them to her cave. Once there, Broch and Kace started a fire and Belia worked to get them something to eat and begin to pack.

"Where is it you're going?" asked Belia.

"What?" asked Kace.

"You said you're going back. Back where?"

"We heard that the illness hit a lot of tribes. Once we knew it was out of control, we all split up and went to separate areas. The people who were not sick," explained Kace.

"You split up?"

"Yes. Our memories told us that when the illness kills more than three people, we go out in groups until it's time to return."

Broch interjected, "I lost my brother to the illness." He reached into his pack and drew out a pair of small shoes. "He was very young…. Juliac. We all took shoes of the dead…." Broch became silent in his grief.

"I don't understand," said Belia, kindly.

Kace explained, "We hung the shoes at night when we camped. When they moved on their own, we knew it was time to return home. Our memories told us that through Tac'kana, our Healer. So a few days ago, the shoes started to move. We're going back home." Belia gave them some food. "Thank you. Our canoe broke on the shore during a storm. We thought it was Mishi Bizi who demanded our copper. So we buried whatever copper we had and maybe that's why you were there to save the child."

Broch admired her painting. "Nanabozho?"

"Yes," replied Belia.

"Excellent," Broch said.

"Thanks. So you're traveling back to your home?"

"Yes," said Kace.

They ate in silence for a while. Belia began to have her doubts about her decision. "I have red hair."

Both Broch and Kace stopped eating and looked at her. "Yes," Kace said.

"But… I have red hair."

Kace finally spoke up. "I heard that some tribes see red hair as bad luck. Was your tribe that way?"

"Yes."

"What's the name of your tribe?"

"Wikangatra."

Kace and Broch looked at each other. "I'm sorry," Broch said. "We heard of them. You said they're dead?"

"Yes. They made me leave but I think everybody died of sickness. Well, maybe everybody. I don't really know."

Broch took her hand. "You've been with them all your life?"

"Yes."

Kace spoke up, "That's not the way we are. That's … not the way we are. Tac'kana made it very clear many years ago. We can't be like that and remain human."

"I'm sorry," Broch said.

Belia snatched her hand from his and stood, defiant again. "I don't need you to be sorry! Why are you sorry?"

To Belia's surprise, Broch stood just as defiant as she was and she backed down, confused. "I'm sorry. That's all. I choose to be human, that's all. And that's all I'll say about it." He sat back down again.

Belia stayed standing for a moment, then sat down. "All right then."

After a while in silence, Kace said, "Thanks for the food. What's your name again?"

"I didn't say it in the first place." Belia felt she needed to stand for herself but didn't know how. She sulked.

Kace looked at her and said, "Well, this is fun."

"I'm going to sleep," said Broch. "You mind if I stay in here?"

"We stay in here?" Kace interjected.

"That'll be fine." The two men settled down. Belia cleaned up a little and then went outside.

After a short while, Kace whispered, "So what do you think?"

"I think I finally found my mate," Broch whispered back. "She's fantastic."

"Oh shok," Broch said the next morning as Belia finished packing. "I can't hardly open my eye."

"Let's see it," said Kace. He looked closely at Broch's eye, poking it a little with his finger. "Oh, this is bad. You need me to carry you or you think you can walk on your own?"

"Shut up," Broch said as he bumped Kace's hand from his face.

The morning was cool as they traveled north along the spine. Belia picked herbs and flowers as she walked. There were many deer paths from which to choose and Belia found traveling pleasant with good company. The more she was with the two men, the more she found she liked them. They treated her as equal and she reveled in the utter lack of oppression and debasement she'd known all of her life. The first night, she made a poultice from the herbs and flowers she found whilst walking and placed it on Broch's eye, and her hand.

"This should help with the pain and swelling," she said.

"Thanks," replied Broch.

"My name is Belia."

"Belia the beautiful," Broch said. Kace snickered and Broch looked at him to shut up. Kace just smiled and pretended to look away.

Belia made them some tea that she placed in some herbs for pain. "I'm sorry I hit you," she said softly as she gave him some in a wooden bowl.

"I'm not," Broch replied. Belia didn't know what to say or how to react with that. "What I mean is, you had every right to protect yourself. And I can't think of a better way to say hello." All three laughed, and Belia found herself feeling closer to them than she'd ever known except for Maelys.

"What she really means, Broch, is she's sorry she hurt her hand." They quietly laughed again. "Nice to meet you, Belia." Kace held out his hand, and when Belia took it, he gently drew her hand close to him and looked closely at it. "Don't worry." He felt her bones and suddenly grabbed and sharply pulled. It hurt Belia, but she very soon realized that her hand felt right again.

"What is this?" Kace asked, pointing to the loom.

"I make tapestry," replied Belia.

"Are you any good at it?" asked Kace.

Belia smiled. "Yes."

"Do you have anything I can see?"

"No. My work was always for somebody else. I did take a bag I made, but I buried it when I painted the thunderbird on the wall."

"Oh," said Kace. "It must have had copper in it."

"Yes, it did."

"We buried all of our copper after the storm."

"That's what you said. I mean. Oh, I'm sorry."

"It's okay. It's not really ours anyway. We take it from the earth, and when Mishi Bizi wants some of it back, we just put it back into the earth. It seems to keep things in balance. We were very grateful that none of us were hurt in the storm."

"Kace is one of the best copper trackers we have," Broch said.

Belia did not give out hardly any information about her past tribe or her life. But the two men could feel that her life was stifled. They said nothing and did not pry. But they chose to not assume she knew information.

"I'll show you tomorrow if you like. If I can," Kace said.

"That would be rega!" Belia replied.

"We need to hunt a little for food tomorrow too," Broch said.

"Okay," Kace replied.

The next day, they woke to hoarfrost. As they packed for travel, Kace said, "Maybe we can see where the copper is." They traveled north and soon, before the sun melted the hoarfrost, Kace stopped and pointed. "You see where the frost is gone? Over there. It's like a line of no frost."

"Yes. There's copper underneath?"

"There's copper there. Copper breathes warmer and the hoarfrost on the plants doesn't take hold."

"I didn't know that copper will breathe," exclaimed Belia.

"He's alive. No doubt about that. Sometimes you can see patterns on the earth where there's copper underneath. Like moss or mushrooms in patterns. Even the movement of rainwater can tell us where."

"Nobody ever tell you this?" asked Broch.

"No. I stayed near our hut all the time. I just worked."

"You'll have more freedom now," Broch said. "It's not right to make a person do what you want all the time."

This gave Belia hope that perhaps her life will change. They arrived on the banks of what is now known as Lake Medora. They found a ring of ash. Kace examined it. "Haol and the others were here just last night. We're not far behind. Let's stay here tonight."

"Okay," said Broch. He dropped his pack and took his bow and arrows. "We don't need much. Let's hope for Nanabozho's happiness." He went out to hunt while Belia and Kace set up camp. Unlike the other nights, they decided to use their bedding. Some time after they made a fire, Broch returned with two geese. They all plucked the birds, gutted them for the four-leggeds and insects, and laid them to cook on stones they built in the fire ring.

The food lasted the two days more traveling to the Woodland tribe. Belia was amazed how large the compound was, nearly covering the north shore of what is now Lake Fanny Hooe. Most of the compound was located where Fort Wilkins is today. The lake was located about eight hundred yards from Lake Superior where there was a small cove in a harbor. They kept several canoes on the shore. The huts were large and sturdy and made the same as were Belia's tribe. The tribal members greeted them warmly. But they told them to stay apart at two arm's length until Tac'kana, their Healer, told them differently. They said that Tac'kana relied on memories and hanging shoes that would stop moving when it was safe again.

Broch and Kace were the last of the people to return to the tribe, so that night everybody sat together, distanced apart, outside. Kace found Tac'kana, Jokan, and Shoria and told them what he knew about Belia. The center hearth was on the north side of the lake and people sat facing the hearth and the lake. Broch and Kace found Haol, Narsa, and the others, and they could sit together and be together without restrictions, just as the other groups who left together stayed together. The tribal members had no problem following Tac'kana's decree because they knew their purpose was to protect each other. The tribe relied on memories Belia's tribe had forgotten. Broch and Kace expected and wanted Belia to stay with them until Tac'kana told them otherwise, or gave people a choice. Everyone was happy to see and be with everyone else after being apart during a long spring and summer.

Jokan, the Leader beside Healer, stood and addressed the tribe. "Grandmother Earth has reminded us. If all the trees and plants die, we die. If all the four-leggeds and winged people die, we die. But if we die, nothing of the earth will die. We are reminded of who we are. The sickness has reminded us of our obligation to protect the earth and each other. We have lost too many people who died of the majimanidoog sickness. But we are together again. When the manishoes stop moving, we can live again as we did before. If nobody becomes sick, we can be together again. Meantime, stay with your groups and rest. When it's time, we can celebrate."

Everyone rose to go to either a hut or to stay outside. Kace, Broch, and Belia decided to stay outside near the center hearth. They used their packs to sleep. Belia dropped her pack near theirs. When she looked up, she saw Wandago smiling at her. She nearly fainted with sudden anxiety.

Chapter Ten: Spring

Only one person noticed that Belia looked at Wandago and turned ghost-like. Shoria knew that she must do something to help Belia. Shoria didn't like Wandago. He carried a negative energy so pronounced that she knew him to be out of balance. She thought that he was loud and laughed loudly. But she also felt a mean streak within him. Positive and negative energy had nothing to do with cruelty; that is a human characteristic. But if a person is off-balance, negative energy could influence his or her caliber of character.

The next day, Belia was told to speak with Tac'kana. Shoria led her into her hut where Tac'kana and Jokan were waiting. The light was very dim, but Belia could see a pair of shoes hanging from the ceiling. They were constantly moving. Belia was nervous and Tac'kana did not help by stepping up to her. Tac'kana was the Healer of the tribe and dressed with a great deal of feathers in her hair and her clothing, with her deeply lined face painted red, brown, and black. Her tunic had the thunderbird painted on one side and Mishi Bizi dragon painted on the other side. She looked at Belia with interest.

"Tac'kana, help the poor woman," Jokan said. To Belia, he said, "Don't let her scare you. She thinks she's being funny." Tac'kana laughed and moved away. She told Belia to sit down, and they all did, the three facing Belia. "Kace says your name is Belia," Jokan said.

"Yes," Belia replied. "My tribe was killed by sickness."

"Everyone?" asked Tac'kana, knowing the answer. But Belia could not speak of Wandago, so she said nothing. She felt like crying.

"We are the Woodland people. You are welcome to become a member of our tribe," Shoria said.

Belia looked down and stuttered. "I … I have … red hair."

Tac'kana leaned forward and looked closely at her. "Yes. Yes, you do."

There was an awkward silence. Then Belia said, "You don't understand. I have red hair."

"What does that mean?" Shoria asked.

"I am majimanidoog. I have evil in me."

"How do you know, Belia?" Shoria asked.

Another silence. Then Belia said, "I have red hair." She could not speak of Inda's death, but it loomed over her.

Tac'kana thought for a while, looking at Belia and Belia tried to avoid looking at anyone. "I have been waiting for you," Tac'kana said. "I have known you were coming for a long time."

"How?" asked Belia, confused.

"Everything that I know, I learned from watching and listening. Grandmother Earth and I are great friends. I see the earth. I see the water. I see the sky. Anybody can. These are sacred acts. And if you look closely enough, you can see the heart of a human struggling to become."

"I have … done … terrible things," stammered Belia.

"Terrible things have been done to you, child. So go with Shoria and Jokan."

"What?" asked Belia.

"Shoria and I would like you to come to our hut to stay with us. Is that all right?" Jokan asked.

Belia was frightened and confused. "But I am majimanidoog. I don't belong …"

"You are not in balance, and that is all," Tac'kana said.

"Come on, Belia. It'll be all right," Shoria said.

Once outside, Belia thought she was back being a slave again. "What do you want me to do?" she asked.

"Right now, we want you to stay with Kace and Broch and their group until we can live together. It won't be long," said Jokan.

"Then … then what?" asked Belia.

Shoria stopped Belia walking. "Look at me. We know who the Wikangatra tribe are. I think I know how much they made you a slave. But your red hair doesn't matter here. You are not bad luck to our tribe. We want you to do what you want to do. But we also want you to give us a chance and for you to stay with us until you know what you want."

Belia was confused. She didn't know why trust was so difficult. It took some courage to try to trust them, mainly because somewhere inside of her, she wanted to trust them. So she accepted. "Good," Jokan said. "Broch is looking at you. So go have some fun."

Belia started toward Broch but turned back. "Thank you," she said. Shoria and Jokan just smiled at her.

She slowly walked up to Broch and Kace and wondered where Wandago was. "Well?" implored Broch.

"They accepted me into the tribe," Belia said.

"Oh good," said Kace. "You're one of the crazy people now."

"Don't scare her off, Kace," Broch said laughing.

"Oh, I think she's stronger than that!" Belia blushed at that. She was not used to praise or teasing, but she liked it.

"I'm to stay with Jokan and Shoria when we can all get together."

"Really?" Broch asked. "That's a great honor, Belia."

"It is?"

"Oh yes," said Kace. "It's all good news."

Kace and Broch were walking and Belia was with them, but she did not know where they were going. Once outside the compound and into the woods, Belia realized that she did not have control of where she was. "Where are we?" she asked.

Kace answered, "Thought you'd like to see some of the mines being worked."

"Oh. Okay."

"Have you ever seen people work a mine?" asked Broch.

"No. I've seen them work the copper, but I've never been to a mine."

This stopped Broch with concern. He turned to her and looked at her with compassion. "They didn't let you do anything, did they?"

"No.... But it seems as if I'm doing what I want now," Belia said, smiling. Broch stood awkwardly, not knowing what to say. Kace sat down on a log. "Broch, it doesn't matter," Belia said. "Not anymore. As long as you don't hurt me, I think I can live here."

"I'd never hurt you, Belia. Never!" Broch said with urgency. Now it was Belia's turn to stand awkwardly.

After a few moments, Kace said, "You two finished?" That broke the silence and the awkwardness of the two.

Kace stood and said, "Okay, the mine's a ways off this way." He then led the way to the mine.

Kace and Brock took Belia to the pits where people of his tribe found ribbons of copper in rock. Although considerably filled in, a couple of the pits can be seen today near Copper Harbor at Fort Wilkins. The Keweenaw is structured as a "finger," with a spine as the higher terrain running along the midsection of the peninsula and sloping down on both sides to Lake Superior waters. The eastern slope is steeper than the western slope. Ancient peoples began to pit-mine near the water, and mined up toward the spine. They often threw dirt and shards of stone into the already worked pit behind them. This kept the water that might otherwise be trapped in their working pit from impeding their work as well as a natural place to throw the debris. Later miners filled in the pits even more. The pits near Fort Wilkins were some of the last of the pits the Woodland people mined, and being high on the spine explains why they were not completely filled in like the others. It also explains why they are so prominent today. There are thousands of ancient pits in the Keweenaw. Unlike later nineteenth and twentieth century mining, the PaleoIndian peoples did not seek to extract as much copper as possible. Instead, they sought copper that could be worked with the technology of their day: cold-hammering and annealing. They had no possibility of working large masses of copper, having stone hammers and flint knives. According to *Prehistoric Copper Mining in Michigan* by John R. Halsey, confirmation of their inability to work large copper masses was found in the South Pewebic Mine (later the Atlantic Mine) where ancient people dug a pit twenty-two feet deep and abandoned it when they found large masses of copper at the bottom of the pit. The Woodland tribe sought sheet copper up to an inch thick so they could work it.

They came upon a few men trying to break a rock in a mine pit. The pit was only about six feet deep sloped up at one end, and they had extracted quite a lot of small pieces of copper by just digging the pit. Belia noticed a few chisels and a wooden paddle-shaped shovel to remove debris. Wooden bowls containing copper pieces were also near the pit. The larger wooden bowls may have also been used to bail out water that seeped into the pit. Pottery, including bowls made of pottery, was well-established in the Keweenaw and upper Wisconsin by 2000 BCE. However, during this time of 5000 BCE, pottery was unknown. Strewn about were copper as well as stone chisels, gads, and pikes. Belia saw wedges made out of both stone and wood to help pry the copper from the rock and remove the copper from the pit. A little further was a ladder made of a tree that had been carefully trimmed so that the cut branches could serve as handholds and footholds. They even built scaffolding out of wood to help raise the rock out of the pit. The technology had been used for several hundreds of years and would continue for several more. The site was as cluttered as any construction site today.

Kace explained one way they used to break open the rock. "If we can't break a rock any other way, we get a lot of wood and place it against the rock. We make sure air can get at the bottom of the wood. We have long copper straws and we tip the straws with clay or we wrap leather strips so we don't feel the heat. We blow into the straws, so we can make more air go under the wood to make it very hot. We have to do this for a very long time. Then when it's time, we throw water on the rock. Sometimes the rock breaks and sometimes it doesn't." An example of broken rock for prehistoric mining is near the Delaware Mine in the Keweenaw.

"Seems like a lot of work," Belia said.

"It is. That's why we don't do it very often," Kace replied.

Nearby, Lena was painting a Mishi Bizi dragon on a round, smooth hammerstone. The tribe picked up hammerstones near Lake Superior. The glacier and water shaped them to be round and smooth. The hammerstones of the Woodland tribe were similar to prehistory hammerstones around the world, whether working a mine, flint quarry, or processing food. *Wonderful Power* points out that the hammerstone had little, if anything, to do with contact amongst differing cultures, but developed from a common need to use its force to achieve ends. To nineteenth century Daniel Wilson, such use evidenced humankind's mental unity. Technology grew from need, and the use of primitive tools were derived from perception and creativity.

Near Lena and hovering over the men in the pit, Dosh paced, mainly because he had nothing to do. His broken arm was wrapped tightly with bark fibers around straight sticks and resting in a sling. "What happened to you?" Broch asked.

"Oh, shokack here made me hold the chisel when he swung the hammerstone. He missed," Dosh said.

"Depends on your point of view," Lena muttered.

"What?" Dosh asked.

"Nothing."

"I'm sorry! How many times do I have to say I'm sorry?" Flep asked.

"Seven tens," Dosh replied, raising his voice. "And you can keep track of it."

"What really happened," Flep said to Broch and Kace, "is he couldn't hammer in the chisel, so he held it ... ALL BY HIMSELF."

"Idiot," Lena said, under her breath.

"What?" Dosh asked.

"Nothing."

"Not nothing. I heard you!"

"She said you're an idiot," Flep said.

"Then you just be quiet!" Dosh said to Lena.

Kace nudged Broch. "Oh this ought to be good."

"Why?" asked Belia.

"They're mated," Kace replied quietly.

"What did you say to me?" asked Lena, standing.

"Nothing," Dosh replied, backing off.

"You don't tell me to be quiet!" Lena said, coming close to Dosh. As she spoke, she poked his hurt arm. "You know better."

"Mishi Bizi ..."

"Mishi Bizi had nothing to do with this," she interrupted, poking. Dosh kept backing up as she advanced. "I don't know what it is with you men, but you always think nothing you do will hurt you. So you just *(poke)* don't *(poke)* think *(poke)*."

"Lena! Stop it! That hurts!" Several things happened at once. Belia giggled. Dosh lost his footing and started to fall backward into the pit. And Lena grabbed his good arm and helped him regain his balance. He pulled her against him. "Thank you my dear."

"Come on," she said. "I'll make you some tea to help with the pain."

"Um, teeeeeeaaa."   They walked back to the compound together. "It does hurt," Dosh said, fading into the forest.

"I know, dear. I know. I'll make it feel all better."

The anthropologist, Margaret Mead, saw a true beginning of civilization when examining a healed broken leg bone.   Instead of pointing to tools or domestication or the creation of civil law as signs of civilization, people caring for other people when hurt marked our becoming civilized. She looked at a 15,000-year-old femur that had healed and knew that other people had to care for the person when healing; without it he or she would have died of a broken leg. Caring for others when in need is a fundamental human characteristic buried deep within our hereditary psyche. We can ignore it, but humankind can't survive without it.

Flep took the hammerstone and wrapped it several times with a fiber rope. His hammerstone was very heavy and had been pecked. Pecking means someone made very subtle dents in the stone to make rough patches. This way, the smooth hammerstone had friction places, usually at the apex, so its binding will catch and stay. Flep's hammerstone had pecking places both at the top and at the bottom, to keep the rope in place. It was also rilled, which means it was pecked in a line to further keep the rope in place. "Hey, Kace, go and pound in that chisel with that hammerstone over there," Flep said. The rock was too heavy to be pulled out and broken, so they had decided to try to break it still in the pit.

"Okay." Kace walked down the wall with the help of a secured rope. He placed both hands on the rock and said as a ritual, "We see the beauty within you. We want to take it and transform you to your full becoming.

Thank you for your gift." He then tried several times to pound the chisel into a crack in the rock. The hammer Kace used was different than Flep's. His was smaller, and grooved instead of pecked. The grooves kept the stick handle in place, wound by leather strips. The grooves were at the center of both sides of the hammer and were parallel to each other. This hammer lasted a long time, so the effort of creating grooves was worth it.

"You can just go ahead and hold the chisel while I use this," Flep said, swinging the hammerstone on the end of a rope. Broch laughed loudly.

"Don't you dare!" Kace proclaimed. He finally was able to hammer in the chisel on top of the rock in a small crack. He made sure it would stay upright. He then scrambled out of the pit. Flep held his hammerstone with both hands and said the ritual, "Your strength will break rock. Thank you!" He then took the end of the rope with the hammerstone and swung it several times until he felt the stone within his control. He hit the chisel and broke the rock with a boom! Flep then jumped down into the pit and examined the broken rock.

"Oh, this is nice," he said. "Lots of copper ribbons in here." He examined the hammerstone also. "This will hold up quite a lot too. Lena did a good job with the painting." People used ten to fifteen different kinds of stone for the hammerstone. They were difficult to break when worked and easy to discard when they did. By the time the Woodland people lived, they knew what kind of hammerstone would break which kind of rock. They also knew which hammerstone would work best when grooved and which worked best with a handle instead of swinging a rope, as they could read the grain of rock.

No tribal member was forced to mine copper. Each person contributed to the life of the tribe according to individual wants and competency. Kace was excellent in finding signs of copper by studying the terrain. Broch did not mine, but hunted for the tribe. Nobody received compensation; they simply lived together. Two thousand years later, ancient Egypt would force people to work the mines at Nubia, containing a moderate amount of copper (compared to the Keweenaw) and some gold. But the Keweenaw's PaleoIndian people did not use people. The Wikangatra tribe's worldview included oppression caused by superstition and fear, but they were by far the minority of PaleoIndian culture of this time. The life of the Woodland tribe was not utopian by any stretch of the imagination; living was too difficult and fraught with danger for that. Mining and working copper was a way for the tribe to trade for items like flint that was not in the area. They needed flint to make fire.

Humankind discovered long before Clovis that their ability to make items depended on the resources in their terrain. No one group or tribe of people could have the resources to make everything. Such is the origin of trade. The unique resource of the Keweenaw was copper, so they extracted it to trade once they traveled south for the winter.

Broch and Belia walked back to the home compound. Unknown to them, Wandago was following them and keeping out of sight. Belia constantly looked for him without telling Broch or anyone else of her fear. Once near the compound, she scanned the area but did not see him. Stepping out of the forest, she once again scanned the compound. People were still separated into their groups, but either sitting and talking together or working.

Many tools and artifacts were strewn around the compound to dry meat, tan leather, make drums, and what seems to be an infinite number of things. Two men were working a large tree to make a canoe. They used logs to roll it into the compound. The summer day was not hot, but the mosquitoes were annoying. Belia saw people making a repellent to keep them at bay.

Belia enjoyed being with Broch and Kace. Nearly every day, they would go out and hunt for the tribe. Broch seemed more interested in her than Kace, so he tended to stay within sight of her. She wasn't with the tribe very long when the sun was hot and the breeze was cool.

One cool day, Belia was focused on the task to bring back much needed food for the tribe. She stopped in a cache of pine trees and noticed the beauty of the earth. But neither Broch nor Kace were close by, and she could not hear them. She felt relaxed and content.

But then suddenly she felt cold to her core. Turning, she was hit hard and she fell onto the mossy forest floor. Wandago took her by her tunic and lifted her up. He blocked her vision with his face and whispered, "You belong to me, not them." He smelled badly to her.

"Let go of me!" she yelled. She tried to speak more, but his hand clamped around her neck. He pushed her against a large tree.

"You don't belong with this tribe. You only belong to me."

"My evil will enter you if you do this," Belia croaked.

"I won't let THAT happen," he said. "I can have anyone else. But you will be with me and you will work for me. Nothing's changed for you."

"Never!" she whispered.

"Never?" he mocked.

"Broch and Kace won't let you take me."

"They can't stop me. I will kill them, both of them. And nobody will be able to find them. You will be mine or both of these men will die. Do you understand now?"

"No! You can't!"

"I can and I will. I'm stronger than anyone in this useless tribe. I'm stronger than them. I'm stronger than you. I'm better than you. I'm smarter than you."

"Why don't you just kill me?"

"I don't want to kill you. What's the fun in that? You'll take care of me, won't you?" Belia remained silent. "I'm going to Tac'kana and Jokan and tell them you're my mate. And you will agree. If you don't, I'll kill your friends."

Truly afraid, Belia shook. Wandago held her closer to him. "Yes, yes," she whispered.

Wandago then let her go and said, "Then go kill something and show everybody how wonderful you are." He then faded into the forest.

Belia couldn't move for a long time. She had not realized until then just how corrupt Wandago had become. He protected nobody except himself. For him to tell her to go kill something sickened her. That's not in balance with anything, especially not with Grandmother Earth. The four-leggeds sacrificed themselves so humankind could live, and a heart that kills to demonstrate his or her power or ability misses the mark. She knew that she looked at a man who will no longer Become, but stay hidden for the rest of his life. Wandago was truly lost. And she also felt lost and knew despair again.

Broch had no luck gaining food for the tribe that afternoon. He ran into Kace who was carrying a buck on his shoulders. "Looks like you got lucky."

"I did! Isn't he beautiful?" Kace stopped and placed the deer on the ground. "Take over for a while, will you?"

"Sure." Kace took Broch's weapons and then helped him lift the deer onto his shoulders.

"Thanks," Kace said.

"It's a big one!"

"Yeah. Where's Belia?" asked Kace.

"I don't know. She was with me and I turned around and she was gone."

"Do you think she ran off?"

"I hope not." They walked through the forest in silence for a while.

"Narsa said she'll be my mate," Kace said.

"My sympathies for Narsa," Broch said.

"Yeah!" Kace then hit Broch who stumbled and fell face down with the buck on his head. Kace laughed loudly.

Pushing off the deer, Broch complained, "I coulda been hurt!!"

"Woulda been funnier then," Kace said, lifting him up.

Broch brushed himself off. "Oh, you're maji," he said.

Kace picked up the deer and carried him for a while. "I saw an injured bear yesterday. Big male."

"Why didn't you take him?" Broch asked.

Kace stopped and looked at him. "Really?" he asked, adjusting the deer.

"Oh."

"Want to go tomorrow? It'll be an adventure. Maybe Luko and Danuku will come too."

"Okay. Belia too."

"Of course. And Narsa. I want her to have a new bear skin. If Nanabozho is willing, and the bear is willing," Kace said.

"Where is he?" asked Broch.

"Around Mikusandaku Point," he replied. Kace was referring to the tip of the Keweenaw. Between 1964 and 1971, it was used as a rocket range by NASA and the University of Michigan for meteorological data collection. Today, there's a commemorative monument at the site.

"That's a ways out. How long were you gone?" asked Broch.

"Four days, Broch. I've been gone four days. Thanks for noticing."

"Anytime."

Dark feelings blanketed Belia as she walked toward the compound. To desire what you know is a powerful thrust toward a particular state of living. The consequences of trauma, the loneliness and despair felt safe to her. Her darkness felt safe. Belia did not understand what she felt, but she knew she had to survive now. So she longed for the dark, even though it kept her from experiencing her present. She found herself rejecting Broch and Kace and Jokan and Shoria's kindness toward her because she could no longer see them as kind. Their actions were alien to her. The trauma she knew all her life damaged her thinking and she just wanted to cry. She no longer felt safe with the people of her new tribe who were bound to protect her. Wandago triggered her damage.

Belia no longer wanted to be nothing, but to return to the way her life demoted her. Her oppressor was back in her life, as far as she knew, and she deserved to be an object again. She even thought that although the people in this tribe would not, she wanted them to hurt her so she could feel safe. The experiences with this tribe do not generate the darkness. Suddenly, Belia could smell the musk of the earth and that turned her away from her thinking. "Grandmother Earth!" she whispered. "I have forgotten the voice of Grandmother Earth." She looked down and discovered that she had wandered into a small stream. She could feel the water's pressure against her legs and once again she felt herself enter a spiral. Nearly blind, she stumbled out of the water. She fell asleep on the ferns beneath the trees.

When she woke, her damaged thinking was muted, but she still felt despair. The sun had set and the darkness disoriented her; she found herself lost. But an owl flew near her from tree to tree. Belia didn't know why, but she followed the owl until she found the compound. "Thank you, sister," Belia whispered.

Broch, Kace, and Narsa saw her emerge from the forest and ran up to her. "Are you okay?" "Where have you been?" "Are you hurt?" But Belia could not answer any of their questions. She didn't know how. What she did know was the utterly stark difference she felt with them near her. She did not know it, but their presence helped heal her mind. She felt confused, but the foundation of her thinking was morphing into something foreign to her. The experience of kindness was healing her.

"Come on," Broch said. "The manishoes have stopped moving and Tac'kana says we can be a tribe again!"

Narsa took her arm and pulled her close as they walked into the compound. "We're celebrating! Come on!" That is when Belia noticed the sound of the drums and the vocable song of the tribe. People were dancing, eating, sitting, and talking. Belia had never been permitted to be amongst people the way she found herself in the moment. She felt herself healing but did not know how to interact. She stayed close to her friends and looked around for Wandago.

She sat next to Narsa, but Broch was attentive. He brought her food and water and sat next to her. "How are you doing?" he asked.

"Fine," she replied. "I mean, it's all so new and strange to me." She watched people dance in a circle around the center hearth and listened to the drums that seemed to relax her. "Broch, why don't you have a mate by now?"

Broch could tell that she was serious and even kind when asking the question. So he settled back and held his knees with his arms. "I did. A long time ago. Maca. She was beautiful to me. I had just gone through my manhood ritual and decided to move into her family hut. She said it was all right, but it wasn't really. She said she wanted me, but she didn't. I was so stupid back then."

Kace and Narsa were listening and Kace interrupted, "You okay Broch?"

"Yeah, I'm okay," Broch replied.

"We're here for you, me and Narsa."

"I am too, Broch," Belia whispered. Broch smiled at that and he felt close to her.

"There was another man named Plegor. He wanted Maca, and she wanted him. I didn't know it at the time. I mean, they didn't tell me. But Maca became mean to me and I didn't even know why. She would say that she'd do something and then not do it and then blame me. She said she didn't understand. She'd lie to me. She told me I was ugly and stupid. I don't know what happened. This beautiful woman became ugly. I moved out of her family's hut and back into mine. I would see her around, but she just looked at me mean-like or laughed at me. Then one day I went hunting and I saw them together ... you know ... together. That's when I knew. I got angry ... at both of them. I grabbed her and said things I've never said before. I knew it wasn't me at all. It didn't have anything to do with me and all that time I blamed myself. I thought I was doing wrong. I just didn't know what. So Plegor and I fought. Kace came and saw it all. I don't know how, but I caught myself from falling by holding onto a tree. Maca came and hit me in the head with a rock, and Plegor threw his spear. All at the same time. But instead of me, he hit Mega. He killed her. She stepped in the way to hit me again."

"What happened then?" asked Belia.

"We faced the elders and told them what happened. Plegor tried to lie, but Kace was there. So the elders banished Plegor and we haven't seen him again. We left him behind when we traveled to our winter home down south and we think he died."

Belia sat and thought whilst listening to the drums. "I'm sorry, Broch," she said. "Why did they do that?"

"All I know is they forgot the voice of Grandmother Earth. They forgot Pacara."

"What's Pacara," she asked.

"Pacara," he replied. "It's how we treat each other. It's how we see Grandmother Earth. It's how we see our four-legged brothers and sisters and how they sacrifice themselves so we can live. It's relationships. It's balance. Everything is Pacara."

Belia sat in silence for a long time, wondering if she's going to hurt Broch like he was hurt before. Looking around, she saw Wandago talking to Jokan and Shoria. Jokan nodded and he and Shoria talked to Tac'kana and a few others of the tribe. Then they saw her and walked over to her. "Wandago wants to speak with the elders," Jokan said. "We need you to come too."

"Okay," she said. "Now?"

"No. Tomorrow morning," he replied. Shoria touched her shoulder before they left.

"I wonder what that's about," mused Kace.

"I don't know." But Belia felt a lot of different emotions and her anxiety spiked. When Narsa and Kace rose to get something more to eat, she turned to Broch. "Listen. If things go wrong, please don't believe everything you hear."

"Why?" asked Broch. "What's wrong?"

Belia hesitated. "I don't know that anything's wrong. I ... I just want you to know that if things were different ... you and I... I mean ... Broch, just don't believe everything you see and hear. Okay?"

Broch replied, "Okay." They were silent again, but this time Broch's anxiety spiked. He felt very protective of Belia, and the more he was with her, the more he liked her. "Let's sleep out here tonight."

"Okay."

The next morning, Belia and Wandago sat with Tac'kana, Jokan, Shoria, and the rest of the elders in Tac'kana's hut that was oversized enough to accommodate several people. They sat in a circle, with Jokan between Wandago and Belia. Shoria sat next to

Belia, and Tac'kana sat across from them. Many of them smoked and covered themselves and others with smoke. It was a time for slow reflection and deliberation.

To the Woodland tribe, smoke was sacred. Smoke was a conduit that helped them go from the physical world to the spirit world of the ancients. They could be connected to all of life and living and were careful to think positive thoughts because their thoughts were shared with the spirit world. Being connected this way, they could discern the truth of a situation or action – or words.

"What is it that you want to ask us, Wandago?" asked Tac'kana.

He paused and chose his words carefully. "I ask to build my own hut and live there with my mate," he said.

"Where?" she asked.

"Next to Luko."

The elders looked at each other and nodded. More smoke. More silence.

"You may build your hut next to Luko," Tac'kana said quietly.

Wandago grew tired of the silence. "With my mate," he said.

"Who is your mate?" Tac'kana asked.

"Belia." Belia looked down throughout the meeting and felt despair.

After considerable silence, Tac'kana asked Belia, "Are you his mate?"

"Yes," answered Wandago, too quickly.

Tac'kana looked hard at Wandago and it made him nervous. "I did not ask you the question. Belia, are you his mate?"

"You do not have to agree, Belia," Shoria said. Belia remained silent.

"Who are you to say?" asked Wandago to Shoria, impatiently. "Is this tribe led by women? She is my mate. Aren't you, Belia?"

"Yes," Belia said quietly, not looking up.

"There. Then I'll build my hut. Belia is my mate."

Silence. The silence was impossible for Wandago.

Tac'kana continued to smoke. "No," she said.

"What?"

"No. You will not pretend that Belia is your mate," said Tac'kana, with a razor's edge. Belia looked at her, surprised.

Wandago stood, suddenly angry. "Jokan, are you leader here? Are you weak?"

Jokan stood and faced him. "Sit down," he said, quietly. Everyone looked at Wandago in silence. He sat down and Jokan sat down.

"Why are women leading here? Why do they even have a say? They are not warriors." They sat and smoked and said nothing, knowing Wandago will reveal more of his true self. They did not offer smoke to Wandago. Wandago could not contain himself. "I can kill," he said. "I'm stronger than any of you. I should be leader!"

"You have the power to kill all of us," stated Jokan.

"I do. Of course I do," replied Wandago.

"You have the power to use women."

"Look at me!"

"You have the power to take from the earth."

"Yes! I said yes! How many times do I have to say it?"

Nobody was surprised by his words and showed no anger. Jokan spoke, "If we give in to the power that we have, how will, how can, we strive to become who we are meant to be? Even I can tell this world is young, and we are young. As a people."

"It's the same with women," Tac'kana said. "We cannot become when the focus is on our power."

Wandago looked at her with grave disrespect. "Women have no power. I am Man. I can do anything I want. We're stronger than women," Wandago said, with ice. "Even you."

"So you want to shift what it means to be a man?" asked Jokan. "To no longer protect but just use? We give in to this and we will no longer lie beside her, look into her eyes, and see ourselves. She might continue to like us, maybe even love us, but as long as we embrace power over her, we will never know love for ourselves. We will be corrupted. And not even know it."

Wandago looked around at the elders and said, "I have lost everything. Everything! I only have Belia –"

"Belia is not an object," Shoria interrupted.

"She told you she was my mate!" he exclaimed.

"No," said Tac'kana. "You may stay in the tribe and build your hut. But you will not break our laws."

"Your laws," mocked Wandago angrily.

"We see our lives as having obligations," Tac'kana said. "We protect each other. We protect the four-leggeds, the plants and trees and rocks, and all that we see. That is our obligation and our purpose."

Wandago did not understand a word of it. He stood, looked at Belia, and left without saying anything more.

Chapter Eleven: Becoming

All Belia could do was to sit and look down. The elders continued to smoke and be silent. Finally, Shoria spoke up. "We still want you to stay in our hut if you would like that."

Without looking up, Belia quietly said, "I do not deserve … this … you …"

"Why?" asked Tac'kana, quietly. "You are human."

"I've done terrible things," she replied. "I am majimanidoog."

"What have you done?" asked Shoria with sympathy.

Silence.

"Did Wandago threaten you to say you're his mate?" asked Tac'kana. Silence. "You need to answer, but know that we will not hurt you."

"Yes. He said he'll kill Broch and Kace if I didn't."

"We understand," said Jokan.

Belia became frantic and stood in front of them. "No! You don't. He'll kill them! He can! He can kill any of you!"

"Sit down, Belia," Jokan said, sternly. "We needed to know his threat." Belia sat back down.

Tac'kana moved and sat next to Belia and placed her hand on her hand. "Belia, why do you say you're majimanidoog?"

Finally, Belia gained enough courage to tell them. "I killed my mother."

The elders were careful to not react. Tac'kana said, "This is a story that needs to be told. I don't think that what you did is the only story here. We know that the Wikangatra tribe was superstitious and did not know pacara. We know that Wandago is violent. What happened to you, Belia? What was your life like?"

Belia looked up into her eyes and then down to focus on Tac'kana's hand. "It wasn't always bad," she said. "I had Maelys and she had me. But Wandago killed her. I don't really know why." Belia then described her life, trying to not make them feel pity. She told of the days when the illness came, how she left, taking care of Inda, and then the last moments. Belia tried to be as honest as possible. "She told me that she was my mother. I never knew until then. But something broke inside of me and I killed her. It happened so fast and I was so surprised... So I'll leave, unless you want to kill me."

The elders were silent once again. "We will not kill you or hurt you, Belia," Tac'kana said. "You are a member of our tribe. We want you to live, probably for the first time in your life."

"I don't ... I don't ... understand," whispered Belia.

Shoria said, "You don't have to understand. You just have to step into the truth of today. Know the truth of today. We're asking you to be a warrior and seek truth so that its beauty will shine in the faces of our children. We're asking you to hear the voice of Grandmother Earth and to let us help you do that. None of us can do it alone."

Jokan rose and said, "And nothing meaningful happens quickly. So let's go get your pack. You'll share your home, our home, with Shoria, me, Tac'kana, Piesta, and Quekatra. It'll be fine." All of the others rose and touched Belia before leaving the hut.

Belia and Jokan walked over to where Kace had stowed their packs. Jokan explained to Kace and Broch that Belia would stay with them, but to be sure to not stop their activities with her. He then told them to watch out for Wandago.

"Me, Broch, Belia, and some others are going for an injured bear tomorrow," Kace said.

"Where?" asked Jokan.

"Mikusandaku Point," replied Kace. "We're taking a couple of canoes and a tipi to stay quite a few days."

"Mind if Shoria and I come along?" Jokan asked.

"That would be great!" Kace replied.

"Yeah, you and Shoria can brain the hide," Broch said smiling.

"That would be fine," countered Jokan, smiling. "See you tomorrow." Jokan then grabbed Belia's pack and took it with him to his hut. Belia stayed with Kace and Broch for a while and told them what happened. She also told them about Inda, and they talked about common experiences of trauma for a couple of hours. Belia realized that everybody experienced pain some time in his or her lives. That humbled her and helped put her own life in perspective.

The next day, the eight people took three canoes partly laden with poles and skins to make a tipi as well as taking their packs. The poles were tied to the outside of the canoes and rested in the water. They also brought the items and tools they needed to process their kill. They needed two if it was a usual sightseeing trip, but they were out to hunt and needed the room. Fun and adventure was in the air. All of the tribes' canoes were in a cove near the compound, carried up far onto the land so inclement weather would not take them. The cove opened to what is now known as Copper Harbor that opens out into Lake Superior. The sky was clear and the air cool in the morning dew.

Wandago watched them as discretely as possible. He considered following them, but a canoe would be seen, and the brush within the tree line on the shore would impede his progress too much. Besides, he thought, he needed to build a hut, and if he didn't, the elders would become suspicious. So he stayed to build his hut.

They packed up the canoes. Luko and Danuku were in one, Jokan, Shoria, and Narsa in another, and Kace, Broch, and Belia in the third. Kace gave his paddle to Belia, moved to the middle of the canoe, and set up the packs to make himself comfortable. "I didn't sleep well last night," he announced. The others just smiled.

Belia marveled at the beauty of the land and water. The trees looked packed with brush, but she knew that deer paths throughout the forest made walking the land possible. Once outside into Lake Superior, they stayed close to the land. They knew that Lake Superior could be dangerous and change conditions quickly. Up to what is now known as Horseshoe Harbor, Belia saw mostly rocks as the shoreline. Lake Superior was not quite as high as today, so the shoreline extended out a little ways than today. Nevertheless, it would be difficult to step on land. Once past Horseshoe Harbor, beach and rock were more prevalent. Right before High Rock Bay, they found enough of a sandy beach to make it to the land. Broch used his paddle to drench Kace who woke with a start. "Ahhrc!" he yelled. "Thanks a lot."

"You stink," Broch countered. "You need a bath."

They had plenty of daylight to secure the canoes, set up the tipi, and get a fire going. The night fire stirred ancient memories of safety and belonging. They gazed at the stars and marveled at the Milky Way. The moon rose in the distance and Belia once again felt comforted by her presence. They talked of ancestors, for they were aware of past and present. Their ability to see patterns helped them perceive future.

"Look," said Luko, looking at the stars. "There's the great Thunderbird." "And there's the snake manitou," Narsa pointed out. Ancient cultures all around the world looked at the stars, saw patterns, and created a wide array of stories in the star patterns. The Woodland people were no exception, and their creative imagination helped explain their world. Also, mystery was as much a part of their lives as were the four-leggeds and trees. Instead of fear, mystery stimulated thought and curiosity.

"Yeah," Narsa said. "Grandmother Earth was lonely, so she sent snake down from the sky. Snake manitou helped make the world. He carved out the rivers and lakes. Fox got jealous and said, 'I want to help too.' So Fox dug the earth and made the hills and mountains and valleys. Beaver pitched in and said 'I want to help too.' And Beaver brought trees up from the water. And from trees came all other plants. Then bear, deer, porcupine, and wolves decided that this was a good place to live. But it was still dark, so the eagle said 'I will go and get the sun.' So the eagle got the sun but it was too hot. So together, crow and eagle made the sun track across the sky so night would come. But then it was too dark at night, so the owl said, 'I want to help.' So the owl flew high into the black and made the moon. But the Fox wanted to make trouble and made the moon different every night so one night in her circle the dark would return. Grandmother Earth smiled on the world and was happy for all the work they did. But she said that it is not finished. So she took some mud and made man. Then she took a feather from the eagle and from the feather grew woman. Then it was finished."

The others sat silently for a long time after Narsa's story. They had heard it before, but it was never old to them. It helped them know themselves and their world.

Looking at the stars, Danuku said, "It's good that our ancestors watch us."

"I think so too," Shoria said. "Just as deer and bear and the rest of the four-leggeds and winged people do not die but change into something sacred, so do we." They pondered the stars in silence.

"I wonder what they really are," Kace mused, meaning the stars.

"What do you mean?" asked Jokan.

"Well, maybe they're like the earth and rocks but they're too far away to know," he replied.

Kace's thoughts were against the standard beliefs of their culture. But the others knew Kace, and did not argue with him. He had a curious mind. Throughout the history of humankind, individual men and women used their creative thinking and moved knowledge and philosophy forward, sometimes at a price. It took a few hundred years more for cultures to not only discourage thinking against the norm, but eliminate the offenders in one way or another, from exile to death. But Jokan was a leader who knew the meaning of a corrupted use of power and refused to follow it.

"Maybe it's just vapor," Broch said.

Kace looked at him hard and replied, "Everything's vapor to you."

The smoke kissed each of them in turn and helped keep the mosquitoes away. They felt that they could see through time. They gazed at the moon and the stars and wondered at the changing seasons and the coming of a new day. They felt peace being both together and alone on the beach of the Keweenaw. They could smell the smoke, the trees, the moss, and fern. It was as sweet as perfume and they could both feel and smell the damp air. Life was remarkable.

Suddenly, joy and gratitude descended on the group. "Come on," Narsa said. "Let's dance." Broch got a log and a stick and beat the rhythm. The others except Belia got up and sang and danced. Once in a while, they threw a stick into the fire to make the embers shoot up to the stars.

Belia thought it all was exciting. But she felt left out. She knew that the others accepted her, but she was unable to accept herself as part of them. They made it clear that she was a member of the tribe and their friend. But, still, Belia felt as if she was standing on the outside looking in. She had never in her life known a friend except Maelys and did not know how to live this new life. She was constantly afraid that if she said or did anything they didn't like, that they would reject her. So she observed them sing and dance and wished that she could do that too. Her mind was still imprisoned in the trauma of her oppression. Because they wanted Belia to be with them, the others did not see Belia's challenges.

They sang and danced long into the night. Then they sat close to each other. Eventually, they went into the tipi and slept. Jokan, then Danuku kept watch throughout the night.

The next day was the day for the hunt. Kace was up early and found deer paths in the woods. All wanted in on the action, and after a bite to eat of dried meat they brought along, traveled carefully together with their spears, bows, and arrows. Kace and Broch led the way. They saw deer, but they were after bear. They hoped they would come across the injured bear Kace saw. Eventually, the group distanced themselves in smaller groups. Kace and Broch seemed to separate from the others, and Belia found herself with Shoria and Jokan.

At midday, the three stopped to rest and eat by a small creek. Shoria decided to clean herself in the water. "Come into the water, Belia," she said.

"Why?"

"You'll feel better if you do," replied Shoria.

"Well, okay." Belia took off her shoes and stepped into the water. "Feels like water," she joked. The water was warmer than she expected.

"Yes, but if you stop and concentrate, you'll see more," Shoria said. Jokan decided to nap and leaned against a tree. "The earth will do the teaching, so we need to be aware and listen to the earth. Look, I'm washing my body, but when I wash my body with this water, I wash my mind. Doing that helps heal the mind, and everybody needs to do that once in a while."

Belia sat on the bank with her feet in the water. "Is it magic?" she asked.

"No," Shoria replied. "It's just the way it works. Look at the water. It moves and doesn't return right here. It's alive. But more than that, it doesn't end. The water still flows."

"Does that mean something?"

"It means that water has memory. Water does not end. You drink it and it becomes a part of you. Water is within you. Its memory also becomes a part of you. The four-leggeds drink the water and it becomes a part of them. Everything in this world, the trees, animals, birds, grass, has their own manner of being. Each has a spirit that makes it what it is. So do we. But some things connect us, and help us be connected. Water is one of those things. So is air and earth. But water holds the memories. All of our ancestors drank the same water as you and I do. Water came into them and then moved on, like this stream here. When the rain comes, we say thank you for remembering, because water is memory. Sometimes people see water and don't know what they see. But water is alive, water is life, and if you be silent in the water, our ancestors' memories will heal your mind."

"I ... I didn't know," said Belia.

"When you enter water, your mind opens up and you can be healed. Water helps your own memory move on down the stream. You become aware of something outside yourself, you become connected with yourself and everything else. You belong."

"How do I do that?" asked Belia.

"Sit down in the stream. Be quiet and concentrate. Let yourself remember and let the ancestors help you. You will drift off into a sacred dream." Belia moved into the middle of the stream and sat down. "Listen to your breathing and let your mind go. Don't think about anything. Just be quiet," Shoria said.

Belia closed her eyes and tried to focus on her breathing. She knew she had to open her mind, but deep down she was afraid and tried to resist the process. But the water carried her and caressed her mind, probing her memories with gentle fingers. She saw Inda, Wandago, Kandra, and Maelys. She watched them eat while she was hungry. She saw Allotar throw stones at her when she thought she was her friend. She saw herself trying to walk for the first time and Wandago kicking her over and laughing. She held Maelys in her young arms when Maelys was just a baby. Down down down.

Then, suddenly, the memories vanished and Belia saw a white owl fly over to her and rest in front of her. For a time, the owl said nothing and did not move. The owl and Belia just gazed at each other. "What do you want?" the owl asked.

"I don't know," she replied.

The owl just blinked. "What do you want?"

Belia became uncomfortable, as if she was about to break through a wall. "I don't know."

Silence. Belia could feel her heart race.

"What do you want?"

"I want them to kill me," Belia burst through. "I want them to kill me." She felt broken. She was broken.

"But they do not want you to die. I do not want you to die. I want you to live."

"How? Why?"

"Look closely, Belia," said the owl. She then showed Belia and Inda by the stream. She saw Inda slap her across the face. "Don't you dare call me mother. I have paid a terrible price because of you. Every woman deserves to say what is to be done to her. Every woman has a right to her own body. Every woman has a right to say no. Every woman! But he put his hands on me. Then he put evil inside of me. I struggled. I screamed. And now, every time I look at you, I see that evil." Belia watched as Inda stepped up close to her. "I'll find a tribe and you won't be coming with me. You are evil. You don't deserve it. They will never accept you. I don't want you. I never wanted you. You're a freak! You're worthless!" Belia saw her knife striking upward into Inda who gasped. Soon, Inda fell dead into the river.

Belia turned dead and said to the owl, "Why did you show me this? Don't you know I can't forget it?"

"Look again," said the owl. The scene played again. This time, the owl directed Belia's focus. This time, Belia saw Inda move close to her and she saw that Inda drew her knife. Belia realized that Inda was going to kill her. *Death, then Transformation.* If she hadn't killed Inda, she would be dead.

"She was going to kill me!" said Belia.

"Yes," replied the owl.

"Why?" asked Belia.

"Because you finally knew her secret, and nobody could know her secret."

"But why did I kill her?" Belia asked, in shock.

"She was killing you. She's been trying to kill you all your life. Her constant betrayal affected your mind. Besides, you knew she was going to use her knife."

"I did?"

"Look at your left hand," said the owl. The scene repeated. Focusing in even closer, Belia saw Inda draw her knife and right before Inda could strike, Belia's left hand knocked Inda's arm. "You are so used to surviving, you don't even think or see it. You just protect yourself."

"I still killed her. It doesn't change anything," Belia said.

"It changes who you are." A window opened within Belia's mind. "You belong here. You belong to the earth."

Belia was overwhelmed. She cried the kind of cry that tastes like vomit. The owl faded in her sight and she woke, crying, still in the stream. But Jokan, also in the water, was holding her against his chest to protect her from going underwater. Shoria also was with her in the water. Belia looked as she sat up, and she saw a fire burning on the bank of the stream. She couldn't look at Jokan or Shoria. She just cried and released the pent-up fear and remorse. She realized that none of what happened in her life was her fault. It didn't even have anything to do with her. But she also realized that she'd been paying the price all of her life.

Shoria took some water and wiped her face. Then she and Jokan helped Belia stand and sit by the fire. Finally, Belia was able to stop crying. She noticed that it was mid-afternoon. She looked at Shoria and Jokan and thanked them. She told them everything she saw whilst in the water, and they talked long and hard while becoming dry and warm. Late afternoon, they put out the fire and returned to camp.

Broch was worried when they entered camp. "I was hoping you'd be with Shoria and Jokan," he said.

"Yes," replied Belia. "Everything's fine."

"We got a deer today," he said. "I'll get you something to eat."

"Thanks." The group had gutted the deer far in the woods, knowing they could not use all of him. What they did not cook that night, they placed in the cold water of Lake Superior to keep it from spoiling.

The group talked together as the moon rose. Around mid-day, Kace and the others had come across bear tracks, but could not find the bear. "Shoria and I will stay here tomorrow," Narsa announced. "We'll work the deer hide while you all go and play mighty hunter among the trees."

"Well, I'm sure Shoria will be doing all the work," Kace said, teasing her.

"While you don't do anything," Narsa replied. Broch laughed.

The next morning, Danuku decided to stay and help Shoria and Narsa while the others looked for bear tracks. The three stretched and secured the deer hide on the ground and then processed it the same way their ancestors had done for thousands of years.

Kace led the way through the trees to the last place he found tracks. They felt embraced by their surroundings and it was exciting to hunt for food. They also felt a camaraderie with each other that deepened their friendship. They traveled as far as the west side of Schlatter Lake, as it's known today, when they came across rocks that had been rolled. Then they saw bear scat.

"Look," said Kace. "There's scat here and there and there. He's come back here a lot."

They then saw tracks. They could not get as far as the lake due to plant life blocking their way. But they could see far enough to see a large black bear at the southern tip of the lake near a tributary.

"You been here before, Kace? You know the land here?" asked Jokan.

"Yeah," replied Kace. "There's a small clearing near where he's at by the creek. Don't get into the lake where the creek goes into the lake. It's too soft and you'll sink and get stuck. Okay?"

"Okay," Jokan and Luko replied.

"The bear won't go there either," Kace continued. He grabbed a few dry grass and leaves to test the direction of the wind. "Good. The wind is coming from the north.

Let's hope for Nanabozho's happiness. Okay. Let's prepare."

They made mud and streaked it across their faces. They then raised their arms to the four directions without standing so the bear would not see them.

Brother bear, thank you for helping us.

You will not die.

Your spirit will fly to your bear ancestors.

Brother bear, we are all connected.

They gathered their bows, arrows, and spears and moved closer to the bear. Kace told them that they will surround the bear against the lake. So Broch and Belia moved to the bear's left, Luko and Jokan to the right, and Kace center. Closer to the bear, they could see his wound. A spear was embedded in his right shoulder and bleeding. Just a short, broken handle was seen. Jokan was upset. "Who would do this?" he demanded. "This is not the way to honor Grandmother Earth!"

Very slowly, they moved closer to the bear who sat and scratched himself. He could not reach the spear. The bear faced away from the water, and the warriors knew that he would enter the lake when they attacked. Everyone paid attention to Kace as they slowly moved closer to the bear. Kace gave a signal to stay, so they all put down their spears and loaded their bows. Once ready, Kace gave the signal to attack.

Suddenly, they all stood and shot the bear. The bear reacted with rage and moved backward toward the water but to their surprise, did not go in. He didn't run away at all. The warriors then picked up their spears and moved to try to finish the job. The bear rose on his hind legs and bellowed. Jokan threw and hit him under his arm. He then moved close enough to the bear to retrieve his spear. Meantime, Belia, Broch, and Luko threw their spears, seriously injuring the bear. But they did not kill him. He went down on all fours and attacked Kace who planted the end of his spear and let the bear run into it. Jokan threw again while Belia, Broch, and Luko retrieved their spears. The bear caught Kace and tried to bite his head off when Broch struck the bear's head. The bear released Kace, but not without swiping his shoulder. Kace went down and Belia ran back to her bow and arrows and was able to shoot the bear several times. Jokan grabbed Kace and moved him away from the fight while Broch and Luko continued to throw their spears. Luko then jumped onto the bear's back and struck him several times with his knife until the bear threw him off. Broch's last effort with his spear found the bear's heart. The bear stood in front of the warriors in his raging weakness, then lay down as if he was going to sleep. Before death, Jokan took the chance and moved to the bear and placed his hand on the bear's head.

"You are a great warrior," he said. "I'm sorry you were in such pain. Now you can go to your ancestors until you live again."

The bear died. They all sat on the ground to recover, and Belia and Broch tended to Kace's wounds. There wasn't much they could do right then except clean it with water from the nearby creek. Jokan cut open the bear with his knife and cut out part of the liver. One by one, he offered the liver to each person who took a bite. It was difficult to bite through a piece of raw liver. Finally, Jokan ate a piece of liver. "Now this warrior bear will live through us until he finds his way," he said.

They all cleaned up at the stream and set to processing the bear. Belia was delighted and grateful to be as competent as the rest of the company. They were all proficient at skinning and processing because they had done it all their lives. Kace didn't do much because of his pain and watched. "Anything to get out of work," Broch said to him.

"Of course," Kace replied. He had open wounds on his shoulder and no way to stitch them. He knew that they brought fishbone needles and sinew with them, but that was back at the camp.

"You doing okay?" asked Belia.

"Yeah, I'm fine," Kace replied.

They rolled up the skin and cut quite a lot of meat. Luko stayed with the remains and continued to remove organs whilst the others carried pieces back to the camp. Kace also carried a hunk of meat.

Once back at the camp, they placed everything in the cold waters of Lake Superior. At the camp, the three had processed the deer as much as possible and were finished for the day. Narsa ran to Kace as soon as she saw him, asking what happened. Danuku took his cache and put it in the water while Shoria got the items to stitch him up. Kace explained with a great deal of emphasis on himself. "I managed to grab his teeth in my hands to keep him from killing me," he said.

"Sure," Broch said. "That's the way it happened." He then slapped Kace on his back. Kace just grit his teeth so he wouldn't show pain, but he shot Broch a killing look. Shoria stitched him up while both Narsa and Belia held his hands.

Broch stood next to Jokan, looking on. "Some guys get all the luck," Jokan quietly said. "Well, let's go back." Jokan got a hammerstone with a handle and a chisel to help separate the joints. Jokan, Broch, and

Danuku returned to the bear and further processed. By the time they got to the lake, Luko had gutted the bear and placed his bowels and some organs in the forest away from the water for four-leggeds and birds to have. He also cleaned the bear as much as possible. "Good job, Luko," Jokan said.

They made a few trips back to the camp until they had taken all of the bear they intended. One trip was to carry the head back so they could use the brains to tan the hide, keeping the fur intact. Using the chisel, Brock cut off several claws, enough for everyone to have one. Once back at the camp, he handed them to everyone. They would bore a hole through it and add it to their necklace. That helped them be connected to the bear and it also was a remembrance of their adventure.

The group had plenty to eat and a lot to do before going back home to the compound. Nobody had to tell anyone else what to do; every person could see what each other was doing and just helped. Shoria found herbs to help Kace heal and he healed well and reveled in the attention. Although the work was sometimes hard, they all felt as if they were on vacation.

Jokan spoke to Shoria and they asked Belia to help them gather wood for the fire. Once deep in the forest, Jokan and Shoria sat down and asked Belia how she was doing.

"This has been the best time of my life," Belia said, also sitting on a log.

"You know you belong here," said Shoria.

"Yeah. Nobody's talking about me or angry with me. I feel as if I can be myself."

"What will you do once we get back home?" asked Jokan. "I'm thinking about Wandago."

"I don't know," she replied. Suddenly, she became afraid.

"Belia, there's a way to handle Wandago," Jokan said. "Would you like to know how?"

"Yes. Please!"

"Okay. Look at Shoria for a while. Make sure you don't look at me."

"Okay."

Belia and Shoria sat in silence for a while and Belia wondered what was going on. Then Shoria told her, "Now look around and try to see Jokan." Belia rose and looked through and around the trees.

"Where is he?" she asked.

"I'm right here," Jokan said as he stepped next to Belia.

"But ... Where were you?"

"Next to you," replied Jokan. "It's a way to kind of ... camouflage. We'd like to teach it to you if you'd like."

"Yes!" replied Belia. "I'd like that."

"You'll have to learn and that'll take time. But you'll be able to do it. With practice."

"Okay."

"You have to connect to the earth, so always be in touch with Grandmother Earth." Jokan then explained that she will have to learn to meditate and at the same time always honor and respect the earth. "We are all connected and we are all affected by what we do and say. The air we breathe, our feet on the ground, what we think, and all of pacara determine who we are and our obligation to walk our path to becoming by focusing outside ourselves." Jokan taught her the importance of observation and awareness, not only of what affects us but what affects the earth and all our brothers and sisters living on the earth. "Life is in and through everything, and what we see today, we also see yesterday and tomorrow. Just placing your hand against a tree isn't enough. Just placing your hand against a tree will not achieve anything without caring about the earth, without caring about the tree. It's more than a lifestyle. It's who you want to be."

He put his palm against a tree. "You place your hand on the side of a tree," continued Jokan. "Then close your eyes and move your spirit outside yourself. Allow the tree to help you focus and connect to the tree. Remember, the tree is just as alive as you are, but with a different voice." Belia then placed her hand on the side of the tree. "Now quiet your mind and focus on your breathing. You'll fall into a trance-like state. When you're completely quiet, then focus on the tree and you and the tree will be connected."

Belia focused on her breathing and tried to quiet her mind. She did not care about Wandago anymore but felt the tree through her hand. She felt the energy of the tree, that to her worldview meant the spirit of the tree. She felt the energy move into her hand and then throughout her body. By focusing on the energy of the tree, she was able to move herself to outside herself. She felt herself first grow upward as tall as the tree. Then she felt herself grow downward and knew it was her roots. She had never felt such a thing before and it did not frighten her.

Then, in the midst of this experience, the white owl once again stood in front of her. "What do you want?" the owl asked. Belia felt herself surrounded by love. "What do you want?" repeated the owl.

"I want to belong," replied Belia.

"You belong to the earth. You belong to me," said the owl. "You have always belonged to me. I have been with you all the days of your life."

"I don't understand," said Belia. "Where were you? Why did they hurt me every day?"

"You're alive and now's the time for you to live. You belong to me, but you can belong to the tribe and to the people in your life now. Past is present is future, and you are on the path you were meant to be."

Belia then felt overwhelmed and time felt eternal. The next thing she saw was Shoria and Jokan next to her as she lay on the ground.

"What happened? Are you okay?" asked Shoria.

Belia got up and sat back down on the log. Shoria and Jokan sat next to her. "The owl came again," she said.

The two relaxed, relieved that Belia had, indeed, connected to Grandmother Earth. "Oh, that's fine then," Jokan said. "You did well."

"I don't understand though," Belia said. "The owl said that past is present is future and I'm on the path I'm meant to be."

"Belia, you need to realize that your past experiences made you who you are today," Jokan said. "That's why we don't really feel sorry for you. You are an amazing person that you wouldn't be without those experiences."

"That's true for everyone, Belia," Shoria said. "Jokan and I have lost all of our children. When I think about it, I'm terribly sad. But then I remember them with honor and I realize that I am my past, right here, right now and I'm grateful for it."

"You want the pain?" asked Belia.

"No," replied Shoria. "But it happened. It is. And now, I am."

"It isn't just the painful experiences," Jokan said. "It's the wonderful experiences of your past too. Like with Maelys. It's even the mundane experiences. It's all of it."

Belia sat in silence for a while. She could smell the musty perfume of the earth and trees embracing her. "Why are you helping me like this?" she asked.

Without hesitation, Shoria said, "Because we love you."

Belia felt confused and overwhelmed. "But why would you do that?"

Jokan said, "Because you're worth it." Belia looked stunned and Jokan laughed a little. "Broch loves you too, you know."

"He does?"

"Yes," Jokan and Shoria smiled. Jokan continued, "Focus outside yourself and you'll see it. To do that, Belia, you need to accept your past and enter your present. Like connecting to the tree, you have to move outside yourself to focus on other people. This is how you become a warrior and how to think and act like one."

"Oh. Okay."

Jokan rose and said, "Let's gather some wood and go back." They picked up an armful of wood and returned to the camp. Belia had a lot to think about.

Once back to the camp, Broch came up to Belia, took her wood, and threw it near the fire. "I'm glad you're back," he said to Belia. Once he was free of the wood, she took his hand and Broch lit up. Narsa put some bear meat on stones in the fire as well as some roots and greens she found that day. For the rest of the night, Broch and Belia sat together, sometimes talking, sometimes in silence. Belia realized that Broch was a true warrior. He was gentle, and being gentle and kind were the weapons of Grandmother Earth.

It rained that night as well as the next day. The rain stimulated the smell of earth, and they all stayed in the tipi relaxing, talking, and sleeping. The next few days were cold but beautiful. The sunlight turned Lake Superior a dark blue and they marveled at the beauty in front of them as they finished what they needed to do to return to the compound. Soon, the tribe would leave the Keweenaw. The tribe journeyed south to live during the winter months, and returned to their compound and huts in the early spring.

It snowed a little before they woke, but the wind was calm and it warmed up quickly. They saw that the color of the trees had changed. They packed up canoes.

Kace took the bear skin and gave it to Narsa. "This is yours," he said, smiling.

"What?" she asked. "Really?"

"Yup." The others gathered around and affirmed the gift. Narsa took the bear skin and threw it onto the ground. Then she grabbed Kace and pushed him onto it and fell on top of him, kissing him all over. Everyone else pretended to do something away from them and out of sight.

"We're mated now, you know," she said.

"Well it's about time," he laughed. After a couple of minutes, Kace called to the others. "Come on! What are you waiting for? Let's get home!" They finished packing the canoes and went home.

Unloading their canoes at the cove, they noticed that Wandago had built a small, oval hut next to Luko. "Oh great," said Luko. "Just what I wanted." Other members of the tribe came to help them as well as greet them. The new canoe was finished.

Tac'kana came to Jokan, very glad he was back. "It's nearly time to leave and go to our southern home," she said.

"Do we have enough food?" asked Jokan.

"No," she replied. "We need to dry what we have and make sure we have enough." She noticed Kace's wounds. "Kace! Come here!" He did and she examined his wounds. "Does this hurt?" she asked while poking him.

"Ow! No," he replied.

"This is Shoria's work," she said. "It's good. It's good enough."

"Thanks," Kace said. "I'll heal."

"Humm, you've already healed a great deal."

"Thanks Tac'kana," said Kace and then joined the others to move he and Narsa into her family's hut.

Belia looked for Wandago but did not see him. "I'll protect you," Broch said, noticing.

"We'll protect each other," she replied, taking his hand.

That evening, Jokan and Tac'kana announced to the tribe to begin preparing to leave for their winter home. Besides preparing food, there was a lot to do. They needed to reinforce the fence around the compound and fix their huts if needed in order to withstand the coming snow. Like today, it snowed about two hundred to two hundred and fifty inches during the winter. They did not want creatures to take over their huts, although if they did, the tribe's attitude was to accept it. The fence would be a detriment to creatures coming in, but it wasn't tall enough to keep the four-leggeds from stepping over the top of the fence when the snow was deep enough. To keep the raccoons from invading their discard pit, they filled it in with dirt and stone.

Everyone prepared to leave. They put all of the copper in leather bags, and dispersed the bags amongst all of the canoes. They also placed all of their tools they used for copper in leather bags and buried them in their huts for safe-keeping during the winter. The larger tools like wooden bowls and shovels they stored off the ground on rocks in their huts. All of the canoes were inspected as well as the paddles. If needed, they reinforced them, or replaced the paddles. Some tribal members went hunting whilst others dried their catch and processed the hides. Once in a while, Wandago came into the compound carrying a deer. He dumped the deer near the center hearth without asking anyone to process it. Some people saw Wandago as a great warrior whilst others were disgusted with his behavior. Nobody complained, as that was for the leadership to deal with.

Shoria helped Tac'kana take cleaned, dry, intestines and place different medicines in them to take on their journey. She wrapped them in stomachs to keep water out as much as possible. Then they placed them in leather bags. It was very effective. They inspected their traveling tipis to make ready for the trip, as each day was colder than the day before and they needed shelter during the several-day journey. As the days passed, snow was becoming more prevalent and sticking to the trees. Leaves fell, leaving the snow to stay on every twig. It was beautiful. But winter had not yet come, and the snow melted by the afternoon.

One day, Belia and Broch went hunting, and that day, they found themselves separated from each other. Belia did not think much about it as she was hoping for something smaller than deer. Perhaps a beaver would be good. And she could carry that herself.

Her focus was on the hunt and did not notice that Wandago was near. Indeed, he had been stalking her for a long time, and this was the first time he found her to be alone. Suddenly, an arrow grazed her leg, and when she turned around, she saw Wandago. She tried to run despite her wound and he quickly caught her and pushed her to the ground.

"I'm going to kill you, and then I'm going to kill Broch and Jokan. But you, I'm killing slow," he said. He picked her up and she kicked him in the knee.

"Get off of me!" she cried.

In pain, he dropped her and she tried to run again. He grabbed her by her hair and she turned around and she kicked him again, making him bend over. But he took her by her clothes and was able to hit her hard enough to make her ineffective. He hit her over and over and he kicked her. She had been beaten before, but this was different. This had true malice. He lifted her by her hair and planted her against a tree, his body pressing against hers.

"Look at me," he said. "If I can't use you, then nobody will."

"You think you're a man? You're stronger than me and that makes you a man? You've been living a lie all your life."

"Shut up!"

"You're nothing! You're less than nothing! You contribute nothing to the world."

"You're worthless!" he said as he hit her again. "I can't believe how completely stupid you are." She fell and he stepped away from the tree. Suddenly, two arrows and three spears found their mark. Jokan and the elders stepped into view and Broch came, out of breath. Jokan stepped up to Wandago who was lying on the ground and pulled one of the spears out of his body.

Still alive, Wandago looked at them. He laughed. "You would kill one of your own? I'm the greatest warrior here," he said.

Jokan looked at him with pity. Belia and the others waited and watched. "You never knew the voice of Grandmother Earth. You are not human. You are not a member of the tribe. You are nothing."

Realizing his fate, Wandago put up his hands. "Wait! Wait! I didn't mean it! I can do a lot for the tribe. Grandmother −" Before he could finish, Jokan speared Wandago in his heart and he died.

Broch and the others tended to Belia. She stood with difficulty and inwardly checked herself for injuries, as she had done all of her young life. "What are you going to do with him," she asked Jokan.

"Leave him," he replied. "Let the four-leggeds have their way with him." This emphasized just how much Wandago was not human.

"I didn't see anyone here," she said.

Smiling, Jokan said, "Camouflage. We've been following you since you came back home. We knew he would try to kill you."

Belia was once again overwhelmed. "Thank you," she said, crying. "Thank you."

"I'm sorry it took too long to get here," he said.

"You saved my life," Belia said. Looking around, she said, "You all did. Thank you!"

They helped Belia return to the compound, and she took days to heal enough to seem herself again. Tac'kana and Shoria cared for her with medicine, water, and the healing rituals of their kind. Broch tried to help by being with her all the time and caring for her, but he was often in the way, to the delight of both Tac'kana and Shoria. All in all, it took about a month for them to complete their preparations for their journey.

The day came when all their preparations were finished and it was time to celebrate. The tribe prepared a large feast of the meat and greens and berries they had not dried. That late afternoon, everyone sat around the center hearth. Each family sat together. They had brought a short log and set it near the hearth. It was large and secure enough to stand on. Near dusk, every person one by one stood on the log and declared their family heritage. If they were mated, they would stand together and speak in turn. "I am Kace of the Woodland Tribe. My mate is Narsa. My near ancestors are Kallie and Doriga. My far ancestor is Ontona'a. My sky ancestors are Heirta, Piryta, Utria, Mewilis, Juliac, and Tarvia. I have no ashiwanee. Yet." People smiled, but this was an important event to the tribe. Nearly everyone had spoken when Jokan and Shoria stood on the log. They looked at Belia, and then turned to the tribe. "I am Shoria of the Woodland tribe. My mate is Jokan. My near ancestor is Tac'kana. My far ancestors are Piesta and Quekatra. My sky ancestors are Oumi and Nakka. My ashiwanee is Belia, if she will have me." Jokan also said that Belia is his ashiwanee if she will have him.

They stepped down and it was Belia's turn. Belia's heart raged within her with gratitude and surprise. She said, "I am Belia of the Woodland tribe." She then paused and looked at them with a seeing she had not known before. "My near ancestors are Shoria and Jokan. My sky ancestor is Inda. I have no ashiwanee. Yet." She smiled at Broch and stepped down. She sat near Shoria who took her hand. Broch moved next to Belia and took her other hand. Belia could not in any way understand why they wanted her, but their declaration to the tribe forged an unbreakable bond. It took her a long time to trust that they would not change their minds and throw her away, but time healed that fear.

Now was a time for celebration. They ate what the earth gave them with deep gratitude. They looked in each other's eyes and they could see each other. The smell of smoke brought to awareness her own primal memory that was forged by generations of generations of humankind. Suddenly, she felt the spark of new life within her. Awareness molds perspective, and her awareness of family belonging forced Belia to enter a spiral that changed her from becoming to being.

That night, tribal members beat their drums and sang their ancient chant, kin to the first language, which helped Belia experience death and transformation. Members of the tribe danced while Belia looked at them in wonder. The echoes of the drum vibrated within her and she in turn vibrated with Grandmother Earth. All of creation is made of stardust traveling with Light, and, unknowing, she felt that too. Born anew, primal memory became enhanced by the memory of water within and throughout her body, and it touched and became one with her mind.

Identity and purpose are inextricably connected, even though she did not understand. But Belia realized that she had a power beyond her understanding. She was not insignificant, for she vibrated to the echoes of the drum residing within Grandmother Earth and through Life itself. She realized that she was significant. It is like water: still water carries her reflection and little more. But act by throwing a stone and the water reaches out, ripples, and touches others beyond her knowing. A small stone thrown into a lake still makes ripples. It's the quality of living that determines significance. But the quality of living is itself determined by empathy and our ability to see the needs of others and act. Her awareness was both humbling and exciting.

For the first time, Belia knew Love and now knew that she was not evil. That was a lie and an illusion. She knew that she needed to see outside herself, to protect the tribe, to see the needs of other people, and to see needs of creation shown to her by Grandmother Earth. Indeed, her purpose paralleled the purpose of Humankind. Her purpose was to contribute to the greater good within this new realm of Love. Her purpose was to be kind, knowing what it really meant to harm. She knew she must act according to her abilities and circumstances.

She knew that she loved Broch and he loved her. She knew she would mate with him and have a child with him. She realized that the child she would have would be in her care for but a little while. Then, she must lose her, for the child would Become and carry her memory as well as the memory of her ancestors. Her memories will be embedded within generations to come. The awareness of loss and death and pain stimulate the will to live and is part of the sacred dream she must continue to walk.

Belia felt happiness. She was happy. She vibrated in tune with Life itself and Belia rose and danced with the others. She danced.

The dance is not yet finished.

Other Books by Debra Bruch

Fractured Mind: The Healing of a Person with Dissociative Identity Disorder (2016)

Christian Drama for the Worship Service (2013)